ATTACK ON

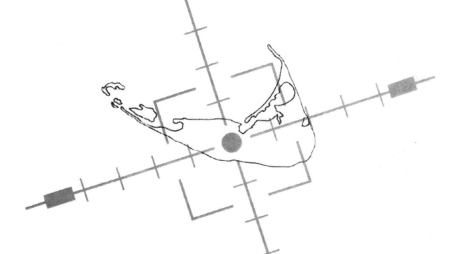

NANTUCKET

THAD DUPPER

Kilshaw Press
Castle Rock, Colorado

Attack on Nantucket
by Thad Dupper

Published by
Kilshaw Press LLC
717 Golf Club Drive
Castle Rock, CO 80108
www.attackonnantucket.com
attackonack@gmail.com

ISBN: 978-09983476-0-8

Library of Congress Control Number: 2016920001

Publisher's Cataloging-In-Publication Data
(Prepared by The Donohue Group, Inc.)

Names: Dupper, Thad.
Title: Attack on Nantucket / Thad Dupper.
Description: Castle Rock, CO : Kilshaw Press LLC, [2017]
Identifiers: LCCN 2016920001 | ISBN 978-0-9983476-0-8 | ISBN
   978-0-9983476-1-5 (ebook)
Subjects: LCSH: Presidents--Assassination attempts--Massachusetts--
   Nantucket--Fiction. | Qaida (Organization)--Fiction. | Terrorism--
   Massachusetts--Nantucket--Fiction. | United States--Armed Forces--
   Fiction. | Nantucket (Mass.)--Fiction. | LCGFT: Thrillers (Fiction)
Classification: LCC PS3604.U66 A88 2017 (print) | LCC PS3604.U66
   (ebook) | DDC 813/.6--dc23

Content editor: Jennifer Fisher

Copyedited by Eileen G. Chetti

Cover design: Austin Hollywood

Interior book design: Deborah Perdue,
www.illuminationgraphics.com

Book production coordinated by Gail M. Kearns,
www.topressandbeyond.com

Printed in the United States of America

*To my devoted aunt
Sister Maryeugene Gotimer, SC,
professor of English,
College of Mount Saint Vincent,
who taught and encouraged me to write
when I was truly incorrigible*

Yip Harburg wrote:

"Words make you think thoughts.
Music makes you feel a feeling.
But a song makes you feel a thought."

To me, Nantucket makes you feel a thought.

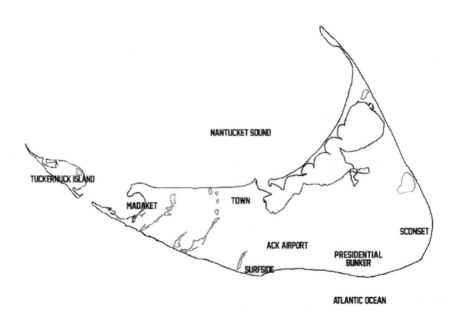

MAP OF NANTUCKET

PRINCIPAL CHARACTERS

Andrew Russell: President of the United States (POTUS); call sign Monsignor

Kennedy Russell: First Lady of the United States (FLOTUS); call sign Mendham

Andrew Russell Jr.: twelve-year-old son of POTUS; call sign Minecraft

Katie Russell: ten-year-old daughter of POTUS; call sign Missy

Stu Jackson: Commanding Officer (CO), USS *Jimmy Carter* (SSN-23)

Mike "Jeb" Bartlett: Lieutenant Commander, VX-23, *Salty Dogs* and US Navy Test Pilot

Kristin McMahon: Deputy Director, National Security Agency (NSA)

Sterling Spencer: POTUS Chief of Staff

Brian Jacobsen: Admiral, Commander, U.S. Fleet Forces Command (COMFLTFORCOM)

Dale Carmichael: CIA agent stationed in China

Amy Lu: Chinese Ministry of State Security (MSS) agent

Knute "Rockne" Burduck: Lieutenant Commander, SEAL Team 2

Dan Nicols: Chief of the presidential Secret Service detail

Lauren La Rue: Managing Director of Oasis LLC, Dubai, United Arab Emirates (UAE)

Abdul Er Rahman: Sheik, leader of the Islamic Front, Riyadh, Saudi Arabia (KSA)

Jack McMasters: Vice President of the United States

Chris Tate: Chief of Detectives, New York Police Department

Prologue

Lauren La Rue was thirty minutes into her morning spin class when her iPhone started to vibrate, interrupting her playlist. A quick glance at the screen and she knew this was a call she had to take. With perspiration rolling down her face, she slowed her cadence and pressed the microphone button on her earbuds.

"Yes," answered Lauren.

Dispensing with any sort of greeting, the voice on the other end of the line asked, "Is everything in order?"

Lauren La Rue, the managing director of Oasis LLC, based in Dubai, responded, "Everything is in order, but the payments have not been made yet."

Dismounting from the exercise bike, she made her way to the patio that overlooked the modern skyline of Dubai's business district, where La Rue's offices were located.

The voice on the other end of the line was that of La Rue's boss, a Saudi billionaire, Sheik Abdul Er Rahman. In addition, and unbeknownst to La Rue, although she did have her suspicions, the sheik was also the anonymous leader of the Islamic Front, the largest benefactor of Al Qaeda. The sheik, who was based in Riyadh, in the Kingdom of Saudi Arabia, ran much of his empire via companies based in Dubai, United Arab Emirates (UAE). His style was notoriously abrupt and demanding of the people who "served him," which was the term the sheik used, rather than "worked for him." His calls were to be returned within minutes, if not seconds. He didn't care if it was the middle of the night. This was especially the case where women were concerned.

The sheik would often say, "Women's role is to serve men. It is their highest calling." That was a commonly held belief in the male-dominated world of the Middle East. But La Rue, his banker and the person in charge of his business affairs, was a smart professional, and as a result he treated her with a modicum of respect. Respect La Rue had worked hard to earn.

"Make sure everything is ready and there are no slipups," the sheik barked.

La Rue had cooled down enough to be able to speak more clearly.

"The teams have arrived and our friends are also in place. The only thing left is to make the payments—and I want to talk to you about that."

The sheik replied, "We will discuss that later" and abruptly hung up.

La Rue returned to her workout, but her heart wasn't in it. Instead of her legs going a mile a minute, now it was her mind. She was going over in her head the steps that had gotten her to this point. She was exceedingly bright and extremely competent, for which she was splendidly compensated, but she knew for the first time that she was crossing a line that would change her life forever. Why she was willing to go this far, she wasn't exactly sure.

❖

Kristin McMahon slowly awakened in her Potomac, Maryland, home. As she stirred she felt the arm of her "boyfriend" reach out and pull her back to him. The word "boyfriend," a term he used, seemed so adolescent. In fact she was a thirty-three-year-old professional woman and he was her thirty-four-year-old partner.

"Don't go," came the plea from the well-toned man that lay next to her.

"I have to, "Kristin replied as she wiggled out of his grasp.

"What could possibly be more important than staying here with me," he chided.

"How about keeping the country safe from terrorists," she replied as she made her way to the bathroom.

"Huh," he let out, "I thought that was my job."

Kristin smiled. She couldn't help herself where Mike Bartlett was concerned—Lieutenant Commander Mike "Jeb" Bartlett, US Navy test and evaluation pilot. She was in love with him and she knew it.

Bartlett was on his second tour as a test pilot having just come from a fleet department head tour. Bartlett was assigned to the Test and Evaluation squadron VX-23, the Salty Dogs. His duty would be to work on the carrier suitability program, where Navy test pilots test all the ship systems to ensure they are ready to be deployed in the fleet.

It was at the beginning of that assignment when he met the deputy director of the NSA, Kristin McMahon, at a friend's wedding in Annapolis. That first meeting had led to many more.

Bartlett walked naked across the bedroom on his way to the bathroom, where McMahon was already in the shower. Bartlett looked at her figure through the steamy shower door and said, loud enough so she could hear him, "Target acquired, I have tone, Fox Two." And with that he swung open the shower door. They were going to get a late start for work this morning.

Thirty minutes later, as McMahon was putting on her makeup, Bartlett asked, "Anything happening today?"

McMahon replied, "No, not really. It's pretty quiet with the president on vacation up on Nantucket. Are you flying today?" she asked Bartlett.

"Babe, I'm a naval aviator. Of course I'm flying," he said with that sparkle in his eye, almost the same sparkle he'd had when he opened the shower door earlier that morning.

"'Babe'? Really? I earned a masters in international studies from Georgetown just so some fighter jock could call me 'babe'?"

That was one of things Bartlett loved about McMahon—her sass.

"I beg your pardon, sir," Bartlett replied, saluting her. "I mean Madam Deputy Director, sir."

She laughed and thought, *God, this guy gets to me.*

Kristin McMahon was attracted to men who were self-confident and successful—those traits tended to go hand in hand. She'd dated a couple of Wall Street, corporate executive types. The problem was they often lacked that certain magnetism that kept her interested in the relationship.

There had also been a couple of professional athletes she'd "known." They were fun and held a certain appeal—but eventually she had to converse with them, and that usually ended it.

It was no surprise, then, that she was naturally drawn to naval aviators. And being in Maryland, she was close to the Naval Academy and the Pentagon, where pilots tended to rotate through, as well as the Naval Air Station at Pax River.

Lieutenant Commander Bartlett was just the sort of man who attracted Kristin McMahon—bright, self-confident, and physically fit, and on top of all that a US Navy fighter pilot. The icing on the cake was Bartlett's Hollywood good looks.

"Well, keep the world safe. I'll see you tonight," Bartlett said as they left the house and kissed goodbye.

"You be safe," she admonished as she got into her Audi sports coupe.

"Copy," intoned Bartlett as he slipped into his pristine 1985 Porsche 911. Fighter pilots cared for their cars almost as much as they did their jets—almost.

❖

"Officer of the Deck, make your depth 150 feet, ahead two-thirds. Comms, let the flagship know we are taking up station off Sconset," ordered Stu Jackson, captain of the USS *Jimmy Carter* (SSN-23), a Seawolf-class attack submarine.

The officer of the deck repeated Jackson's command, with the pilot, who replaced the diving officer on Virginia and Seawolf class subs, responding, "I have the dive."

Stu Jackson was the real deal. A Naval Academy grad, Jackson had joined the submarine force directly out of the academy and had quickly risen to his present command.

Jackson's success wasn't because he was the smartest CO or possessed the best fitness reports. He was simply revered by his crew for his leadership.

His leadership style was a combination of keen intellect and an almost uncanny ability to read his crew, along with a healthy dose of swagger, which enabled him to get the best out of the officers and sailors who sailed with him.

When his crew was asked who they would like to put to sea with or who they would like to have with them on a risky mission, the answer was almost always Jackson.

And that's why Commander, Submarine Forces (COMSUB-FOR), the sub boss for the US Navy, a three-star vice admiral, had personally selected Jackson to command the Navy's most expensive and mission-capable fast attack sub.

The Seawolf-class submarines were intended to replace the beloved and feared, yet aging, Los Angeles fast attack subs. But at more than $3.5 billion a copy, they were exorbitantly expensive, which explained why there were only three in the Fleet.

The *Carter* was unique, as it was roughly one hundred feet longer than the other subs of her class, USS *Seawolf* (SSN-21) and USS *Connecticut* (SSN-22). This was because of the insertion of a top secret additional section just aft of the sail known as the Multi-Mission Platform (MMP), which allowed for the launch and recovery of a Navy SEAL team for shallow-water incursions.

Being the commanding officer of the USS *Jimmy Carter* in the post-9/11 world meant his sub was almost always in demand.

Post 9/11, the skipper of an exceedingly quiet killing machine needed to be capable of more than stalking Soviet subs or tracking the impossibly quiet Chinese diesel-electric subs.

Now the skipper of the *Carter* needed to complete missions with the added difficulty of fighting an enemy like Al Qaeda or ISIS.

Due to the addition of the MMP, the *Carter* frequently had one of the Navy's eight SEAL teams on board, ready to provide a rapid insertion into a crisis situation. All too often, those missions meant providing protection for US cities. And that explained the *Carter*'s current assignment—stationed off the shores of Nantucket. In the event anything should happen to the president, they were ready to go.

Book I

Chapter One

Presidents Bush 41, Clinton, and Obama made presidential vacations to New England de rigueur. Presidents Clinton and Obama's favorite spot was Martha's Vineyard, while 41 preferred his family's estate on the Maine coast at Kennebunkport.

And, of course, long before that, JFK made the Kennedy Compound in Hyannis the center of power and glamour for US society.

While other presidents and first ladies had visited Nantucket, it was President Andrew Russell who made the tiny island located thirty miles off the coast of Massachusetts his vacation destination.

Even though many on the island feigned nonchalance or even disdain at the arrival of the first family, there was always an air of excitement when President Russell arrived in Siasconset, or Sconset as the locals called it. After all, he was the president of the United States.

POTUS and his family were just beginning their four-week vacation on Nantucket, which typically commenced in early August and ended after Labor Day.

The home on Low Beach Road in Sconset where the Russell family was staying was the property of a social media CEO. Rather than Baxter Road, which represented old money, the newer money preferred the south side of the village, along Low Beach Road, which afforded sweeping views of the dunes and scrub oak bordering the Atlantic Ocean.

The White House Communications Agency or WHCA, with the homeowner's approval, had upgraded the systems in the house at an unspecified cost to taxpayers. In addition to the communication upgrades and state-of-the-art security, the Secret Service also added radiation detection and bioprotection systems.

The Secret Service liked the Low Beach Road location because just a few hundred yards down the road was a recently idled Coast Guard station.

LORAN Station Nantucket was once known as "the Power Behind the Pulse." Built at the height of World War II, the LORAN station had been a critical navigation tool for mariners and aviators. Yet the advent of Global Positioning System (GPS) satellite technology eventually rendered LORAN obsolete.

Remaining at the Coast Guard station was a collection of buildings including a single-story structure used as a dormitory as well as a few Cape Cod–style houses for the officers and their families. In addition, the Coast Guard station had a helipad. The US Secret Service took over the entire facility during the presidential hiatus.

Medical facilities on the island of Nantucket were provided by the Cottage Hospital, which, in spite of advances in recent years, lacked a state-of-the-art operating room and as such was not able to meet the needs of a presidential visit.

To remedy that situation, the US Army 9th Mobile Medical Command detached the 254th medical field unit to Nantucket whenever the president visited. The Army field hospital was also situated at the Sconset Coast Guard station.

Another attractive security feature of Nantucket was the bunker built at the height of the Cold War by the Kennedy administration. Decommissioned for many years, the bunker was in the neighborhood known as Tom Nevers, which was located conveniently between Sconset and the Nantucket Airport. The bunker had only recently been recommissioned and brought up to today's standards in order to support President Russell's annual visits to Nantucket.

If necessary, the US Secret Service could deliver POTUS and his family to the bunker in less than seven minutes. It was the presence of the bunker and the nearby Coast Guard station and the fact that it was an island that ultimately made Nantucket an acceptable choice in the eyes of the Secret Service for protecting POTUS.

The call sign the Secret Service assigned to the president was Monsignor, a nod to his Catholic faith and his beloved uncle, who was a monsignor in the Brooklyn Diocese. Keeping with tradition, the call signs for the first lady as well their children would all begin with the letter *M*, modeled on the president's.

Kennedy Russell's call sign was Mendham, after the town where she grew up in New Jersey. The children's were Missy for Katie and Minecraft for Andrew, given his devotion to the video game.

Change was something not embraced on ACK, as the island was known, referring to its airport code. Nantucket had some of the strictest zoning laws in the country, and its Historic District Commission, the HDC, wielded veto power over all exterior design on the island. It was well-known that the HDC infuriated builders and masters of the universe alike with their unrelenting enforcement of design appropriateness.

However, while Nantucketers reveled in resisting change, even Nantucket couldn't resist the gravitational pull of the iPhone. So it wasn't surprising when Nantucket, after epic battles and endless debates, eventually erected three microwave towers.

The first tower went up at Eel Point—an area that had become the hot location for new development on the island. The second cell tower was located in town, disguised in the steeple of the Unitarian Universalist Church on Orange Street. And the third cell tower was located in the center of the island, near the ACK airport. Three towers notwithstanding, cellular service on the island was spotty, especially outside of town.

❖

President Russell was the fourth US president to graduate from a military academy.

Ulysses S. Grant and Dwight D. Eisenhower graduated from the United States Military Academy at West Point, whereas Jimmy Carter and Andrew Russell graduated from the United States Naval Academy at Annapolis, Maryland.

Furthermore, President Russell was only the second naval aviator to become president. The first, of course, was George H. W. Bush, who famously flew TBF Avengers in World War II.

Being a naval aviator often defines a person, and to a large extent it defined Andrew Russell. His competitiveness, his self-confidence, the way he carried himself—these traits were all by-products of his fighter pilot core.

During his Navy career President Russell flew off three carriers – the USS *George Washington* (CVN-73), USS *John C. Stennis* (CVN-74) and the USS *Harry S. Truman* (CVN-75). When Russell *"fleeted up"* he flew with fighter squadrons VF-143, VFA-41, and VFA-32. He began flying the F-14B Tomcat with VF-143, *the Pukin Dogs*, off the *Washington*. He later transitioned to the F/A-18 Hornet with the *Black Aces* (VFA-41). After serving in VFA-41, he was selected for fighter command and then served as XO and CO of VFA-32, the *Swordsmen*.

When he first met his future wife, Kennedy was a marketing director at a New York City Internet company. He was a Navy F/A-18 fighter pilot—and the embodiment of a *Swordsman*.

It was 2003 when newly promoted Commander Andrew "Rudy" Russell and his fellow pilots were in New York City for Fleet Week and found their way to Tortilla Flats, the legendary bar on West Twelfth Street in the West Village.

The Navy encouraged its personnel to wear their uniforms during Fleet Week. So it wasn't really fair to the other male patrons when Russell and his squadron mates entered the bar. Kennedy's friend Harper took one look at them, then turned and said, "Ken, look what just walked in."

Andrew Russell and his fellow naval aviators surveyed the bar like they did everyplace they entered. It wasn't long before Russell and his fellow fliers had Kennedy and her friends on their radar.

Kennedy sauntered over to the bar. It didn't take long.

"Excuse me, ma'am," said Andrew Russell. She cringed when she heard the "ma'am."

"'Ma'am'? Are you talking to me?" she asked.

"Well, I guess I have to call you ma'am because I don't know your name," said Commander Russell.

Noting the gold wings on his uniform, she replied, "Flyboy, you're going to need a better line than that in this city."

"See, that's just it," complained Russell. "My squadron mates and I don't know a lot about Manhattan," he said, flashing his smile.

Of course, that was totally ridiculous because he clearly had a New York accent, but she was willing to play along.

"Isn't that what the USO is for?" replied Kennedy.

"Sure, the USO is fine for getting Broadway tickets and MetroCards, but my friends and I would like to meet some real New Yorkers," he said, adding quickly, "You know, the Navy encourages us to do that. It's good for morale."

"Whose, yours?" shot back Kennedy.

In addition to her looks, Andrew Russell was attracted to her quick wit.

"Well, sailor, good luck on your mission." She smiled and turned to rejoin her friends.

Andrew Russell looked over at his fellow fliers, who were laughing at Kennedy's brush-off.

Just then one of the bartenders yelled, "Do we have any birthdays?" A roar went up around the bar.

At Kennedy's table it was, in fact, Harper's birthday.

As is the custom at Tortilla Flats, all the birthday celebrants line up as a waiter brings each a sixteen-ounce can of beer.

Not wanting to miss out on the fun, Russell's wingman joined the birthday line, even though his birthday wasn't for months.

The crowd clapped and hollered as each participant chugged their beer.

The Navy pilot easily downed his can and then turned to watch Harper begin her turn.

Halfway through, Harper had slowed considerably. Russell's squadron mate noticed her dilemma and offered to finish it for her.

As the aviator drained Harper's remaining beer, one of the Flats bartenders, who are well known for playing music that fits the moment, put Berlin's "Take My Breath Away" on the bar's sound system.

As the music played, Russell's and Kennedy's eyes met. Not breaking eye contact, the Navy pilot re-approached, this time simply saying, "I'm Andrew Russell."

"Nice to meet you, Andrew, I'm Kennedy Preston."

Their romance was a peripatetic affair—a year later they were married in a small ceremony on Coronado Island in San Diego with his squadron mates in attendance. Russell's uncle officiated at the wedding.

Soon after getting married, Russell finished his command tour and retired at fifteen years of service. After leaving the Navy he became the congressman for New York's Eleventh

Congressional District in Brooklyn. Andrew Russell had grown up the third of four children in Bay Ridge, Brooklyn, a well-to-do enclave of tree-lined streets with a view of Manhattan and New York Harbor.

He was mentored and encouraged to run for office by Anthony Faris, the powerful senator from Wyoming. Russell had met Faris, the ranking member on the Senate Armed Services Committee, during an assignment at the Pentagon.

Russell's persona was shaped not only by his career as a Navy pilot and his upbringing in Brooklyn, but also by his twelve years of Catholic school preceding his appointment to the Naval Academy.

It was these three factors that had the biggest impact on defining the person Russell had become: Brooklyn born, which meant he had the typical New Yorker scrappiness; trained as a Navy pilot, meaning he was ultracompetitive; and Catholic, which gave him his humanity and spirituality.

His path through Congress was like his naval career—focused and fast. He was decisively elected the forty-sixth president of the United States after twelve years in Congress by a country yearning to be led by someone who embodied Russell's qualities.

He was perhaps best epitomized by his campaign slogan, which usurped the famous Robert Bolt line: "Andrew Russell—A Man for All Seasons." Some on his staff vehemently argued that the use of "A Man" would alienate female voters. But Andrew Russell rarely, if ever, failed to appeal to the female portion of the population. Russell carried 68% of the female vote when he was elected president.

To the White House he brought his young family: a son, Andrew, twelve, and a daughter, Katie, ten.

His wife and young children, along with his Navy career, gave the White House a flavor like that of the Kennedy era's Camelot—albeit now with a slight New York accent.

Chapter Two

Friday in Sconset

One entered Sconset under a canopy of trees, on the main road, which terminated at a small circle at the center of the village. There stood a small collection of businesses—the historic post office, Claudette's Sandwich Shop, and a bistro named Sconset Café, which was well-known for three things: its exceptional cuisine, its BYOB policy (the Sconset liquor store was next door), and its policy of frowning on children in the restaurant. Also located in the village was Sconset Real Estate.

Ensconced in the real estate office, catching up on paperwork, Cassandra Wilson called to her assistant, in this case a summer college intern, "Becca, make sure all the packets are complete, please."

"They're done and I'm getting ready to drop off today's changeovers." Becca Stevens was an attractive coed from Boston College who lived with her parents at their vacation place on Shell Street. Cassandra referred to her as 'Becca from BC.'

"Good." Cassandra exhaled. "Today won't be too bad, but tomorrow's going to be a nightmare, with twenty places turning over. Saturday is always a killer."

Cassandra liked working for Sconset Real Estate. Her passion was selling multimillion-dollar homes to the wealthy, but her day-to-day job involved the less glamorous, yet lucrative, task of renting homes to families who wished to spend their summer vacation on Nantucket. She was well-known on the island for being the go-to real estate agent for Sconset.

Becca, with her youthful energy and enthusiasm, was immune to the stresses that Cassandra felt. She called out as she grabbed her tote with the four welcome packets, "I've got the packets for Broadway, Shell Street, Codfish, and Baxter."

Cassandra nodded as her iPhone buzzed with a text indicating that one of her rental's washing machines was broken.

As Becca put her bag over her shoulder and mounted her Vespa, she heard Cassandra on her phone pleading with her handyman, "Harry, I need it fixed now, not tomorrow."

Becca made her way to her first rental, a cute cottage with dark green shutters on Broadway. She knocked on the door and called, "Anyone home?"

No one answered. She carefully opened the front door and saw that there were several bags in the living room. She guessed the renters had arrived early, dropped off their bags, and then went for a walk around the village.

As she placed the welcome packet on the table, she noticed that one of the pieces of luggage had an Emirates tag, which she noticed having just watched a recent vlog of of Casey Neistat's, the famous YouTube vlogger.

As she turned to leave, she ran into a group of four young men who were approaching the front of the cottage.

As she stepped outside she pulled her Ray-Bans down and smiled. "Oh, hello. I'm Becca with Sconset Real Estate. I just dropped off your welcome packet."

The four men, who appeared to be of Middle Eastern descent, looked alarmed to see her coming out of the house. The leader of the group tersely said, "Why were you in the house?"

Becca, not used to such an unfriendly demeanor—after all, they were in Sconset on a beautiful Friday in August—replied, "I'm sorry. I just dropped off your welcome packet with all the information you need about the island and the house. If you need anything, just let me know," she said with a flash of her smile, which had always worked for her in the past.

"We don't need anything," said the leader abruptly as he brushed by her.

With the awkward welcome over, Becca headed for her next stop, at a house two blocks over on Shell Street. As she scooted away she had the thought that these guys were not the typical friendly Sconset renters. She didn't know it, but Becca had just met the four members of the Hijra Al Qaeda terrorist team.

❖

On this Friday, the president had a 10 a.m. tee time at the Sankaty Head Golf Club, located on the edge of Sconset. As was often the case, the president used his round of golf to mix work with leisure. Keeping with that practice, his first nine holes would be with his chief of staff, Sterling Spencer. Then, at the turn, their foursome would be filled out by the CEO of GE and Ben Stiller, a frequent summertime resident of the island, who was a terrible golfer but whose company the president enjoyed.

On the fairway of the par-five fourth hole, the president got to the topic of China. "Sterl, you know we have the UN vote on the Spratly Islands issue coming at us in November."

"Yes, Mr. President, it is our highest-profile issue for the upcoming G8 meeting as well."

"Sterl, China is basically constructing man-made islands in the South China Sea, to the concern of all our Asian allies, not to mention the Europeans. Not only that; these islands are little more than military bases. It could tip the balance of power in the area."

"Mr. President, China's making a power play with the Spratlys, no doubt. But their real goal is larger. China is desperate to be seen the equal of the US as a superpower. Zhang is driven to attain that status." Spencer was referring to the Chinese president, Wei Zhang.

"Yes, it comes through with every interaction I have with him. He suffers from superpower envy. There are easier ways for Wei to achieve his goals than forcing this Spratly issue, though," stated the president as he selected his rescue club from his bag to get him out of the short rough two hundred sixty yards from the fourth green.

As the two men prepared for their second shot, Spencer added, "At this point, if China backed away from the Spratlys, they would see it as losing face. And you know how important that is to them."

The president then concentrated on his second shot which landed sixty yards from the cup. "Yes," exclaimed the president. "Sterl, in my Navy days that shot would have elicited hoots and hollers from my squadron mates."

"Mr. President, I am sure the Secret Service would prefer *not* to hear any hoots or hollers coming from me."

"Even Ben Stiller would have appreciated that shot," the president said, laughing.

But the president knew Sterling Spencer didn't have that sort of personality. They had met while they were both congressmen, Spencer being the four-term representative from Colorado.

Though Spencer wasn't an aviator, the president had chosen him as his chief of staff because his style and skills complemented Russell's. As a result, they worked well together.

The president continued, "Anyway, the Chinese aren't the real enemy. Like the Russians, they are too tied to us via trade, banking, the Internet. The bigger threats are North Korea, Iran, ISIS and Al Qaeda."

Spencer, who at this point had lost focus on his golf game, replied, "Without a doubt, sir, our biggest threat is from someone with nothing to lose, like the Islamic Front, or that man-child in North Korea, or Iran."

The president nodded. "And I don't trust the Saudis either. Never have."

Over the next couple of holes they discussed domestic issues and the upcoming G8 meetings in Rome.

❖

If a business could be loved, the Sconset Market was. Located in the center of Sconset, the Sconset Market was in many ways not only the center of activity for the village but its heart and soul.

It was Friday, August 11, around noon, when young Andrew Russell entered the Sconset Market with his sister, Katie.

"Katie, what flavor do you want?" he asked.

Katie, who was not one to be rushed, replied, "I have to look first."

They walked over the well-worn wooden floors to the ice cream cabinet. In spite of $8 ice cream cones and cereal that cost three times the price on the mainland, everyone, from vacationing CEOs to ten-year-olds, loved the Sconset Market.

The children's Secret Service detail hovered near the doorway, keeping an eye on the other patrons in the store as well as the staff.

"Mint chocolate chip," decided Katie. "In a cone," she added.

"Mom says we should get a cup, not a cone," retorted Andrew.

After getting their order, they walked outside to sit in the small brick-paved park adjacent to the store. They looked at the old elm they had climbed when they were younger.

Andrew said, "Let's take the footbridge back."

Katie nodded. The footbridge, another Sconset landmark, was a small wooden pedestrian bridge that spanned Gully Road.

As the children got up from their bench, a black van with "Cape Finished Flooring" written on its side pulled into the parking area.

The Secret Service agent accompanying the children noticed that both the driver and the passenger looked Middle Eastern. Profiling is morally questionable, but in this day and age it was a reality and a very effective tool. The agent nodded to her partner as the driver and passenger, both men, got out and entered the Sconset Market.

As the president's children made their way to the footbridge, two agents went with them while the other two agents of the detail lingered at the store.

One of the agents went over to the van and looked in the passenger window while the other agent followed the van's occupants into the store.

As the new arrivals walked down one of the two aisles grabbing some food, the Secret Service agent purposely bumped into one of them.

"Oh, sorry," the agent said.

In his mid-twenties and of slight build, the man didn't say anything; he just nodded.

The agent, wanting to engage, went further, saying, "Are you guys from around here?"

The man just shrugged and said in a low tone, "Just working."

The Secret Service agent stared directly into the man's eyes. His earpiece, his physique, and the bulge under his shirt gave away the fact that he was police, military, or a government agent.

For a few seconds there was a standoff as the two men looked hard at each other. It wasn't a friendly moment.

A few seconds later the Secret Service agent disengaged and left the Sconset Market.

Once outside, he nodded to his partner and they left to catch up with the Russell children.

The other agent said, "I got the plate number."

The lead agent nodded, his sixth sense still tingling, warning him that something about the men in the van was wrong. He was tempted to go back and engage the two again, but without anything concrete to work with, he instead moved on.

Life is all about opportunities—some realized, some missed. As it turns out, the Secret Service agent would have been well served to have put a bullet in each of the men.

❖

During the first family's Nantucket vacation, it was not unusual for Admiral Jacobsen to be accompanied by his wife, Ann, who would often join Andrew and Kennedy Russell in Sconset. Kennedy liked Ann and looked forward to the couples' informal dinners.

In fact, Ann had rented a house in Sconset on King Street for a couple of weeks, which allowed the two families to share their vacation time.

The Jacobsens had three children, ages eight, eleven, and thirteen, who got along well with the Russells' ten- and twelve-year-olds.

Ann and Kennedy would sit either poolside at the Low Beach Road house or on the beach at Sconset or Surfside.

That Friday afternoon, while the president was playing golf, Kennedy and Ann planned a trip with the children to Surfside Beach. While at the beach, Kennedy confided to Ann, "There's a lot to like about being first lady, but I worry more and more about security. Do you know that this year the Secret Service inserted a tracking chip in Andy, me, and the kids?"

Ann looked startled. "A tracking device?"

"Yes, they call it a SPID, and it has some sort of transmitter that they can use to track us."

"Did it hurt? Is it large?" asked Ann.

"No, it's tiny. It was like getting a shot, basically. Anyway, I am glad we have them, but I find myself rubbing my shoulder where they inserted it. It's a constant reminder to me about the threats to my family's safety. Between you and me, I can't wait until Andy is out of office so we can resume some sort of normalcy to our lives."

As Kennedy said that, she looked over and saw her detail of Secret Service agents scanning the beach around them.

"That said," added Kennedy, "Andrew is doing important work, and I know he is counting on me for my support. And he has it."

Ann Jacobsen just nodded sympathetically.

Kennedy then changed the subject. "Ann, wouldn't it be great if Brian got assigned to the Pentagon? Then we could see each other more than just while we're on Nantucket."

Ann replied, "Well, Brian has mentioned that to me. His assignment in Norfolk is just about up, so a Pentagon assignment would be the natural next step. If it happens I would appreciate your input on area schools if you have the time."

Kennedy smiled and came back with, "That would be a pleasure. Everyone in Washington has an agenda, and it would be nice to just have a friend close by."

They then both got up to cheer the kids riding the waves on Surfside Beach.

Soon after, they started to pack up to return home and prepare for Friday night dinner.

❖

Every night at 6 p.m. when President Russell was in residence—weather permitting—two F/A-18 Super Hornets (call sign Rhinos) would conduct a 2-ship flyby down Sconset Beach as a salute to POTUS.

They would start their run at an altitude rarely much higher than three hundred feet and fly a north-to-south run from the Sankaty Head Lighthouse to Tom Nevers at 350-400 knots.

It never failed to put a smile on the president's face or his children's, not to mention the faces of any guests in attendance.

So low and fast did the F/A-18 Super Hornets fly, they routinely set off car alarms along Codfish Park, located below the bluff in Sconset.

The flyby became a Sconset summer tradition; people would go to the beach or stand with cocktails in hand along Front Street and watch the F/A-18 Super Hornets. This year the mission fell to the pilots of VFA-11 *Red Rippers*, VFA-136 *Knighthawks*, or VFA-211 *Checkmates*, with a big AB painted on their vertical tails, designating them as part of Carrier Air Wing 1 (CVW-1), to conduct these crowd pleasing daily airshows.

While locals were aware of the Hornets, there was additional military assets in the area as well. The US Air Force, which rightfully prided itself on the protection it provided for Air Force One, had also contributed a squadron of F-15C Eagles, sixteen jets in all, to support the president's vacation. They were stationed at the Otis Air National Guard Base on Cape Cod with standing orders to provide a Halo Ready Alert CAP (HRAC) within minutes over the island.

The Army was not to be left out. They had two Apache gunships loaded with Vulcan miniguns and Hellfire missiles sitting on the tarmac at the Nantucket Airport (ACK). Also at the airport were two CH-53E Super Stallion Marine helicopters.

From a military perspective, one could say the tiny island of Nantucket was ready for almost anything. And that was a good thing—because no one could have predicted what was about to happen.

Chapter Three

More on Friday

Kristin McMahon was at her Langley, Virginia, office with her team finishing up their daily update. "Kevin, what's on the board?" she asked, referring to the global threat board.

Kevin Mannix was her team leader.

"There is some violence in Syria, mounting political pressure on the president of Brazil to resign, unrest in Nigeria over low oil prices, and the president is on Nantucket—where I wish we were."

"Thank you, everyone. Keep me apprised if anything breaks," said McMahon as she closed the meeting.

Mannix stayed behind. He was scheduled to give McMahon a debrief on a project he was working on.

"Okay, Kevin, this is about Oasis, correct?" questioned McMahon.

"Correct. As you know, I have been putting together a book on Oasis LLC." A "book" was NSA parlance for an in-depth analysis.

Up came the first slide in his presentation. "Lauren La Rue is the managing director of Oasis LLC. She has an undergraduate degree from the University of Wisconsin–Madison and an MBA from the Stern School of Business at NYU."

"What made her go to Dubai?" asked McMahon. "She should be working for Goldman Sachs or one of the hedgies."

"We believe her boss is Sheik Abdul Er Rahman of KSA," Mannix continued, using the shorthand for the Kingdom of Saudi Arabia.

"Ah, so the plot thickens," McMahon said. The sheik was high up on their watch list. They didn't have anything firm on him, but he was under suspicion. It also spoke to Saudi Arabia's increasing importance for the US.

"The Israelis tell us that Oasis LLC is a cover for the Islamic Front. We don't have anything definite on that, but you know how accurate the Mossad is on topics like this."

McMahon just nodded.

After a few more slides and additional explanation, McMahon asked Mannix for his recommendation.

"In a perfect world I would like to make Oasis LLC a class A intelligence priority. For now, I recommend we put them on the CIA Priority List and contact the CIA KSA country head to alert them that we are increasing the profile on Oasis."

McMahon responded, "Kevin, put the paperwork together for the director's signature. I'll be meeting with him on Monday."

❖

Stu Jackson stood in the control room of the *Carter* studying the navigation charts of Nantucket Sound. As long as the president was in residence on ACK, the *Carter* would be patrolling off the eastern tip of Nantucket in the waters off Sconset, Great Point, and Surfside Beach.

On board the *Carter*, in addition to its standard crew complement of 130 officers and sailors, was a SEAL Delivery Vehicle (SDV) and its team of commandos, referred to as SDVT-2 and based out of Virginia when not on board the *Carter*.

SDVT-2, better known as SEAL Team 2, was led by Lieutenant Commander Knute "Rockne" Burduck.

Standard SEAL teams are typically led by a command structure of a lieutenant with two ensigns and a chief petty officer. In this case, because of the anticipated interaction with the US Secret Service and CIA in conjunction with the president's vacation, the Naval Special Warfare Command in Coronado made the decision to assign Rockne an O-4 lieutenant commander to lead SEAL Team 2 for this op.

That meant Lieutenant Mahoney would be in charge of the tactical aspects of the team, with Lieutenant Commander Burduck focusing on interservice coordination. That was unless any shooting started. There would be no keeping Burduck from participating in a mission if the proverbial shit hit the fan.

Since the president had started vacationing on Nantucket, the Commander, United States Fleet Forces Command, or COMFLTFORCOM, always deployed a carrier battle group to the waters around Nantucket for a round of workups and training at the same time. The admiral's rationale was, "They need to train anyway—so why not have them train off Nantucket?"

As a result, on the Atlantic Ocean side of the island, in addition to the USS *Jimmy Carter* was the aircraft carrier USS *Theodore Roosevelt* and its escort ships, together known officially as Carrier Strike Group 12 (CSG-12).

The USS *Theodore Roosevelt*, CVN-71, was named after Teddy Roosevelt, whose foreign policy was summed up as, "Speak softly, but carry a big stick." Fittingly, the nickname for CVN-71 was "The Big Stick."

Carrier groups rarely, if ever, go to sea with a full four-star admiral on board. Typically they embark with a rear one- or two-star admiral.

However, Admiral Brian "Chain" Jacobsen, an academy classmate of the president's, made it his practice that while President Russell was on Nantucket, he would embark on the *Roosevelt*.

Having COMFLTFORCOM on board the USS *Theodore Roosevelt* was no one's idea of fun, least of all that of the commander of Carrier Strike Group 12, or COMCARGRU-12, Rear Admiral Mark Singer, but it wasn't open to debate.

Chapter Four

Still Friday in Sconset

Of the four homes rented and one home owned in Sconset by Oasis LLC, three were staging homes—meaning these were homes where the Hijra, Amina, and Kiswa team members, eleven trained commandos in all, would stay.

The leader of the three teams was Karim Hamady, a twenty-eight-year-old Saudi. He was intelligent and well trained, with a worldview based in radical Islam.

Karim, the man the Secret Service had run into at the Sconset Market, spoke to his team from the living room of the rented house on Broadway.

Karim instructed them, "Go to the two big houses and make sure all the weapons are ready." He was referring to the two locations the teams referred to as armory houses. The year before, other teams who had traveled to the island had hidden weapons there.

The team split into two groups of five each and drove to the Baxter Road house and the Hedge Row Road house.

Twenty minutes later, in the Sconset Landscape pickup truck they had purchased for the mission, Karim followed the team to the Baxter Road house to check up on them.

He began with a prayer. "We praise Allah for giving us the strength and means to attack the American infidels."

At the Baxter house, his team removed vinyl bags hidden in the house the year before, when it was rented by Oasis LLC. The weeks of that year's rental purposely did not coincide with those of the president's holiday.

The Baxter Road house was a good choice because of its quantity of custom woodwork. The panels around the staircase and the built-ins were perfect locations to hide an arsenal of weapons. By installing false bottoms in the window seats and built-ins they were able to hide an assortment of AK-47s, RPGs, smoke grenades, and extra magazines.

The Baxter Road home was located high on the Sconset Bluff. The houses along Baxter Road were owned by powerful blueblood families of generational wealth. Possessing spectacular ocean views, these homes had an Achilles' heel. During the last fifteen years the surf and undertow had waged a war of erosion on the Baxter Road bluff, which was cleaving at an accelerated pace and, as a result, was threatening the stability of many of the homes.

Design and location-wise, the Baxter Road house was a very appealing property to Oasis LLC. It had what amounted to a clerestory on the top of its second floor. Surrounded by windows on all sides, it would function perfectly as a lookout, providing a 360-degree sweep.

The house was owned by John Munson, a Marine and Vietnam vet, and his wife, Carol, a New York City banker, as an investment property.

John was well-known in Sconset and rented a small house on Park Lane. Munson wore many hats, as did many of the people who resided on the island year-round. He tutored children and wrote books, and on the side he bought and sold houses.

Over the years he had settled into the comfortable rhythms of Sconset. But the old joke still applied—there is no such thing as an ex-Marine.

Once Karim was satisfied with the progress of the Baxter house team, he left for the other armory house on Hedge Row.

The Hedge Row house, located on the other side of the village near Low Beach Road, had been purchased by Oasis LLC via a Bermuda shell company eighteen months ago. At Hedge Row, Karim conducted the same ritual, including the prayer to Allah.

❖

At the NSA, Kevin Mannix had just returned from his noontime workout. He settled in front of his five screens, which were arranged in a two-over-three configuration. Mannix still had Oasis LLC on his mind from his earlier discussion with McMahon. Using sophisticated and proprietary software, he was now mining transactions that Oasis had completed via the international SWIFT wire transfer system.

Those transactions were then linked to various accounts and scanned for any relationship to known terrorist organizations or individuals.

A family tree would then be created that showed entities that were doing business with Oasis LLC. This family tree could be manipulated to show relationships by company, geography, and time frame.

The analysis wasn't yielding anything new or actionable, but Mannix continued to stare at his screens, tapping his mouse and moving from one view to the next. On the wall were three fifty-inch flat-screens showing CNN, Fox News, and the BBC. (The people at MSNBC would be livid to know they had been replaced by the BBC on the screens at the NSA, but the NSA liked the international perspective the BBC provided.)

The CNN broadcast, with closed captioning enabled, was showing a clip of the Russell family vacationing on Nantucket. Mannix was looking at the CNN broadcast—had he expanded the view on his computer screen, it would have shown that

Oasis LLC had rented several homes on Nantucket over the last three years and had also purchased one via a shell company. The Oasis rentals had never been during the same weeks as the president's visit—never, that is, until this year.

❖

It was now early afternoon and Lauren La Rue had just finished making the fifteen SWIFT transfers for US$1 million each through the sheik's Deutsche Bank account. The payments went to a list of international banks, including Emirates Bank NBD, HSBC, BNP Paribas, Sumitomo, Société Générale, and Royal Bank of Scotland. As she logged off the banking system, she received a WhatsApp text message.

The text read, "Everything appears to be in place for your friend's holiday. Please consider visiting us soon though."

The message, she believed, was referring to the impending operation on Nantucket. She replied, "I would love to but work won't allow it."

A second later came the response: "You are working too much and need to take a break—soon."

On the other side of the world, the members of the Hijra, Amina, and Kiswa teams were also receiving texts, informing them that their money had been deposited to their individual accounts. That money would be moved to two more accounts in the coming days, making the electronic footprints harder to trace.

Acts of terrorism were always said to be done in the name of Allah. Back in 2001, that might have been the case, but today, despite the cover of religious zealotry, most terror work was done for one reason—cold cash. No one wanted to admit it, but money was the motivating factor in many of the terror attacks that had occurred in recent times. That was why cyber sleuthing was one of the areas of greatest investment at the

NSA. Tracking the money was one of the best ways to track down potential terrorists.

As the Oasis money transfers were completed, a red icon started to blink on Kevin Mannix's bank-monitor screen, indicating an alert. Oasis LLC had just transferred fifteen "sticks," or fifteen individual $1 million payments, to private accounts.

The sum was not the tell—Oasis LLC regularly moved hundreds of millions of dollars in transactions. What generated the flag was the short succession of time during which Oasis had made the fifteen equal payments.

Kevin's eyes fixed on the blinking icon. He clicked on it, and opened a list of the fifteen transfers. He spent the next thirty minutes trying to identify and map the owners of the fifteen accounts—he could confirm only nine. He ran their names with a click of the mouse against every known terrorist database. Knowing this would take a couple of minutes, he walked off some nervous energy and went to the restroom.

Upon his return, his eyes widened—three of the account holders got positive hits in the terrorist database. With that intel in hand, he lifted the handset, pressed a button, and said, "Kristin, I need to see you at once."

A minute later he was in McMahon's office. "What's up?" she asked.

"We just picked up three sticks transferred to three known individuals on the Priority One terrorist list," said Mannix.

"Do we know the location of the terrorists who received the funds?"

"Not yet, but the transfers originated with Oasis," replied Mannix.

McMahon called out to her assistant, "I need to speak with the director, priority."

Before Mannix left McMahon's office, he told her he wanted to elevate the surveillance on Oasis and La Rue to a Priority One status, something he had held off recommending earlier in the day.

McMahon thought about it for a second, then nodded, saying, "Call Wayne Macklem at CIA. He will get you some in-country eyes."

When Mannix got back to his desk, he called the NSA's liaison at the CIA. Mannix and Macklem knew each other, which made the call easy and to the point.

"Wayne, Kevin Mannix. How's it going?" opened Mannix.

"Hey, Kevin, what's up?"

"Listen, we're calling to get some eyes on someone in-country."

"Sure, what's the rundown?"

"We have a high-value target in Dubai, an American woman—Lauren La Rue. She runs a front called Oasis LLC. We picked up some money transfers that got hits in the terrorist database."

"How much money are we talking about?"

"She moved $1 million to fifteen different accounts—three of them got hits on the P-One list."

"Sounds like Al Qaeda is getting ready to commence an operation. Do we know the location of the three?"

"Not yet. I've been following Oasis LLC for a long time and I'm pretty sure it's a cover for the Islamic Front."

"Kevin, what do you need from the CIA?"

"We are requesting the CIA make La Rue and Oasis LLC in Dubai a Priority One intercept. We want the CIA to start a tail on her. We may want to pick her up in a hurry if this thing develops."

"A snatch and grab on La Rue in Dubai, copy." Wayne Macklem then hung up.

Macklem sent an encrypted priority message to the CIA's UAE country chief requesting they put one of their best in-country assets on the job—trusted undercover agent Aziz Mahmood. The request went further, specifying that Mahmood should locate and follow La Rue but not pick her up.

Chapter Five

Friday Evening

Dale Carmichael was stationed in Beijing, China, where he worked for the CIA. A career agent with expertise in Asia and China in particular, he was a graduate of Manhattan College.

Carmichael was viewed as a senior operative for the US in China, having been stationed there for more than seven years. Dale was fluent in Mandarin, which was a sine qua non for being successful in China.

Over his years in the country he had met many of the ministers of the various government departments. Dale had also met many of his Chinese counterparts, who represented the Ministry of State Security, or MSS, China's equivalent to the CIA.

The MSS's primary mission was purported to be the collection and analysis of foreign intelligence—simply put, they were spies.

One such MSS agent was Amy Lu, an attractive, smart, and dangerous Chinese national.

Carmichael, like most agents, was an adrenaline junkie and liked to live on the edge, and that meant taking risks. It was not beyond Carmichael, who was a thirty-eight-year-old bachelor, to sleep with an MSS agent if he found her attractive. This, of course, was a clear violation of CIA policies, but agents like Carmichael were hard to come by. As a result, his superiors tended to look the other way at his venial indiscretions.

And that is how Dale Carmichael found himself in bed with MSS agent Amy Lu this Friday evening in his Beijing apartment. Chinese women of a certain education and sophistication enjoyed being romanced by US men because of their physicality and their superior lovemaking.

Both Amy and Dale knew they were using each other for their individual pleasure and professional advantage, but that didn't mean they didn't enjoy each other's company—they did. After a rather rigorous session, Amy asked, "Dale, how much longer do you expect to be stationed in China?"

"There hasn't been any talk of a transfer. You know I like it here, and I certainly am not an office type. Like you, I want to be in the field."

Amy listened and said something that took Carmichael by surprise. "I was just wondering if there is a future for us."

Carmichael was taken aback at seeing a side of Amy that she had never shared before.

Unsure how to respond, he said, "Well, we enjoy each other's company. Why don't we just see how our relationship develops?"

Amy didn't look thrilled with that response. But she snuggled closer to Dale and drifted off for a short post-workout nap.

A few hours later, Amy awoke and nudged Carmichael out of his sleep.

"Wake up, sleepyhead. How about something to eat?"

A short time later, as they sat at his kitchen table eating a light breakfast, she brought up work.

"By the way, we have been picking up some chatter between Al Qaeda cells indicating that Nantucket might be an upcoming target for an attack."

Like everyone, Carmichael knew President Russell spent August on Nantucket. Putting down his chopsticks, he asked,

"Just how good is your intel, Amy?"

"How good is it usually?" she replied flatly.

Dale knew it was almost always one hundred percent right and that she wouldn't be sharing this with him unless it was cleared at very high levels within the Chinese government.

"Details. Come on, Amy, I need some details."

"We have an unusual amount of traffic coming from suspected Al Qaeda cells. In addition, we have noticed a recent increase in fund transfers from known businesses that are fronts for Al Qaeda. I would say that there is *a clear and present danger* mounting, and all indications point to Nantucket as the target."

Amy then stood up and, taking her dishes to the sink, said she needed to take a quick shower and get back to her apartment before flying the following morning to Sanya.

Carmichael sat at the kitchen table processing the data he had just received. Sanya was the location of the Chinese Yulin submarine base. It was China's equivalent of Groton, Connecticut—the center of the US Navy's submarine force. In addition, the Nantucket data was red-hot.

Why is Amy going to the sub base? he wondered. Admiring her lithe body as she moved past him, he grabbed her and pulled her back down onto his lap.

"Easy, Romeo, I've got to get home to get ready for my flight," lilted Lu.

Carmichael thought about protesting but knew Amy had to leave, plus he wanted to report the Nantucket intel to Langley ASAP and see if anything unusual was happening at Sanya. He let her go with a smile and a slap on her rear, which earned him a lusty smile in return.

❖

Admiral Jacobsen called the captain of the USS *Theodore Roosevelt*. "CO, ready a Seahawk, I'm going to Sconset."

The captain got the wheels in motion to ferry COMFLTFORCOM on the short trip to the Sconset Coast Guard station's helipad.

This evening the admiral had been invited to join the president along with his Chief of Staff for dinner at the Summer House, the classic Sconset restaurant, just three-quarters of a mile from POTUS's Low Beach Road digs.

On occasion Jacobsen would bring along the CO of the Roosevelt, Captain Tom Fraser, since Fraser had flown with the president back when he was the CO of VFA-32 on the USS *Harry S. Truman*.

Then commander Russell took a liking to Lieutenant (junior grade) Fraser, who was on his first deployment. However, the fact that Fraser was a personal friend of POTUS's had no bearing on Fraser's career. Fraser was now high on the promotion list to get his first star and eventually command a carrier group of his own, based on his merits, not his circle of friends.

Tonight's diners were just POTUS, Sterling Spencer, and Admiral Brian "Chain" Jacobsen. Over dinner at the Summer House, the president asked Admiral Jacobsen, "Brian, what do you think about this Spratly Islands situation?" The issue was a high priority for him, given the current tensions between the United States and China.

The president was referring to a group of islands, more aptly a collection of reefs, that China had staked a claim over the objections of many of the countries in the region.

"Mr. President, it's a clear act of aggression. As you know, we have a carrier based out of Japan, but given this Spratly business we are going to have to deploy another forward-based carrier either out of the Japan or somewhere nearby. It's going to stretch us thin, sir."

Sterling Spencer said, "Admiral, under strict confidence, we are in discussions with the Philippines about re-opening and expanding our naval facility in Subic Bay. In addition, we are considering creating a new major base in Vietnam. Having both Subic and a new base in Vietnam would provide us the necessary presence in the region to respond to the Spratly Islands issue."

"You know, Chain," said the president using the Admiral's callsign as aviators often did even after they retired, "naval aviation has no better supporter than me, but at $14 billion per deck, these carriers are getting expensive. What do you think if we were to station a couple Zumwalt destroyers permanently out of Subic?"

Jacobson wasn't sure if the president was baiting him with the question or if he really thought the new Zumwalt destroyers might be the best solution to the Spratly situation. This was one of those subtle—but crucial—dialogues with the leader of the free world that could leave an indelible imprint on one's career. Everyone thought these dinners with the president were strictly social—but they weren't.

"Mr. President, a pair of Zumwalts is certainly a viable solution, but given the Spratly situation, the carriers give us a more flexible deterrent."

Spencer added, "Many on the Senate Armed Services Committee are impressed with the capabilities of the Zumwalts."

Jacobson finished strong. "Fight power with power. In my opinion, sir, we will need another carrier in the South China Sea."

The president thought about Jacobsen's answer and then said, "Chain, what do you think of this wine?" indicating that the policy discussion was over for now.

The president, always the gracious host, would entertain his guests, often quoting Yogi Berra. Russell would adapt Yogi's line about how he wanted his pizza cut to ordering cake for dessert, quipping, "You'd better cut it in fours. I don't think I can eat six pieces."

Once dessert was finished Russell would then work the main dining room at the Summer House, stopping at every table, which in the age of the iPhone inevitably meant taking a lot of selfies.

More than once, though, the president's staff heard him say, "You know, Derek Jeter doesn't allow any camera phones at his place in New York City."

He would go on to describe the basket Jeter purportedly had at the door of his Manhattan penthouse, where everyone had to place their cell phones before entering.

On occasion the president would say to his Secret Service detail chief, Dan Nicols, "Dan, let's put out one of Jeter's baskets tonight," which meant the Secret Service would ban all photos and smartphones. But tonight wasn't one of those nights.

❖

Later that Friday night Cassandra Wilson's assistant, Becca, was at Cru, the new "it" place in town.

Becca's friend Lexi noticed three good-looking guys at the bar.

A few minutes later Becca and Lexi were talking to Josh Wagner and his fellow members of the US Secret Service detail assigned to the POTUS children.

As they talked, Becca told Josh she worked at Sconset Real Estate. Of course the topic of the president came up.

Josh said to Becca, "Well, you know, I can't say anything about that."

"Even a little?" flirted Becca.

"Well, can you keep a secret?" asked Wagner as he leaned close to Becca's ear. "You know, the children . . . they like— ice cream."

Becca, realizing she had just been had, said, "Just for that, you can buy the next round."

It was over her sea breeze that Becca told Josh about the four foreign-looking men at the Broadway house. Because he was a Secret Service agent, she also mentioned the Emirates luggage tag.

That piqued Wagner's interest as he recalled the run-in he'd had earlier in the day at the Sconset Market.

❖

It was about 11 p.m. and Karim was getting ready to turn in. But before he did he wrote a message to his parents using an encrypted and disappearing-message app called Cyber Dust.

> Dearest Father and Mother,
> Tomorrow I will make a stand for Allah against our
> enemies. I am in the United States surrounded by the
> decadent Americans. I may not speak to you again but
> I want you to know everything I do, I do in the name
> of Allah.
> A package will arrive at your house soon with
> instructions. Please follow them and see to it that
> Amok is taken care of.
> Wa-Alaikum-Salaam,
> Karim

As midnight approached, armory houses one and two had been prepped with their arsenals of firepower.

The other three homes in Sconset were where the terrorist teams were staying. Eleven men stayed at rented houses on Broadway, Shell Street, and Gully Road in Codfish Park.

The next day, the Hijra and Amina teams would load their weapons into beach and umbrella bags and pile into their recently purchased Land Rover and Ford Explorer. Both vehicles had been bought on the island a month earlier, using cash, by a guest staying at the Wauwinet—the island's world-renowned hotel.

The Hijra and Amina teams would drive down Low Beach Road until they reached the turnoff that led to the beach.

This beach access path was well-known to locals. It was a tricky drive because the sand was so soft. Drivers needed to let the air out of their tires and maintain momentum or they would soon be calling the island's only tow-truck guy, George, for a pullout.

Once on the beach, the Amina and Hijra teams would open the tailgates, put out blankets, set up some fishing poles, stage their bags, and then wait until the appointed time.

Two members of the Hijra team made their way to the Hedge Row house in the Sconset Landscape pickup to wait until the specified time.

The Kiswa team's assignment was to man the Baxter Road house.

Chapter Six

Saturday Morning

The president looked out the window as dawn was breaking. It was a little after 6 a.m. on Saturday, August 12th, as he pulled on a pair of Asics. He glanced back over at his wife, who was still in bed, and said, "I'm going to go for a run." He leaned over to kiss her, then made his way down to the kitchen.

There the president was greeted by Mr. Hallenbeck, their cook. The cook knew the president preferred to run on an empty stomach, but afterward he would have raisin toast and some Noosa, his favorite yogurt, and maybe a banana.

As the president walked into the family room, he dialed 33 and immediately the phone was answered by the duty Secret Service agent. "I feel like a run this morning. Do you think you can scare up a couple of agents who can keep up?"

"Yes, Mr. President, we are ready when you are," came the crisp reply.

Walking out to the front driveway, the president started his stretching routine. He then cleared the memory on his Garmin running watch as the detail arrived and got organized.

Agent Nicols spoke first. "Good morning, sir. Where are you thinking about heading this morning?"

"How about out to the lighthouse?"

"Yes, sir," answered Nicols, who was already warmed up and ready to go.

As Agent Nicols quietly spoke into his wrist set, the vehicles in front of the compound started to move out onto Low Beach Road. Once on the street, they backed up about one hundred feet and waited for the group to appear and start the run.

The president came out front and walked over the shell driveway, which crunched with every footstep. At the foot of the driveway the shells gave way to a Belgian block apron, underneath which the Secret Service had installed a variety of sensors.

Dan Nicols and another five agents would run in a wheel pattern around the president. On these runs everyone except the president carried Sig Sauer P229s—with two of the younger agents carrying H&K MP5s strapped across their backs. The straps were made to look like CamelBaks, with some of the agents opting to wear a second shirt over the MP5s.

This made the MP5s less noticeable, but it also made drawing the guns more difficult.

Following the runners at a safe distance were two black Suburbans with agents in each one and more firepower, including automatic weapons and additional communications equipment. Following the Suburbans was an ambulance.

"Okay, special agents—try and keep up," the president challenged, as he started up the low rise of Low Beach Road, headed toward Morey Lane and then past the Summer House restaurant. As the detail moved out, they savored the early morning air and the quietness that was Sconset.

It was a beautiful morning, and the president looked out over the grass and dunes to the Atlantic while the rest of his contingent's eyes were sweeping houses and windows, looking ahead for any vehicles, and generally keeping the most powerful and important man in the world safe on his morning jog.

Up past the Summer House, an agent ran ahead to peer into the garbage bins located near the entrance to the pool patio of the Sumer House. The agent thought the bins shouldn't be on Ocean Avenue but instead located behind the restaurant. He didn't understand why a fancy restaurant would have the garbage out front—no one else did either.

They then ran past a parked Mini Cooper with a diagonal red stripe on its door—probably the designation for a crew team from someone's alma mater. They soon approached the landmark footbridge, where a decision had to be made to either run over the bridge or go around it into town. The president went left, bypassing the bridge and entering town past Claudette's Sandwich Shop, as he usually did.

Town was quiet at this time of morning—some workmen were getting their morning coffee from the Sconset Market and a few folks were walking here and there.

Without a word, the detail continued along Shell Street, with the motorcade following about thirty seconds behind, in spite of the fact that they were now going the wrong way on a one-way street. The president had dropped the pace to below eight minutes a mile—he was feeling good, they could tell.

Next they passed the Wade Cottages and made the right turn onto Butterfly Lane for about fifty yards followed by a quick left onto Baxter Road. The president liked to see the old Jeep the owners of the house on Butterfly Lane kept—a 1960s Jeep Cherokee restored to like-new condition.

The residents of Baxter Road loved gardening, and one of the best examples was immediately on the president's left as he turned onto the street. It was an award-winning garden that commanded any passerby's attention, drawing it away from what was happening on the other side of the street, where an ornate and beautiful old house sat in an ever-increasing state of disrepair, an atypical occurrence on Nantucket.

The house had to be tied up in some sort of litigation, thought the president as they ran by. He reminded himself to have his assistant, Alice Ahern, look into what was going on with the property.

The sweat was now running down the president's forehead. He knew he was pushing himself as he passed Rosaly Lane, then Emily Street, both off to the left of Baxter Road.

The president's group was now passing Annes Lane; they passed the Soros house, then the old Benchley place. They could now be clearly seen from the clerestory of the Baxter Road house, where the Kiswa team was standing by.

The Kiswa, Hijra, and Amina teams had planned to be in position every morning, starting today, anticipating the president's run. If he didn't run this morning, they would be ready tomorrow morning. They knew from prior intelligence that the president, when on vacation on Nantucket, never went more than three days without a morning run. So it was just a matter of time. And this beautiful Saturday morning was now the time.

Chapter Seven

Saturday Early Morning

On the bridge of the USS *Theodore Roosevelt* (CVN-71), Captain Tom Fraser sat in his chair overseeing the operations of what amounted to basically a small city. It was Saturday morning and Flight Ops were getting ready to commence within the hour.

Captain Fraser was a year and a half into his assignment as the CO of the *Roosevelt*. The typical tour of a US aircraft carrier CO was two and a half years. It was a coveted assignment among naval aviators and in most cases was a path to getting promoted to flag rank.

Fraser, a charismatic man with a bit of an Irish twinkle, was well liked by his crew. At about six feet and fit, Fraser possessed a keen intellect and warm gravitas.

The CO picked up the phone that hung from the ceiling above his chair and punched the number for Combat Direction Center, or CDC, one of the nerve centers on the ship. "What's on the board?" asked the captain.

"A lone wolf is tracking a Russian attack boat about seven hundred miles away off Newfoundland, sir, but other than that—all clear." A lone wolf was the designation for a submarine operating independently of the carrier group. In this case the lone wolf was the USS *Montpelier* (SSN-765), a Los Angeles–class attack sub.

As he put the handset back in the cradle, the light from the admiral's line lit up. "Yes, Admiral?"

"Captain, can you come down to the admiral's bridge?"

"On my way, Admiral."

"Captain's off the bridge," was the next sound heard as Fraser climbed down the command ladder to make his way to the admiral's flag bridge, which was one deck below his command bridge.

There he met with Admiral Singer and the commander of Carrier Air Wing 1 (CVW-1), CAG, for the next few minutes to discuss the day's operations, the current threat board, and any noteworthy activities involving the president's trip.

The admiral began, "As we discussed yesterday, we will be running a counter-ops drill today, gentlemen." In this drill the attack submarines of the carrier group detach and attempt to penetrate the defenses of the carrier group undetected.

The USS *Jimmy Carter*, along with the USS *North Dakota* (SSN-784), a Block III Virginia-class attack sub, would be the foxes for today's drill, with the USS *Theodore Roosevelt* their target.

The CAG added, "Aye, aye, Admiral we're ready. We'll be launching a Hawkeye and then get the Dragonslayers"—CVW-1's helo squadron—"up. Plus we'll have an Alert 5 ready."

Captain Fraser looked at his watch. "Its 06:15. As planned, we will be ready to commence Flight Ops within the hour."

The USS *Jimmy Carter* was patrolling, submerged, due south of Sconset off Tom Nevers at a depth of one hundred feet. That was ridiculously shallow for a sub, but the waters off Nantucket were not deep and represented a constant headache and hazard for the *Carter*'s navigators.

The CO began, "As you know, the admiral instructed us yesterday to prepare to run a counter-op on the Stick." The XO just nodded. This counter-op was the sort of drill submariners lived for.

Jackson continued, "Navigator, where is the *TR*?"

The navigator responded, "Sir, I have the *TR* thirty-five miles north-northwest of us bearing 033 degrees."

"Plot a sweep course. I want to come in from the north. They won't expect that," commanded the captain.

"Aye, aye, Skipper," the navigator replied.

"Officer of the Deck, I recommend course 042 smartly, depth 250 when the sounding allows, ahead two-thirds."

"Copy, come to 042 smartly, depth 250 on the sounding, ahead two-thirds," were the next words from the officer of the deck.

The captain reached for the handset. "Officer of the Deck on the 1MC."

"Crew of the *Carter*, we are going carrier hunting. We are running a counter-op on the *Roosevelt* carrier group. We will be going ultraquiet in five minutes. Let's go bag us a carrier. Jackson out."

The crew of the USS *Jimmy Carter* jumped to action. After days of monotonous patrolling of the box off Sconset, going after the carrier was just the sort of challenge that would get the crew pumped up. The chief of the boat had gone to the flare locker and gotten a green flare, which he was displaying to the crew as he walked through the sub, making sure everyone was alert and prepared. The USS *Jimmy Carter* was ready.

The *TR* carrier group was just over the horizon about thirty-five miles north of Great Point. Jackson and his XO plotted a speed course to get them within twenty miles of the carrier group, where they would then go ultraquiet and look to breach the perimeter.

Once inside, they would fire a green flare, which traditionally was the way a sub commander let a carrier battle group CO know that their perimeter had been penetrated. In a war setting, there would be no flare. Instead the carrier would have been sunk by the sub.

The counter-ops plan showed just how proactive the commander of Carrier Group 12 was—here only forty or so miles off Nantucket, Singer was practicing a drill that was more likely to take place in the South China or Arabian Sea. No one expected any real danger to take place here off the coast of Massachusetts.

❖

The Secret Service detail running with the president was approaching Bayberry Lane when the first shot rang out. The lead agent in the president's running detail went down from a bullet to the left side of his chest. A second later the other lead agent also went down from a shot to her chest.

The remaining four Secret Service agents quickly joined ranks on the president, with the two agents in the back peeling off their T-shirts to unship their MP5s. Lead Agent Dan Nicols hit the transmit button on his headset and broadcast, "Code Red, Code Red, Monsignor under fire—Monsignor under fire, lock down Eagle's nest."

When a Code Red call is put out on a Secret Service channel, it means that all Secret Service agents move to a priority one, or P1, security state. That sets in motion a series of important actions.

The Secret Service agents on duty at the defunct Coast Guard station immediately sent a Scramble Alert out on all military and police channels. Receiving that alert, the two CH-53E Super Stallion helicopter pilots standing by at ACK picked up their helmet bags and ran to their CH-53Es. Ground crews were notified and they started the APUs, or automatic power units, which would initiate the helos' emergency start engine procedure.

The emergency start protocol called for all cylinders to be primed and revved to operating rpms, regardless of the engine temp, which ran the real risk of damaging the engines. A start like this, used only for emergency purposes, would shorten the life of the CH-53E's engines, but that didn't matter at the moment.

At the ACK airport, the Code Red call required that the control tower implement a ground stop. In addition to the Super Stallions, the two US Army Apache helos based at ACK were now also scrambling on the Code Red call.

On board the USS *Theodore Roosevelt* the Combat Direction Center received an encrypted message from the Secret Service: "This is a Code Red alert, repeat, a Code Red Alert." The COs and admirals were informed of the Code Red immediately.

The captain picked up his handset. "Launch the Alert 5." The pilot, who was already seated in the cockpit, heard the order and started to spin up its engines. As the name implied, the Alert 5 jet could be launched within five minutes. Hammer 11 of VFA-136 would be airborne in a matter of four sweeps around the clock.

As the Alert 5 readied for launch, the officer of the deck turned the USS *Theodore Roosevelt* five degrees to starboard in order to put the wind straight down the flight deck.

The air boss sounded the Flight Ops alarm, and twenty colored-shirt deckhands started to run to their assigned duties, led by the flight directors. The Alert 5 bird was already positioned on catapult 4 for immediate launch.

As the jet blast deflector rose behind the Alert 5 Super Hornet the pilot performed a wipeout of his controls ensuring the control surfaces of his fighter were free. He then was given the hand signals by the shooter to perform the engine run-up of his Super Hornet. The pilot, a lieutenant, saluted, and a second later the yellow-shirt shooter's right hand touched the flight deck and then came back up to shoulder height, which was the signal for the catapult officer to fire the catapult. A second later the catapult fired and Hammer 11, the Alert 5 Super Hornet, was airborne.

❖

A flash was seen from the clerestory of the Baxter Road house as an RPG launched at the lead Secret Service Suburban, breaching the engine compartment and killing the two agents in the front seats. That left Nicols and three remaining agents, who needed to make it to the second Suburban while protecting the president.

As the first shots were fired from the Baxter Road house, one of the Kiswa team members texted all the other teams on the island with the message "It's on."

The two agents with their MP5s now unshipped returned fire, concentrating on the clerestory where the RPG had just been fired.

John Munson, the owner of the Baxter Road house, had decided this morning to ride out to the Sankaty Head Lighthouse and check out his Baxter Road property on the way. Pedaling his bulky boulevard cruiser bike, he was coming up to the president's group when he heard the first shots fired. His next indication that something was wrong was when the lead Suburban blew up almost in front of him. He was stunned for a moment, but his military instincts quickly kicked in. He jumped off the bike and ran past the retreating Secret Service agents, who were surrounding the president, and looked into the burning Suburban.

The passenger doors were blown off, making the grisly scene inside visible. Munson picked up an M4, the standard-issue military replacement for the M16 assault rifle, from the rear deck of the burning Suburban and made his way to one of the two downed Secret Service agents, both of whom were seriously wounded. As he slung one of the agents over his shoulder, he said, "I've got you," and turned to see where the shots were coming from.

Amazed, he realized the shots were coming from his house.

"Bastards," he yelled as his adrenaline kicked in, and he ran to the ambulance, never turning his back on the threat. With the first wounded agent safe, he ran back to rescue the other agent, letting off short bursts of gunfire and cursing the entire way.

Once he reached the second agent, he grabbed her, and again he said, "I've got you—you'll be okay." The agent didn't respond.

As he pivoted back to the ambulance, he felt a burning sensation in his left calf.

"Motherfucker," he screamed.

He had been shot in his leg, but he wouldn't let that stop him. Munson crossed to the shrub line, where he placed the injured agent on the ground.

He yelled to the other agents to get the agent to the ambulance as he started to crawl through the shrubs to the yard of the neighboring house. He had the advantage over the Secret Service agents because he knew the area well and certainly knew the layout of the house—his house—where the shots were being fired.

He also knew he had to be mindful of his ammo. He had only that single magazine in the M4.

He glanced down at his leg and saw the blood but knew it was just a flesh wound. *Oh, you fuckers*, he thought, *I am going to kill every one of you.* Gunnery Sergeant John Munson had snapped back into his combat persona.

Agent Nicols yelled, "Mr. President, get in," as they pushed him into the second Suburban, which had already made a U-turn, gunning right through the hedges on the opposite side of the street.

Nicols was on the radio. "This is Agent Nicols. Bravo, Bravo, execute Bravo." Bravo was the US Secret Service code to evacuate the presidential residence and get POTUS and his family to "Fort Apache," the secure location. In this case it was the bunker in Tom Nevers.

❖

Captain Stu Jackson was in the control room of the USS *Jimmy Carter* planning how he was going to sneak up on the CSG-12 when the Code Red call came in.

"Quartermaster of the Watch (QMOW), cancel the counter-op. I want a speed course back to Sconset," the captain ordered.

"Two hundred degrees, sir," immediately came the reply.

"Helmsman, come right to two hundred degrees ahead flank."

The captain picked up the phone and pressed the button for the engineering officer. "Ronnie, pull the rods, I want all you've got."

"Aye, aye, sir," came the response.

"Officer of the Deck, sound the general alarm. Alert the SEALs to prepare to launch the SDV."

Immediately, the twelve-thousand-ton, 453-foot USS *Jimmy Carter* started to accelerate as its jet-pump propulsion system increased to its top secret max speed.

❖

At the Nantucket Airport, the two Apache gunships were now airborne and headed for Sconset.

"Renegade 06 and 19 are inbound and hot. Requesting tasking," called the lead Apache pilot.

"Hot" indicated the Apaches were armed. "Requesting tasking" is the military term to request a target.

Admiral Jacobsen, who had been conducting a Q and A session over breakfast with the sailors in the enlisted crew mess, quickly made his way to CDC once his chief of staff informed him of the Code Red message.

From CDC, COMFLTFORCOM ordered, "Ready a squad of Marines and get me an MH-60R Seahawk spun up *now*."

Chapter Eight

Saturday Morning, With the Attack Underway

The door burst open to the locker room in the clubhouse of the Congressional Country Club, in Bethesda, MD where Vice President Jack McMasters was preparing for a round of golf with some large Republican Party donors. After all, it was a Saturday morning in August.

Two Secret Service agents quickly approached the VP, saying "Mr. Vice President, we have a situation. We need you to come with us."

They grabbed the VP and rather unceremoniously jostled him out of the locker room and into the waiting car. Outside the clubhouse there were two more agents standing ready with their MP5s drawn.

The VP's motorcade was already alerted, and as soon as McMasters was secure in the limousine, his driver headed off at high speed, with the motorcycles and trailing Suburbans struggling to keep up.

❖

At Baxter Road, a second RPG shell launched toward the now U-turning ambulance but skipped on the ground and missed.

These bastards can't even shoot straight, thought Munson, figuring the distance was only about thirty yards. He pulled himself up just as the RPG shooter was sighting his next target. The shooter never got to pull the trigger. His head exploded in a flash of red. Munson had gotten his first kill.

Next was the RPG loader—he was dead a few seconds later. Munson may have been in his sixties, but, damn, he could still shoot.

Munson's shots gave the ambulance time to complete its U-turn. It was now speeding down Baxter Road. The Suburban carrying the president was long gone, having already made the turn onto Butterfly Lane.

❖

As Admiral Jacobsen approached the Marines standing on the flight deck, Gunnery Sergeant Julio Galleta saluted, as did the rest of his squad. "Sir, we're ready." The salute was unusual because at sea the accepted practice is not to salute. That said, Jacobsen was a four-star and Galleta was, well, a Marine.

The admiral just nodded as they boarded the MH-60R Seahawk helicopter. Once seated, the admiral spun his right index finger in a circular motion, signaling the pilot to take off.

As the MH-60R Seahawk lifted off, a Marine corporal worked with the admiral to help him put on his bulletproof vest and the rest of the tactical gear he would need for their incursion.

The admiral was going into a firefight to support the president, and his friend, Andy Russell.

❖

Having received the text that the operation was a go, the Hijra and Amina teams made their way from their beach positions to the president's Low Beach Road house. The terrorist teams split as they approached the presidential retreat.

Amina was tasked with taking out the upper-floor threats and the sniper on the roof, while Hijra would focus on the ground forces.

With silencers on their rifles, they quickly dispatched the Secret Service agent on watch on the patio near the pool. No one even heard him fall. The next fatality was the Secret Service sniper on the roof—again with one shot.

It was 6:43 a.m. as the fire fights were underway on Baxter Road and at the Low Beach Road house. Hammer 11, the Alert 5 fighter, had just arrived on station, flying over the houses of Sconset at three hundred knots at an altitude of eight thousand feet.

"Hammer 11, Rough Rider, standby for tasking," was the call from the USS *Theodore Roosevelt*.

"Rough Rider, Hammer 11, am on scene and can provide visual cover," replied the pilot.

Captain Fraser, the CO of the *Roosevelt*, was monitoring the calls from the bridge. He picked up his phone and pressed the button for the air boss. "Boss. What is the status of the Alert 15 tanker?"

"Captain, the tanker will be up in minutes. Also we are readying the Alert 15"—Super Hornets—"on cats one and two, sir."

The captain then added, "Boss, also ready an E-2 Hawkeye so we have an airborne platform to monitor the battle space."

"Copy," came the reply from the air boss, whose responsibility was to run the airport that was the USS *Theodore Roosevelt*.

❖

Upstairs at the Low Beach Road house the first lady was just leaving the master bathroom and headed to her daughter's room to see if she was up yet.

The Hijra team was tasked with the extraction of the first family, while Amina dealt with the first lady's Secret Service detail.

Quietly the Amina team entered the Low Beach Road house from the rear French doors overlooking the pool. Once in the house, Amina gunmen stationed themselves at doorways in the kitchen and family room, taking out the president's cook and securing the entire lower floor of the house.

Just then the chief of the first lady's Secret Service detail entered the kitchen for some coffee. She was only able to remove her Sig from her holster before two bullets hit her in the center of her chest. Agent Nicols had allowed the Secret Service agents to dispense with wearing bulletproof vests while on the island.

There was a flurry of motion near the stairs as the remaining agent reacted to Nicols's "Bravo" call.

The agent knew her first responsibility was to secure FLOTUS and her chicks. The agent burst into Katie's room, startling the first lady and scaring Katie.

"Ma'am, we have a situation," said the agent.

The first lady instinctively grabbed Katie with both arms and demanded, "Andy, where's Andy?"

"I'll get him," said the agent as she ran toward his room.

Once in his room, she woke him, saying, "We gotta go, kiddo," as she picked up the twelve-year-old.

They met at the top of the stairs, with FLOTUS holding Katie and the agent carrying Andy.

The Hijra gunmen were stationed below the staircase, all with a clear line of site to the top of the stairs.

The female Secret Service agent, her weapon in her right hand and the president's son in her left, noticed the threats as she approached FLOTUS at the top of the stairs.

In a single motion she spun to her left, placed the president's son against the hall wall, and took aim on the intruders.

There were three members of the Hijra team, all in firing positions, when the bullets started to fly.

Secret Service agent Danni Appleton got off the first rounds, hitting one of the Hijra members squarely in the chest.

As she took aim at her next target, she felt a burning sensation in her left shoulder, then a piercing sharp pain in her abdomen. She fell to the floor, firing her Sig Sauer pistol as many times as she could, but failed to hit any of her targets. As she lay there, her consciousness slipping away, she heard FLOTUS scream as the members of the Hijra team rushed up the stairs with pillowcases and zip ties.

❖

The president's Suburban was now speeding through Shell Street. The driver locked up the brakes as the vehicle entered Pump Square in the center of Sconset. Miraculously, no one was hit, let alone killed.

As the Suburban decelerated, Hammer 11 passed overhead.

Secret Service Agent Nicols was making more radio calls. "Multiple agents down on Baxter Road, POTUS secure. We are headed to Fort Apache."

Nicols tried to contact the FLOTUS detail but got no answer. He put out an all-channel call for any agent at Eagle's nest, the president's house on Low Beach Road, but received no response.

Again he called, "This is Secret Service Agent Nicols. I am not getting any response from Eagle's nest, repeat, Eagle's nest is off the air. Has Eagle's nest executed Bravo?"

That caught the president's attention. "Dan, what's happening?" he asked.

"Mr. President, we can't raise FLOTUS."

With a hard look, the president replied, "Get me to the house *now*." Then he bent over the backseat of the Suburban and grabbed an M4.

"Mr. President, we can handle this, please. We've got to get you to Fort Apache," stated Agent Nicols.

It took only one glance from the president for Nicols to

read his mind. In a deadly quiet tone the president repeated, "Dan, get me to the house now."

POTUS took the safety off the automatic weapon and checked the magazine.

❖

Admiral Jacobsen was five minutes out from Sconset, but he didn't know where to deploy his forces. A call went out: "Marine squad inbound, provide tasking."

The Army Apache attack helicopters came on the air. "Renegade 06 and 19 are inbound, crossing Sankaty Head Lighthouse and requesting tasking."

There was no reply from the Joint Terminal Attack Coordinator (JTAC) who was responsible for inter-service communications to coordinate the Close Air Support (CAS). No one knew where to send the inbound helos or what targets to give them.

Both Navy and Army helicopters could see the smoke rising from the Suburban on Baxter Road that had taken the RPG round, so they headed in that direction.

At the same time, with no response from Eagle's nest, Agent Nicols radioed, "Code Blue, Code Blue, all available forces head to Eagle's nest." The Code Blue call meant a location was under attack.

With the Code Blue call received, Admiral Jacobsen pointed south. "Get me to the house *now*."

The Army Apache gunships were monitoring the Navy radio calls and responded, "Renegade 06 and 19 on your wing."

The Army Apache gunships, their chin turrets already training back and forth looking for a target, were now escorting the admiral's MH-60R Seahawk helo.

❖

The Hijra team had duct-taped pillowcases over the heads of FLOTUS, Andrew, and Katie and zipped handcuffs on their wrists. They were then dragged out the front door of the Low Beach Road house and put into the back of the Sconset Landscape pickup truck, which had just pulled up.

All three were quickly secured to rings on the bed of the pickup by another set of zip strips. As a tarp was pulled over the back of the truck, they were injected with a strong tranquilizer. The Hijra and Amina team members then piled into the pickup with four of the terrorists lying in the back of the pickup with the Russell family. The entire operation took less than five minutes.

The pickup started to slowly drive up Low Beach Road. A moment later it turned left onto Morey Lane, just as the black Suburban carrying the president went speeding past in a blur.

The pickup went only another couple of hundred feet, turned onto Hedge Row Road, then made a quick right into the driveway, which led them to the house that Oasis LLC had purchased. Once they were parked, Hijra transferred their human cargo into the house.

❖

When the Navy and Army helos reached the Low Beach Road house, all was still. The Navy MH-60R landed at the Sconset Coast Guard Station helipad, while the Apaches hovered over the house, looking very much like a rattlesnake coiled and ready to strike. But there was no activity, no movement, nothing.

A moment later the president's black Suburban pulled up.

He and Nicols rushed into the house with the Marines following, but it was empty except for the bodies of FLOTUS's Secret Service detail.

Two of the Secret Service agents were still alive, and they were quickly transported to the field hospital by the Marines.

But two of the Low Beach Road Secret Service team had been killed during the attack.

"Mr. President," said Nicols, "we have *got* to secure you."

"Where's my family?" yelled the president.

"We will find them, but I need to get you out of here *now*."

The president understood what he needed to do, but he was also a husband and a parent. He had to know what had happened to his family.

Not waiting another minute, the Secret Service basically pushed the president out the door. Before he knew it, he was in the CH-53E Super Stallion helicopter that had also landed at the Coast Guard station's helipad. Once the president was on board, the helo lifted up, on its way to the presidential bunker in Tom Nevers.

As the Super Stallion started to gain altitude, the president said, "Screw this. Put this bird down now. We're going to find my family."

The helicopter pilot looked around for someone who would counter the command, knowing full well he had just been given a direct order by the commander in chief.

Agent Nicols just nodded to the pilot, then turned to the president and said, "We are in the process of closing off all access to Sconset, Mr. President."

The CH-53E Super Stallion headed toward the Sconset water tower and landed on Milestone Road, the main entrance to Sconset.

Meanwhile, the MH-60R Seahawk carrying the Marine squad had taken off from the Coast Guard station in Sconset and had now landed at Sankaty Road just north of the village to effect a roadblock there.

Now both main roads in and out of Sconset were blocked by helicopters.

Nicols next called the Nantucket police. "Implement a Hold One," he said to the chief of police. A Hold One meant stopping all modes of transportation both on and off the island.

In a matter of minutes the island of Nantucket was on lockdown.

❖

Because of the Secret Service agents at Baxter Road and ex-Marine Munson, only three of the five members of Kiswa team were still alive. But Munson's ammo was running low. One of the two Secret Service agents remaining at the scene had a Sig Sauer P229 semiautomatic pistol, and the other an MP5 machine gun and his Sig.

Munson rolled onto his back and propped himself up against the lower patio retaining wall. He was near one of his patio tables with its umbrella closed. He reached up, ripped away the strap that held the umbrella, and wrapped it around his bleeding calf.

He then surveyed the house through the rear French doors for motion but didn't see anything. However, with two terrorists dead, he assumed there were likely others on the ground floor.

As he rested against the retaining wall, he heard the approach of a helicopter.

One of the Army Apache helos had departed from Low Beach Road at the direction of JTAC who had been informed by the Secret Service that there was a fire fight underway at the Baxter Road house.

Moments later the Apache emerged from below the bluff as it appeared directly behind the target house. Munson shielded his eyes and tried to look up as the Apache attack helicopter hovered, overlooking the rear of the Baxter Road house.

Munson waved to the gunner in the Apache to make himself known. He guessed the pilot and gunner didn't know what to make of the old man in a Tommy Bahama shirt holding an M4 and crouching behind the target house.

He signaled to the helo to orbit toward the north side of the house, which it did slowly. Munson could see the pilot was talking in an animated fashion to his gunner and on the radio.

"Control, this is Renegade 06. Do we have friendlies on-site at the target?" the Apache pilot was asking JTAC.

"That's affirm, Renegade. There are Secret Service agents on-site and at least one noncom. Copy," came back the reply.

Munson could tell the gunner on the Apache was just itching to unleash his weapons on the house, but this was a situation where a cool head and judgment needed to trump adrenaline.

Munson now saw some movement from inside the house. A figure was crawling along the kitchen floor. His long leaf pine floors, Munson thought.

The person was attempting to make his way to the family room in order to get a better shot at the helo, which was now hovering a short distance off the north end of the house.

"Control, do I have permission to fire?" called the Apache pilot. After conferring with the Secret Service the Joint Terminal Attack Coordinator (JTAC) replied. "Renegade 06 you are cleared hot. Copy."

The Apache pilot immediately replied, "Copy. Control."

In a sudden flash, the Apache gunship let loose with its 30mm canon. The Apache pilot had also detected movement in the house and let loose with the canon housed in its chin turret. Unable to withstand the rapid rate of fire, the whole side of the house disintegrated in seconds. The terrorist who was crawling across the floor was quickly transformed into a motionless pile of flesh and blood.

Just then another figure came running out of the back of the house onto the patio. Munson was in a perfect firing position. The Kiswa team member had turned to fire at the Apache attack helicopter when Munson trained his M4 and fired a burst, running a line of bullets up the terrorist's spine. He fell forward and lay lifeless on the patio.

As this was unfolding, Munson heard more gunfire coming from the front of the house. The remaining two Secret Service agents were engaged with whomever was left of the terrorist team.

The Apache also detected the firefight in the front of the house and orbited to get into a better firing position. The Apache pilot got on the radio. "Control, have the onsite Secret Service agents take cover. We are going to light up the target. Copy."

It took only a few seconds for the Secret Service agents to receive the message and fall back.

The Apache gunner toggled the cyclical control, similar to the stick on a jet, and switched from the 30mm gun to the Hellfire missiles. In a blaze of light, the Apache fired its laser-guided Hellfire missile at the house from close range.

Munson, who did not have the benefit of radio communications, was crouching against the sunken patio when the center section of his trophy home opened up in a huge explosion. He ducked to shield himself from the flying debris but ended up being cut over most of the exposed parts of his body.

He shook his head and wondered what his wife was going to say when he told her about this. As that thought left his mind, he used the M4 as a crutch and helped himself to his feet, staring at a thirty-foot gaping hole in the center of his house.

The Secret Service and Apache waited for about five minutes to ensure there was no more movement or infrared signatures coming from the Baxter Road house.

As Munson made his way to the front of the house, the Apache circled. With the threat now neutralized, the Apache headed back to the Low Beach Road house.

When Munson reached the street, the two surviving Secret Service agents came up to him. "Who are you?" they demanded.

"Munson, John A., Gunnery Sergeant, 2nd Marines."

The lead agent nodded and said, "Well done, Sergeant. Let's get you looked at."

The agent spoke into his headset: "The Baxter Road location is now secure. All nonfriendlies are neutralized. We are in need of an ambulance."

"Copy, ambulance on its way," came the reply from the Secret Service Communication Center at the Sconset Coast Guard station.

With the gunfire over and the Apache helicopter off station, the neighbors of the Baxter Road house started to slowly come outside to lend assistance.

Munson asked, "The president—is he okay?"

The female agent did not respond.

Munson tried again, this time asking, "Your injured agents—any status?"

"No, not yet," said the female agent as she holstered her Sig and added "Gunny, we need to secure the area." The agents started the somber task of securing the site, including the burned-out Suburban that held the remains of the two fallen Secret Service agents. They could hear the approaching sound of the ambulance siren in the distance.

❖

On the *Carter*, Captain Jackson decided it was better to get the SEALs on the island than have them remain on the sub. A few minutes later the SDV detached from the *Carter* and slowly made its way up onto the beach near where the Low Beach Road house stood.

As the SDV breached the waves, its nose came to rest in the dark brown sand. A Navy SEAL unstrapped from the SDV and surveyed the area for 360 degrees, then dropped back down into the SDV. A few seconds later he and the rest of SEAL Team 2, led by Lieutenant Commander Burduck, silently made their way to the Low Beach Road house.

Once at the house, they met with a Secret Service agent who briefed them on the situation. The president was on Milestone Road with Agent Nicols and his evacuation detail, along with the CH-53E Super Stallion crew.

The SEAL commander shook his head and said, "We need to get the president to a secure location. He needs to let us do our job."

❖

The Hijra and Amina teams regrouped at the Hedge Row house. They had all moved into the basement along with their three hostages.

The plan called for one of the Hijra terrorists to drive the Cape Finished Flooring van to the public parking area at Sconset Beach at the foot of Gully Road and park it there.

Before he left the van, he would set the timers on the bombs that would destroy the van and all associated forensic evidence. They were set to go off thirty minutes after they were activated. He would then walk back to the Shell Street house, where he would hide in the basement and wait for nightfall, when he would attempt to rejoin the team at the Hedge Row Road house, if the coast was clear.

The other Hijra terrorists would lay low in the basement of the Hedge Row house until after dark and then leave the island and rendezvous off Sconset Beach with three Zodiac inflatable boats. For now they needed to sit tight and not draw any attention.

❖

The two Alert 15 F/A-18s from the USS *Theodore Roosevelt* were now on station and orbiting over Sconset, as were four US Air Force F-15's from its Halo flight, which had also been scrambled from Otis Air National Guard Base on Cape Cod. The next orders went to the Alert 5 Hornet, "Alpha Papa, Hammer 11, hit the Alert 15 tanker for fuel," came the call from the Strike Warfare Commander watch stander call sign as Alpha Papa. Having received the order, the F/A-18 Super Hornet pilot broke over Sankaty Head Light and headed toward the tanker as ordered.

Admiral Jacobsen was on a satellite phone with the Pentagon from the Low Beach Road house while his squad leader met with the SEAL team to discuss their plans for a search and rescue (SAR) mission.

Everyone—the Secret Service, the SEALs, and the Marines—reasoned that FLOTUS and the children had to still be on the island, but no one knew where, and that was *the* problem.

Agent Nicols was briefing the president as they stood on Milestone Road at the entrance to Sconset. "Mr. President, we need to secure you. We have Secret Service agents, Marines, and SEALs all at the Low Beach Road house getting ready to conduct an SAR. Let us do our job. We need to get you to the bunker. We aren't doing much good standing around here."

Russell knew Nicols was right and a moment later nodded his agreement. An agent took the M4 from the president, and the CH-53E Super Stallion, now call sign Marine One, started to turn up its engines. The Super Stallion lifted for the short flight to the presidential bunker.

As the CH-53E Super Stallion climbed to five hundred feet, the Army Apaches Renegade 06 and 19 took up station on its wing. Above the Super Stallion, four Air Force F-15Cs orbited, providing top cover for Marine One as it proceeded on the short flight to the bunker.

The bunker crew was preparing for the president's arrival and setting up the briefing room. They knew the president would want to get in contact with the White House Situation Room, where the directors of the CIA, NSA, FBI, and Joint Chiefs, along with VP McMasters, were all assembling.

The president's head was spinning as he entered the bunker. He was trying to absorb everything that was happening. He turned to Spencer. "Sterl, my family, where are they?" he asked almost rhetorically.

"Mr. President, the Secret Service is conducting a search for them. We have locked down the island. No one can make it on or off the island without our knowledge. We will find them, sir."

It was the first time Spencer had ever seen the president rattled.

"I need to find them," flatly stated the president.

"Mr. President, let the Secret Service do their job, sir," responded Spencer in an even tone. He added, "They are trained for this."

The president pivoted. "How could this have happened? My family, Sterl. We need more resources on the island."

The president's thoughts were chaotic and jumping around. He didn't know if he should pray or panic or maybe both.

Spencer knew he needed to give the president some time to allow his intellect to catch up with his emotions. He knew they would be on with the Situation Room in a matter of minutes and he wanted the president composed—at least as much as the situation would allow.

As the Secret Service worked with the SEALs and Marines on the SAR plan, they realized they would need more manpower. They called their command and requested three platoons of Marines. Their SAR called for a pincer-type tightening-of-the-noose approach. They would deploy each Marine platoon at the outer edges of Sconset—on Sankaty Road and on Milestone Road—and allow them to work their way inward.

Meanwhile, the SEALs would work from the Sconset Coast Guard station out. A house-to-house search would be slow and dangerous, with many of the houses populated with families on vacation but with a fair amount of the houses vacant. Altogether the SAR plan represented a stark departure from the typical Saturday morning routine of life in Sconset.

Just then an explosion rocked the village. The Cape Finished Flooring van parked at the Sconset Beach parking area had exploded. A detachment from the Milestone Road Marine platoon was dispatched to investigate. It was clear that chaos was winning out this morning and the US government was not in control of the situation.

While the distraction from the explosion continued, the Hijra team worried and waited in the Hedge Row Road house. The time now was 8:35 a.m. and they weren't scheduled to leave the island until 10 p.m. That meant they had a long time to just sit and wait.

Chapter Nine

Saturday Midmorning

Up until now Sconset had been the center of attention. That was about to change.

In this day and age of social media and wireless technology, coupled with a free and open society, if you wanted to create chaos, it was easy to do and it could be accomplished at a cost of only a few thousand dollars. The island of Nantucket was about to experience Terrorism 2.0.

Al Qaeda expected that once the attack was under way, authorities would take down the wireless and landline networks. And while taking down the network would disrupt the terrorists' communications, it would also add to the public chaos, which was about to take hold in unprecedented proportions on the island.

Karim Hamady of the Hijra team and the overall leader of the attack sat in the basement of the Hedge Row house.

Karim called to one of the team members, "Check on the packages."

He was referring to the first lady and the children, who were in the basement, drugged and sleeping on folding cots.

One of the men asked him, "Karim, now that the mission is under way, can you share more of the plan with us?"

Karim's first reaction was to regard the man as insolent. But the questioner was one of his best men, and he knew if this one was asking, the rest of the team had the same question.

"My friends in arms, we are not the only ones on the island fighting for our cause. Our brothers and sisters will start the next phases of our mission soon."

Karim continued, "The Baxter Road attack on the president was always intended as a diversion. Our main objective was the kidnapping of FLOTUS and the children."

Karim spoke well. He had been educated in London and, like many others, had come from a well-to-do family before entering into jihad.

"We have others on the island who will help us escape. Our assignment now is to wait and take care of the packages. We will be successful as long as we stick to the plan," instructed Karim.

❖

Surfside is an area on the island just west of the airport. It was in Surfside that Oasis LLC had rented another house for a young Al Qaeda couple and their two-year-old child.

This couple, code name Umma team, was focused on creating chaos and was unarmed.

The Umma team was led by the father, an unassuming-looking but technically savvy man.

Aided by low-cost, powerful encrypted devices sold by Apple, namely the iPhone and iPad, Umma had arrived on the island a little less than two weeks ago with a technological arsenal.

In their car, in addition to the toys and other necessities for their two-year-old son, were eighty iPads.

For the last two days Umma had traveled around the island placing iPads in brown paper bags in nondescript locations.

They were put behind Dumpsters, in the corners of yards, and even behind headstones at the cemetery. With the help of Google Maps, the locations where the iPads were placed had been carefully designed, with the range of the iPads and the topography of the island in mind.

The network would use the iPad's Bluetooth module to communicate and form its own network. Then standard apps using Arabic would send a flurry of encrypted text messages via Snapchat and WhatsApp.

iPads, with their long battery life coupled with Apple's staunch reluctance to cooperate with US law enforcement regarding encryption, were the perfect device for this task.

The father, who had also received the text message from the Kiswa team that the operation was now under way, ordered his wife, "Activate the network."

At approximately 10 a.m. the wife entered the commands into her laptop, which was acting as a network hub.

As she typed, she spoke out loud. "I have a connection. I am sending the key now. Key accepted. Executing the script. The network is up. The iPads are being set to ping each other."

Umma had spent the last three years working with a group of Al Qaeda-funded programmers and network specialists to design and create the iPad network.

At 10:07 a.m. the iPads started broadcasting random text messages to one another.

The purpose of this network was to distract and confuse the US intelligence agencies, with the goal of hopefully delaying the SAR mission looking for the first family.

Whether it worked or not, the investment was small and the risk negligible.

❖

At the airport there was general confusion created by the ground stop and the fact that the landline and, more important, the wireless networks had been taken down. To add to the chaos, it was a Saturday, when most of the rental homes on ACK turned over.

Families were trying to find out the status of their flights. At this early stage, people were more confused and annoyed than concerned.

The little information they got was coming from CNN, which was doing a live remote from a house in Sconset. Their correspondent, a young reporter who was on the island to cover the president's vacation, was broadcasting via Skype over a satellite phone from her rented house. Due to police activity, she was broadcasting from indoors.

"I am in Sconset this morning and have witnessed a great deal of unusual military activity. The police are telling all of us to remain indoors. I have heard a lot of helicopters overhead as well as fighter jets that were very low and very loud. Clearly there is some sort of military operation under way, but for now that is all the information I have."

In Washington and New York the news bureaus were beginning to pick up coverage of the events on Nantucket. They were having their correspondents reach out to their sources at the White House and Pentagon, but because it was a Saturday morning in August, many of the news bureaus were lightly staffed and those on duty tended to be very junior people. From a media perspective, it was a perfect storm of confusion.

And that was true of the White House staff as well. Most of the senior staff were either on their own vacations or on ACK to support the president's visit. That left the White House with a skeleton crew to deal with the national press corps, which was eager for an update on the situation.

❖

Karim and his team in the Hedge Row house had just completed their midday prayers when Karim shared the next part of the plan.

"Brothers, I did not tell you everything before. We have another team on the island at a place called Madaket. Team Ruku is our drone team. They are going to fly drones over the island to create additional chaos among the population, which will assist us in our safe escape. We are getting much help from our brothers and sisters. Praise Allah."

The Ruku team had also arrived a week earlier. They came to the island via the ferry driving a Ford Explorer and a Volvo station wagon.

In the back of each vehicle were five small drones and two larger drones, plus an array of spare parts.

On the small drones, which were the size of footballs, they installed a single aerosol can that would emit a cloudy white gas. It was just a pesticide, but the white gas was visible and had a distinct odor.

The larger drones, with eight engines each, were fitted with eight aerosol cans inverted and pointing downward.

The Ruku team knew they couldn't launch the drones from their Massachusetts Avenue house because they would too easily be discovered.

Just like the iPad network, the smaller drones had been deployed the night before at preselected locations all over the island.

The iPad network, in addition to generating false messages, would provide communication and flight commands to the drones.

Now a small fleet of drones was ready to take to the air. The ten smaller drones were preprogrammed to fly automatically, having been loaded with a set of GPS coordinates.

The four larger drones would be launched and manually operated by the Ruku operators from the Madaket home.

Those four drones, each about the size of a large suitcase, had also been deployed the night before. Each was placed in the back of a pickup truck covered by a lightweight tarp. At noon, two of the members of the Ruku team, both on bikes, rode by the four pickups and pulled off the tarps. Within minutes after being uncovered, the drones took to the air.

Karim updated his team in the Hedge Row house. "Within the hour, fourteen drones will fly over the island, spraying the inhabitants in town, at the airport, and at the hospital. The panic they will create will keep the Americans from finding us."

When the drones took off, they flew low, at about fifty feet. Eight flew into town, with four stationed over Main Street more or less in a line.

One of the larger drones hovered right over the Hub, the legendary newspaper store, located in the center of town. In spite of what was going on in Sconset, town was busy, which was typical for a summer Saturday. It took only a few minutes for people to notice the hovering drones.

Two drones—one small and one large—were sent to the Cottage Hospital, and another small one was sent to the Stop & Shop at the center of the island.

That left three large drones. One went to the high school, one to Surfside Beach, and one to the airport terminal.

At 11:23 a.m. the drones started to randomly spray short bursts from their attached aerosol cans. At first people thought maybe these were either government or news drones to supply video feeds, but as they started to emit the gas, panic set in.

It was made worse because the operators of the large drones could reposition the drones for maximum effect using the onboard cameras. The Ruku team could actually position the drones to stalk people as they moved down the street.

As people saw the drones and the vapor coming from them, at first they were just confused, but their confusion quickly turned to fear.

On Surfside Beach, one of the island's most popular beaches, people started to gather their things and make their way to the parking lot.

The drone operators had the drones tack back and forth from the beach to the parking lot, emitting random bursts over the panicked beachgoers. People yelled and got into their cars and rolled up windows. Those left outside started to pound on car windows to be let in. It was instant pandemonium.

In town, everyone quickly went indoors. In a matter of minutes the sidewalks of town were empty.

While this was unfolding, a heated debate had broken out between Nantucket Chief of Police Phil White and the Secret Service. Chief White, concerned about public safety, wanted to reestablish phone service to broadcast a reverse 911 message to disseminate information to the public about the drones. The Secret Service was adamant that there be no communications at all.

On a good day the chief was an ornery fellow. But now, with his town under attack and being overruled by the Secret Service, he was apoplectic.

"Damn it," yelled White, and he terminated the conversation with the Secret Service via the police radio.

"Matt, grab the M4s with the scopes," he called.

White was talking to Sergeant Matt Tracey, who was the closest thing the Nantucket PD had to a SWAT team and the best shot in the department.

"What do you have in mind, Chief?" asked Sergeant Tracey.

"We are going to shoot down these goddamn things," barked the chief.

"What does the Secret Service have to say about that?" asked Tracey somewhat cautiously.

"Screw the Secret Service. They have their hands full," replied Chief White, with an M4 in hand as he headed for the door of the Nantucket police headquarters.

Chief White and Sergeant Tracey, both armed with M4s with red-dot scopes, ventured out onto Main Street.

As the football-size drones hovered overhead, Tracey centered one in the sights of his M4 and squeezed the trigger.

It wasn't hard because the drones were just hovering.

When one of the drones crashed nearby, the chief kicked the aerosol can with his boot. The can itself was painted white, but on the bottom the chief noticed a price sticker from Walmart.

"Sons of bitches," yelled Chief White. With that, he got on the police radio and told his police force to start shooting down all the drones.

It took a little more than an hour to locate and immobilize all the drones. By 1:30 p.m. all the drones were down.

That said, the power of suggestion can be very convincing. People who believed they were sprayed with a poison started to exhibit respiratory problems.

Some were having panic attacks, shortness of breath, fainting spells, or even heart attacks. Even the steadiest of people were experiencing elevated heart rates and increased blood pressure.

The Ruku and Umma teams had accomplished their goals. By two o'clock the police and military were struggling to maintain order over the island and its inhabitants.

Once the iPad network was up and operating, the Umma team's job was done. They left their Surfside rental house and drove into town. There they took the water taxi, which was still running as its job was to shuttle people from town to their moored boats, to a blue Hinckley picnic boat named *Doing Well II* that was docked in the harbor.

They would stay on the boat until they could leave Nantucket. Their plan was to motor the boat to Martha's Vineyard, where they would eventually make their way back to Saudi Arabia via JFK, Paris, and Turkey.

❖

The president was in the bunker conference room, where he was convening a call with the Situation Room in Washington. In the Sit Room was the head of the NSA, the directors of the Secret Service, CIA, FBI, and Joint Chiefs, and the vice president.

The president began in a low, slow voice. "Gentlemen, how could they get in my home? *In my bedroom! Where my wife sleeps, where our children play.*" There was silence.

The president next asked, "And what is going on with these drones? Were they emitting a poison? Do we have an anthrax attack on our hands?"

The president's chief of staff, Sterling Spencer, who had talked to each of the intelligence heads before the call, began with a summary for the president, "Mr. President, here is what we know. At approximately 6:35 a.m. you and your Secret Service detail were attacked while you were on your morning run. We believe the attackers were Middle Eastern terrorists. In the subsequent firefight the terrorists were all killed. However, we believe your attack was a cover so that another team could kidnap your wife and children. Then at approximately 8:30 a.m. a van exploded in Sconset near the beach parking lot. We are not sure what the purpose of that was other than to cause a distraction. That was followed about ninety minutes later by the launch of an electronic network that is emanating from the island and sending numerous messages in Arabic. Then at about 11 a.m. a series of drones started to fly over the island emitting an unidentifiable gas."

The director of the NSA, George Riordan, added, "Mr. President, none of the sensors we have installed on the island have gone off. It doesn't appear the drones are spraying anything radioactive or biological."

Next, Lisa Collins, the director of the CIA, spoke. "With regard to communications, yes, we are picking up a lot of traffic that is being generated by some sort of network that has been installed on the island. It is using Bluetooth technology. But beyond that, right now we don't know much else. Our teams are working on deciphering the messages they have overheard."

The president asked, "What is our defense condition and what is the plan to find and rescue my family?"

That was the cue for John Standard, the chairman of the Joint Chiefs, to join the discussion. "Mr. President, we have raised our DEFCON from 5 to 4. We have a platoon of Marines and a Navy SEAL team on the island. As you know, offshore we have CARGRU-12 along with the submarines *Jimmy Carter* and *North Dakota*. Our teams are working on a SAR plan, and we are in the process of getting some Predator drones to the island to help with our surveillance. The drones will arrive within the hour."

"What about the citizens of the island? What is their status?" asked the president.

Dan Nicols replied, "Not good, Mr. President. We are seeing pockets of panic break out as a result of the drone attacks. The local police department is overwhelmed. The Mass. State Police are sending troopers to the island to regain control."

The president understood it was a fluid situation, and he didn't want to add to the confusion.

"Look, there is a lot going on all at once. Mobilize whatever resources we need. Gain control of the island. And keep an eye out for attacks in other locations. Raise the DEFCON to 3. Dan, I want to meet with the Marine and SEAL team commanders to understand the plan to locate and rescue my family."

With that the president cut the line to the Sit Room and went to get an update from the Secret Service on how the search for his wife and children was progressing.

❖

The police were securing the site where two of the larger drones had crashed. As a precaution they were treating the larger drone crash sites as hazmat areas. The modest Nantucket Police and Fire Departments really weren't equipped to handle a potential poisonous gas situation. As a result, things were moving slowly and the problems were overwhelming their resources.

Police Chief Phil White was giving an update to Dan Nicols.

"I have dispatched fire trucks and three police cars to keep order at the Cottage Hospital. People are walking around with makeshift masks over their faces. They have scarfs around their faces like it was January," said Police Chief White.

Even the cable news reporters were broadcasting either from indoors or outside with these ridiculous masks over their faces.

Chief White had contacted all news networks to get the word out that the drones were not harmful and were just spraying an insecticide.

The networks did a good job of putting that information out on a constant crawl on their stations, but people were still concerned and not everyone believed the news.

At 2:02 p.m., the next element of the operation commenced as more explosions were heard going off in Sconset. The Hijra, Kiswa, and Amina teams had planted bombs in all the homes they had rented in Sconset.

In Sconset, two of the staging houses exploded within a short time of each another. Their wooden construction and age caused the fires to spread quickly. Some Sconset residents who had taken refuge in their homes based on police PA announcements now had no choice but to leave.

The Nantucket Fire Department, which has been staffed by full-time firefighters in town, had recently replaced the Sconset volunteer fire fighters with full-time employees. That decision, a controversial change, meant the Sconset fire station on Sankaty Avenue was now staffed with full-time fire fighters in place of the group of dedicated, but aging, volunteers.

Now, with multiple fires raging in Sconset, the recently replaced volunteers of the Sconset fire station didn't hesitate to join in with the full-time firefighters.

The Marines, Coast Guard, and Secret Service personnel on the island didn't have a lot of firefighting equipment. But the well-trained damage-control teams on the USS *Theodore Roosevelt* and its accompanying ships had a lot of firefighting experience, and the equipment to go with it.

Admiral Jacobsen, who was still on the island coordinating the US Navy's response with the president's chief of staff and the Secret Service, acted as soon as he received the news about the fires.

He immediately called the USS *Theodore Roosevelt*. "Captain, we are dealing with multiple fires in Sconset. I want you to start sending equipment and teams to Sconset to assist in the firefighting."

"Copy, Admiral," came the response from Captain Fraser.

The Broadway house fire spread quickly to the nearby homes, some of which were thought to be over three hundred years old. Soon an entire row of houses on Front Street and Broadway were ablaze.

Another challenge was water. The Sconset water tower wasn't designed to handle multiple fires.

Of course, all this was just cover for Hijra to get FLOTUS and her children off the island.

However, the Secret Service, FBI, CIA, and NSA had figured this out. The general pandemonium that had gripped the island was a decoy that made executing the SAR much harder—and they knew it.

❖

Vacationing on the island was the NYPD Chief of Detectives Chris Tate. Tate had just taken a call on his satellite phone from one of his deputy chiefs in NYPD's operations center in Manhattan. Chiefs from NYPD never go anywhere without keeping the NYPD operations center aware of their

whereabouts also are required to carry their badges, service re-
volvers and sat phones with them at all times. The operations
center duty officer told Tate about the Code Red on Nantucket
and that something was going down with the president and
the Secret Service.

There was no doubt Tate was the most senior investigative
expert on the island. Chris looked at his wife, Linda, and said,
"I've got to see if I can help."

She understood and nodded, feeling that familiar mix of
emotions all police spouses feel when duty calls. Not only
did Chief Tate never travel without his sat phone, badge or
his gun—but he also carried with him his police sixth sense,
which had served him as he rose to an NYPD senior-grade detective and beyond.

As he left their house in Madaket, unbeknownst to him not
far from where the Ruku team was staying on Massachusetts
Avenue, he got into his SUV and headed to Sconset. Along the
way he encountered three police roadblocks. Perhaps a better
way to put it was that the three police roadblocks encountered
him. He carried himself as you would expect any thirty-two-
year veteran of the NYPD would.

With some convincing, Tate made it to the Secret Service
Command Center. The on-duty shift leader at the center called
Nicols at the presidential bunker and explained to him that
the NYPD Chief of Detectives was at the center and offering
his assistance.

Normally this sort of offer would be summarily dismissed,
but Chris Tate was not just some beat cop.

Soon enough Chris Tate was meeting with Dan Nicols and
Sterling Spencer.

What the NYPD Chief of Detectives brought to the investigation was the perspective of a street-savvy detective, and
Nicols knew they could benefit from those insights.

Before Tate had assumed the Chief of Detectives assignment, he was considered one of the NYPD's best detectives. Nicols and Spencer accepted Tate's offer.

A few minutes later Spencer was updating the president. The president told him to convene a meeting with Nicols and the SEAL team commander.

"Will do, Mr. President. Also the NYPD Chief of Detectives has offered to help us. He was vacationing on the island and I think he can be of value to us."

Without pausing, the president added, "Sterl, I want to meet him. If he can help, all the better." Having been a congressman from Brooklyn, Russell held the NYPD in high regard. Although he had not met Tate, he was aware of the talent and experience that someone with Tate's title of Chief of Detectives could lend to the task of finding his family.

Within minutes the president had been introduced to Chris Tate and had immediately accepted Tate's offer to help.

"Gentlemen," said the president, "it has been almost six hours since my family went missing, and I am seeing little progress in finding them. I will remind you, we are on an island that is only fifty miles square." The tension in the room was palpable.

"First, do we think they are still on Nantucket?"

Dan Nicols spoke first. "Yes, sir, we don't believe they had time and/or the ability to leave the island. All flights were canceled within minutes of the abduction."

"Okay, if we think they are on the island, do we have a clue as to where they might be? Have we tried locating them via their SPIDs?"

"Yes, Mr. President, we activated the SPIDs immediately after they were abducted. But we haven't picked up anything."

The president asked, "And why is that, Dan?"

"There are three possibilities, sir. One, they are off the island and out of range, which we think is unlikely. Two, they had the SPIDs removed and destroyed, or three, they are still on the island but in a location where the SPID signal is not able to be picked up due to shielding of some sort."

The president sat in contemplation for a minute. "Dan, I agree with your premise that they are still on the island. Detective," said the president, turning to Tate, "You probably have the most experience in the room on a kidnapping—what is your advice?"

Tate wasn't put off that the president had referred to him as "detective" rather than what he was used to being called–"Chief."

"Mr. President, we need a plan. First, what are the priority locations to search and why? Second, we need to start to surveil these locations passively while SWAT, I mean the SEALs, come up with a plan to enter each location. Third, we can't just assume your family is still on the island; we need to consider they may have left. What were the last flights off the island, both private and commercial, and when—"

Nicols interrupted. "We have already done that and only one commercial flight left within twenty minutes of the kidnapping. We have detained the passengers and crew from that flight and are interrogating them now. There are no apparent links from that flight to the kidnapping. No ferries left around the time of the kidnapping either. Obviously we don't know for certain if a private boat departed from the island, but we think it's unlikely given how quickly we put out the Hold One.

"Keep in mind your wife and children were in Sconset, and it is very hard for a boat to come ashore here without being detected. And if they did, the SPIDs would have transmitted. They have a range of about five miles."

Admiral Jacobsen had joined the group a few minutes into the briefing.

"Brian, what can the Navy tell us about boats departing the island around the time of the kidnapping?"

"Mr. President, soon after I arrived on the island I detached the Virginia-class sub that travels with CARGRU-12, the *North Dakota*, and deployed them to the mouth of Nantucket Harbor. Off Sconset we have the *Carter*, which delivered the SEAL team. The *Carter* is still patrolling off Sconset as we speak.

"Mr. President, our subs are monitoring every surface contact, but there are a lot of boats on the sound on a Saturday in August. Can we say with certainty that a boat did not slip by us? No, but I think it's extremely unlikely the kidnappers left the island by boat, sir. We also have a CAP of F/A-18s up along with an E-2 for communications to prosecute any surface or subsurface contact we think is questionable."

"I understand," said the president, "but can we tell if any of those boats have docked near the island since the abduction?"

"Yes, sir, but there is a lot of coast to cover and some of these boats are very small."

"Brian, coordinate with the Coast Guard. I want every boat in a one-hundred-mile radius of Nantucket stopped, boarded, and searched."

"Aye, aye," said Jacobsen, and with that he knew enough to leave and implement the order immediately.

The president turned to Chris Tate. "Detective Tate, do you have anything further to add?"

Tate replied, "Nothing more at this point, sir."

Dan Nicols said, "Mr. President, we are also isolating our investigations. We have a team that is one hundred percent focused on finding your family. We also have other teams working the investigations at the Baxter Road and Low Beach Road locations. In addition, we are bringing in Mass. state troopers to restore order on the island."

Lieutenant Commander Burduck spoke. "Mr. President, we are going to start with a house-to-house SAR beginning in Sconset. The Marines have Sconset locked down. My team will conduct the searches. Before we start I want to get a few Predator drones up so we can surveil the area. They will be essential once it's dark. When the drones are on station we can begin the SAR."

The president immediately asked, "When will that be, Commander?"

"Within the hour, sir."

The president paused and started to look at a map of the island that was hanging on the conference room wall. "Declare an island-wide curfew starting at 8 p.m. until further notice. The only people allowed on the streets are police and military. All others must stay indoors. Commander, I want you to work with Detective Tate on the house-to-house search plan."

With that, the meeting came to an end as the president was receiving a call from the VP, Jack McMasters.

Outside the conference room, Chris Tate motioned to Dan Nicols and asked him about the SPIDs.

"What would be needed to block a SPID signal?" he asked.

"I'm not an expert on the technology, but I think some sort of thick chamber, like several feet of concrete."

Tate asked, "Would the barrier be metal or lead?"

Nicols replied, "Concrete probably. We aren't talking about kryptonite here. It is a radio transmission and either an electronic jammer tuned in to the signal, which would be difficult to do with the encryption keys on the SPIDs shifted randomly, or a thick concrete wall would be my best guess."

Tate replied curtly, "Agent I don't want to be guessing where the president's family is concerned. Who can I speak with who can give me an accurate answer?"

Nicols called Washington to get an answer for Tate using the Secret Service's secure communications channel, which wasn't disrupted by the taking down of the public networks. Within minutes Chris Tate was on the phone with the Secret Service's most knowledgeable expert on SPIDs.

After a short conversation, Tate had gathered all he could from the Secret Service resource on SPIDs. Tate's next stop was to talk with Sterling Spencer. Tate explained that he was not satisfied and that he needed access to the best data analysts the NSA had. Spencer, too, was put out by the NYPD chief's direct style. Normally Spencer wouldn't have even responded to him, but today was different, and as a result he worked to get Tate the SPID tech contact.

Within a few minutes the phone rang in Kristin McMahon's office at the NSA.

"Ms. McMahon, I am the NYPD Chief of Detectives. I am on Nantucket and working with the president, his chief of staff, and the SEALs on finding the president's family," opened Tate.

While listening, McMahon jotted down Tate's name on a piece of paper and waved Linda Hickman, her administrative assistant, into her office. She put her phone on mute and said, "Linda, check out a Chris Tate from NYPD—pronto."

Tate then went on, "Ms. McMahon, I need access to the NSA's best tech on SPIDs and I need to speak to them right now."

Kristin McMahon replied, "Chief Tate, we will get back to you shortly."

"Perhaps you didn't understand me," Tate said dryly. "I said I needed them right *now*—meaning you don't get back to me in a few minutes. You call them into your office immediately or transfer me into the conference room, where I expect them to be assembling as we speak. Are we clear?"

McMahon's first reaction was to step on this Tate person hard, but like Nicols and Spencer, given the situation, she thought better of it and instead said, "Please hold." McMahon then called Mannix in Crisis Room 1 and had Tate's call transferred into the war room. A minute later McMahon pushed the speaker button on the Polycom and said, "Chief Tate, I have Kevin Mannix, our lead data analyst, and his team here. Please go ahead."

Chapter Ten

Saturday Afternoon
to Early Evening

Sterling Spencer was talking with Colonel Tim McKeon of the Massachusetts State Police to get more troopers on the island. McKeon was marshaling thirty troopers from each of his seven barracks to form the force.

That would result in getting over two hundred Massachusetts state troopers to the island within the next few hours.

Nantucket High School would be commandeered by the state troopers to house the force.

Much to the dismay of its executive director, the Nantucket Whaling Museum at 13 Broad Street was also to be taken over by the state police as their command and control center.

Once on the island, the troopers would move the exhibit and replace it with stacks of supplies, including weapons and ammunition as well as satellite phones and Motorola radio sets. The whaling museum's location was ideal, as it was only a block away from the Nantucket police headquarters.

Troopers would be dispatched to locations all over the island, including fifty troopers in town, fifteen in Madaket, fifteen in Surfside, forty in Sconset, fifteen at the Cottage Hospital, and thirty or more at the airport. Fifteen would man the command and control center and twenty more would be sent to the high school.

Admiral Jacobsen's decision for the Navy to help fight the fires in Sconset was paying off. The fires that consumed the Broadway cottages and others in Codfish Park were now under control. The Broadway fire was the most difficult to suppress, having spread to the surrounding houses.

The Secret Service was also making progress restaffing their decimated teams. With four agents dead and four seriously wounded, there was a need to replace them and also send additional teams to augment the investigation of each terrorist site.

The two vehicles abandoned on Sconset Beach by the Hijra team, the Land Rover and Ford Explorer, were also being secured by the Secret Service. Each vehicle had a stolen license plate, but the VIN numbers allowed for a quick search of the Massachusetts Registry of Motor Vehicles databases for the original owners. These people had been identified, but with the communication networks down it was proving difficult to contact them and verify what had happened to their vehicles.

In Madaket, in the house next door to where the Ruku team was staying, was Ed and Joy Maffei. Ed had run track while attending the University of Colorado Boulder and was still fit and regularly ran sub-seven-minute miles, even though now he was a New York City investment banker.

He and his wife, Joy, had bought the house in Madaket a few years back after a big deal Ed was working on closed and he came into some serious money.

Now they were spending their two-week vacation at their house on the island and enjoying some peace and relaxation away from their frantic New York life. Ed was a conscientious homeowner who always checked out the other houses on his block when he and Joy returned to the island. That was how he knew the house next door was owned by the Soules, who now spent most of their time in Florida and rented their Nantucket home during the summer season.

Ed still liked to run, and he regularly got up early enough that most mornings the neighborhood was still quiet when he returned from his run. He would walk up and down the street as he cooled down. It was during one of these walks a few days after they arrived on the island that he noticed the renters at the Soules' house next door.

To Maffei they were just a group of young guys with darker complexions. He really didn't think too much about it, but he did wonder why a group of young guys picked Madaket instead of the Jersey Shore or the Hamptons. But he quickly forgot about them and went inside for a quick shower and then a leisurely breakfast with Joy.

But now that all hell had broken loose on the island, Maffei was a little more curious about the young renters next door. It was almost 5 p.m. on Saturday when his interest finally got the better of him and he said to his wife, "Joy, I am going to go next door and ask how they're doing."

Joy looked surprised. "What do you mean?"

"Exactly that. I am going to go over there as a neighborly gesture and ask if they are doing all right with everything going on."

Joy said, "I'm not sure that's a good idea," as the front door swung shut.

The Ruku team members were sitting at the dining room table working on their laptops when they heard a knock on the door. One of them instinctively picked up a Glock, but another shook his head.

The oldest of the group went to the front door and peered out through one of the front windows. He saw the man standing there, and, realizing he wasn't police, cracked open the door.

Ed said, "Hi. We live next door and I just wanted to check and see if you need anything given what has been going on today."

The leader responded flatly, saying, "We don't need anything."

Ed pressed further and said, "Okay. By the way, where are you guys from?" As he spoke, he came closer.

The leader said again, "Everything is fine—no problems."

Ed looked him up and down and could tell he was nervous and wanted to end the conversation. But Ed kept at it and said one more time, "Well, if you need anything, let me know." He began to move away but then turned around and put his hand on the door and, pressing it a little harder so that it opened halfway, said, "If you need a ride into town or something, let me know." His eyes surveyed the room, noting three men at the table in front of laptops and electronic parts that looked like the pieces his nephew used in the drones he flew.

Ed had seen enough and quickly started backing away from the door. But it was too late. That's when the first shot rang out. It came right through the door, barely missing him.

He turned and ran as the members of the Ruku team came out the door in pursuit, firing randomly. Ed had the advantage. From running the neighborhood over the years, Ed knew the area well.

As the Ruku team members spread out to look for him. Ed knew he had to get Joy to safety, so he doubled back to his house, going through backyards and staying off the street.

He got to the backyard of his house, surveyed the area, and quietly slipped into the house. Joy was anxiously waiting at the door having heard the gunshots.

Motioning her to be silent, he called her over and said quietly, "We gotta go right now." A look of terror came over her face as the next shot rang out.

Ed yelled, "Follow me," and they both ran out the back door as more bullets flew. They moved through backyards, ducking as they ran. They could hear men's voices, but they weren't speaking English.

Just as Maffei was wondering where they should hide, a car pulled up, and out jumped two Massachusetts state troopers. They were part of the augmented team of troopers that had just arrived on the island. The troopers were stationed in Madaket and had heard the shots.

Exiting the vehicle, the trooper pressed the transmit button on his radio, reporting, "Shots fired, shots fired in Madaket near the beach." The next bullet struck him in his neck.

His partner immediately dove behind the car and put out the radio call, "Trooper down, 10-13, trooper down. We are in Madaket on"—he looked around and saw the street sign—"on Massachusetts Avenue."

Next he crawled from behind the car and grabbed his partner, who was wearing a bulletproof vest, and pulled him behind the vehicle to relative safety. The trooper was conscious but bleeding badly.

Joy and Ed were hiding behind a nearby house and could hear additional cars pulling up. State troopers started to sweep the street, coming east from New Jersey Avenue, and that's when the troopers drew their first blood.

A dark-skinned figure emerged from behind shrubs, and a warning shot was fired. The young man froze for a second and then started to run again—it was a mistake. Eleven shots in total dropped him. The state police captain, who had just arrived on the scene, got on his radio. "Do not shoot to kill. Do not shoot to kill. We need to capture the suspects if possible. Copy."

The captain repeated his order, knowing full well that his men would find it difficult to follow his command. "Repeat, we need to capture the suspects alive. *Do not shoot to kill.* Acknowledge. Acknowledge."

The radios started to crackle with troopers responding to the captain's order, as they had been trained.

The next figure jumped from behind a shed, and shots again rang out. Another member of the Ruku team was down. He was wounded but not dead. Next a Ruku team member just gave up and lay down prostrate on the street.

Crouched behind a hedge, Ed and Joy heard the shots and yelling from the troopers. They decided to move away from the gunfire and hide in the tall grass near the waterline. As Ed and Joy started to move, Ed ran smack into the remaining Ruku team member—it was the person he had faced at the front door.

Immediately they grabbed each other and started to fight, with the Ruku member trying to raise his Glock to fire. Ed was bigger and stronger than the terrorist, but he wasn't a fighter. His adrenaline-powered first punches missed.

The terrorist responded with a kick toward Ed's groin that hit more of his thigh than anything else. Ed's next punch didn't miss—he caught the team leader square in the jaw, almost knocking him down. The Ruku team member, now with a broken jaw, staggered backward, which had the effect of creating some room between them.

As the terrorist aimed his pistol at Maffei, a two-by-four came crashing down, hitting the terrorist's forearm. Joy had picked it up and swung it as hard as she could. The terrorist dropped the pistol and fell to the ground, with Ed jumping on him. Ed was still throwing punches when two state troopers rushed over with guns drawn.

One of the troopers grabbed Ed and pushed him aside as the other trooper started to administer his own blows to ensure that the terrorist was incapacitated. It was then the trooper remembered the order: "Don't kill him . . ."

Ed got to his feet, still pumped up on adrenaline. Embracing his wife, he said, "There are four in all," referring to the number of terrorists.

The state trooper nodded and spoke into his radio, "The neighbor is telling us there were four perps in the house, copy."

If that number was correct, then all four were now accounted for, but the lead state trooper told his men to press the three captured terrorists to confirm there were only four.

❖

Dan Nicols entered the president's conference room in the bunker. "Mr. President, we've had a development." He relayed how the state troopers had just captured three terrorists in Madaket.

The president replied to Nicols, "You do whatever you have to to find out what they know about my family. Do you understand, Dan? Whatever it takes."

"Understood, Mr. President," came the sharp response.

❖

Vice President McMasters entered the Sit Room, where the heads of the Secret Service, FBI, CIA, NSA, and Joint Chiefs were assembled.

Once seated, McMasters began to address the group. "I spoke with the president and he wants us to assemble a list of targets who we believe are involved in this attack, even if they are only remotely involved. And we are going to hit them— and hit them hard.

"You have three hours to put this list together." The men stood as he left.

McMasters was right—this unconscionable act would need to be avenged.

McMasters wasn't trying to come off as a tough guy. The truth was, he *was* a tough guy. He was raised in Florida and played college football in the SEC at Ole Miss as a wide receiver. He stood at six-four and weighed at least 230 pounds.When he walked into a room he commanded the space, not just because of his physical presence but also because of his demeanor.

There was some discussion when they were forming the ticket whether or not McMasters would cast too large a shadow over Russell, both figuratively and literally—but Russell was a Navy fighter pilot. He could, did, and would hold his own in any room, oval or otherwise.

❖

Kelly Callahan, a correspondent for NBC, was doing a remote from the island. It was a little before 8 p.m., just before curfew was to begin. There was a strong and visible police presence with the fifty Massachusetts state troopers now stationed at various street corners in town.

As Callahan and her crew were wrapping up their remote, they heard the sound of jet engines. She stopped her report and looked up as the noise increased and saw the jets of Carrier Air Wing One of the USS *Theodore Roosevelt* as they started their first pass overhead.

As the people of Nantucket had come to expect whenever the president was on the island, the US Navy would perform a flyover. This evening would be no different, with the exception that tonight more of the air wing was up.

Tonight's flyover was led by a four ship division flown by VFA-*11 Red Rippers*, followed by another four ship division of the VFA-136 *Knighthawks* in single-seat F/A-18Es.

In total eight F/A-18s flew low and loud in a racetrack pattern around the island for more than thirty minutes at an altitude of five thousand feet. It was Admiral Jacobsen's way of reassuring the people of Nantucket that the US Navy had the watch tonight.

Chapter Eleven

Saturday Evening

Chris Tate had been on a conference call with Kevin Mannix and his team for the better part of two hours. Tate had told them he wanted a list of every building permit issued on Nantucket for the last three years, since President Russell had started vacationing on the island.

They were checking for new pool construction, new building foundations, major renovations and expansions of existing homes—anything that required a lot of concrete. Against that list—the building permit list—they cross-checked purchases of concrete from any of the three main providers on the island—James Rallis Concrete, Walter Blatz & Sons Inc., and Neches Sand & Cement Inc.

With the phones still down, the Secret Service had to literally go to the homes of the owners of these three companies and get the billing data to Mannix and his team.

After about forty-five minutes of work, Crisis Team 1 had produced a map of Nantucket highlighting where any significant amount of concrete had been delivered over the last three years.

Tate took the map and knocked on the door of the president's conference room. He suggested they get Spencer, Nicols, and

Burduck too. Once assembled, with McMahon and Mannix on the conference bridge, Tate explained his thinking and what led to the creation of the map they were all looking at.

"Mr. President, if the SPID signals are not working, it could be because FLOTUS and the children are being hidden in an underground bunker. That would require a lot of concrete, and this map is our target list of properties to check."

Lieutenant Commander Burduck, the SEAL team leader, looked at the list and started to make notes.

Tate continued, "There were thirty-seven identified properties in all. Twenty-one had pools installed over the last three years; the other sixteen had either new foundations, or were new builds or add-ons to existing homes—all required a lot of concrete. Six of the targeted properties were in Sconset, eleven in Eel Point, five in Tetawkimmo, two in Quidnet, three in Squam, two in Madaket, two in Monomoy, two in town, and four in Tom Nevers."

The president listened intently and then turned to Nicols and Burduck. "What do you think?"

They agreed they needed to check each of these properties as a priority.

Burduck said, "Mr. President, my team and I will take the six Sconset homes and the four in Tom Nevers while the Marines start on the other houses."

It was clear the SEAL commander thought the Sconset and Tom Nevers homes were the top priorities.

Nicols agreed but added, "The Secret Service could make some additional technology available to aid in the surveillance."

He was referring to the top secret Alpha2 sensor packs that were being added to the Predator drones that were now on the island.

The president agreed, adding, "Get them ready to deploy."

He then asked Nicols, "What are we learning from the captured terrorists from Madaket?"

"We discovered the Al Qaeda drones weren't carrying anything harmful. In addition, they completely gave up the info on the iPad network—it was just a decoy.

"They don't know anything about the kidnapping, Mr. President."

Nicols went on to tell the president it was not unusual for terror cells to be operationally isolated from one another.

The president just looked at Nicols and said, "Keep interrogating them. I want to know everything they know, Dan—everything."

"We will, Mr. President." With that Nicols left with the SEAL commander and Spencer to debrief.

Lieutenant Commander Burduck had his SEAL team together and was explaining the SAR operation and the targets on the Concrete List, as it was now being called. They called over to the Nantucket Airport, where the SEAL Special Operations Unit had just arrived in their own C-130 and asked how long before they could deploy their Predator drones with the Alpha2 electronics package.

Burduck asked Nicols and Spencer, "Do you think the Predators might create more panic among the public?" The SEALs wanted to have the surveillance data that the Alpha2 package could provide for their Concrete List mission, but Burduck felt he had to first ask the question.

Spencer replied, "No, we will fly them high enough that no one will hear them. Commander, deploy the Predators as soon as they are ready."

❖

Less than a mile from the Low Beach Road house, the Hijra team was in a bunker under the house on Hedge Row Road. They had kept FLOTUS and the children drugged all day, placing intravenous feeds in them to avoid dehydration and to provide some nourishment.

The Hijra team looked at their watches and started to stir. The next phase of their operation would begin soon.

The lone member of the Hijra team still in the Shell Street house was getting ready to move to the Hedge Row house. As he had with the van earlier in the day, he set timers on the bombs that they had installed in the Shell Street house. He then left the location and carefully made his way toward the Hedge Row Road house to reunite with the rest of the Hijra team.

As the Hijra team member approached Morey Lane, he heard the explosion of the Shell Street house. Sconset now had to deal with another fire and more chaos.

❖

At the same time, President Russell was on the phone with VP Jack McMasters. "Jack what do you think about invoking the Twenty-Fifth Amendment?"

The president was referring to the amendment to the Constitution that allowed for the vice president to become the acting president if the president died, resigned, was removed from office, or was otherwise unable to discharge the powers of the presidency.

McMasters responded, "Mr. President, I can do everything you need me to do as VP."

"I realize that, Jack," said the president. "But we don't yet know where this is going, and I'm not certain I can be counted on to put all my attention on the nation with my family missing."

He continued, "Talk to the chief justice and cabinet and put the wheels in motion but hold short of implementing the Twenty-Fifth. Then let's revisit the issue in the next few hours," he instructed the VP.

"Mr. President, I will speak to the chief justice, but I feel confident we can handle the situation together. Invoking the Twenty-Fifth would add to the confusion and would give the terrorists a very public victory," said VP McMasters with as much conviction as the president had ever heard from him.

Russell responded, "I understand, Jack. Speak to the CJ and we will revisit later."

❖

At the Hedge Row house, the Hijra team was emerging from the bunker. They went outside at dusk and pulled two ATVs from the shed. They then attached two iPhones to each ATV with Velcro.

While the Secret Service may have thought the SPIDs were top secret, the Hijra team knew about them. It would be another lesson for the US intelligence organizations that secrecy of top secret technology was critical. It was also a reminder of just how much damage Edward Snowden had caused the nation when he leaked thousands of pages of top secret documents to WikiLeaks.

The Islamic Front, which had hired some of the best techs in the Middle East, had correctly assumed that there had to be some sort of location transmitter inserted in the bodies of the first family. As a result, they had four iPhones that would emit an electronic signal, or noise, across various megahertz bands in order to mask any signal emitted from the SPIDs. Effectively the iPhones would work as jammers.

The Hijra team members brought out a rolled carpet from the home and strapped it from front to back to one of the ATVs.

With two members of Hijra on each ATV, they headed down Hedge Row Road and then darted off the shell-covered street, turning onto the utility road that led to the open space between Sconset and Tom Nevers.

They drove at a slow and steady pace. From the utility road that led to where the old LORAN tower stood. Once there, they veered off and headed toward town, following a series of trails through the scrub oak.

In spite of the curfew, as night fell they turned on their headlights. They were basically paralleling Milestone Road via the trails; they traversed Tom Nevers Road, then passed Russells Way.

They continued past Nobadeer Farm Road and then crossed Tawpoot Road. As they approached Five Corners they slowed their ATVs to a stop.

Not far from the largest traffic circle on the island, but still well off the road and well hidden by woods, the Hijra members dismounted their ATVs, turned off their lights, and unstrapped their bundle.

As they unrolled the bundle, a body appeared. It was Kennedy Russell. The Hijra team then took the four iPhones that were jamming her SPID and placed them on the ground around FLOTUS, each under a small pile of pine needles.

They were getting ready to leave her behind when one of the Hijra team members had an idea.

He spoke to the three other members for a few minutes, and when the conversation ended, two of the men made their way to FLOTUS and started to disrobe her. Once they had all her clothes off, they took pictures of her with their cell phones, including some of the iPhones that were going to be left behind to jam the SPID.

Then one of the Hijra team took a bar of tar they had brought with them and rubbed it over the soles of the first lady's feet.

Another took a piece of a life preserver ring, made of hard foam and painted in the customary orange color, and scraped her fingernails over the preserver several times, making sure some of the orange got under her nails.

They then took her clothes, rerolled the bundle, packed it on the back of one of the ATVs along with the hard-foam preserver, and started back to the Hedge Row house, but at a much higher speed.

❖

Ex-Marine and hero of the Baxter Road firefight John Munson was lying on a cot in the Army field hospital recovering from the wound in his left leg when the president entered. Everyone who could stand did so.

He first spoke with the doctors regarding the condition of the four agents wounded in the attack; then he checked on the state trooper who was shot in Madaket. The Secret Service agents were more critical than the state trooper, who was listed in serious but stable condition.

He then went over to Munson. "Marine, I understand you were a big help to us today," said the president.

"Not really, Mr. President. I did what anyone else would do—or what any other Marine would do."

"I appreciate your modesty, Sergeant, but that just isn't the case. I want to thank you for what you did."

The president then spent a few minutes with the others in the tent, thanking them for their work. A moment later, he left in search of Burduck and Tate for the latest on the progress regarding the Concrete List plan.

But first he detoured to a small house that had been the Officer Residences when the Coast Guard station was active. The president entered the small Cape Cod–style house and went down the stairs to the basement.

There he saw three young men zip tied to plastic patio chairs. Nearby were soaked towels and plastic jugs filled with water. All of the prisoners were passed out. The president turned to the interrogators and asked, "What are they saying about my family? Who is behind this attack?

One of the interrogators replied, "Mr. President, we have

pressed them very hard, but I don't think they know anything about the whereabouts of your family."

"And what about who is behind this attack?" added the president.

"It is clear they are Al Qaeda and Islamic. We haven't gotten details beyond that other than they were trained in Saudi Arabia."

The president repeated the last words, "Saudi Arabia."

As the president turned to leave, he said, "Wake them up and keep at them."

The lead interrogator nodded, cracked open some smelling salts, and placed them under the noses of the three miserable examples of human beings, saying, "Time to wake up."

❖

Outside Nantucket Harbor on board the submarine USS *North Dakota*, the sonar operator called out, "Conn, Sonar. I am tracking a contact coming out of the harbor."

The *North Dakota* CO, Mike Smith, picked up the 1MC, saying, "Sonar, Conn. What do you have?"

"Sir, I am tracking a small contact moving at fifteen knots bearing 023 degrees. It sounds like a fishing boat, sir."

The USS *North Dakota* notified the Brant Point Coast Guard Station. "Dogpatch, Dogpatch, this is Papa Kilo. We are tracking a fishing boat coming out of the harbor. Bearing 023 degrees at fifteen knots. Confirm."

"Copy, Papa Kilo, we have it too. We are dispatching a Response Boat to intercept. Stand by."

The Coast Guard Response Boat vectored to the fishing boat that was coming out of the harbor. The Coast Guard crew turned their two high-power spotlights on the boat and hailed them via the loudspeaker, stating sternly, "Heave to or I will fire on you. Heave to or I will fire on you," as the Coast Guard crew trained their two M240B machine guns on the fishing boat.

Under the harsh glare of the Coast Guard spotlights, the fishing boat immediately reduced its throttle to neutral as the Response Boat came alongside. "Prepare to be boarded. Make no sudden movement and keep your hands up."

This wasn't just a random Coast Guard safety inspection. Given everything that had happened today, the Coast Guard was on edge and all anyone had to do was give them a reason to shoot. It made for a very dangerous time for all involved.

Five Coasties jumped on board the fifty-eight-foot Bertram Sport Fisherman, led by their master chief.

The master chief commanded the four people on the boat to lie down on the deck with their hands in sight and not to move. He then barked, "Where the hell do you think you are going?"

One of the men lying on the deck said nonchalantly, "We wanted to go fishing to pass away the time."

The master chief, in no mood for this sort of reckless behavior, produced zip ties and told his men, "Arrest them all for stupidity."

The men were brought on board the Response Boat, leaving three Coasties on the Sport Fisherman to bring it back to the harbor. The master chief looked at the four middle-aged, well-to-do men sitting on the deck of the Response Boat with their hands zip tied behind them, "Assholes," he said out loud.

The Response Boat updated the Brant Point Station, which passed the information on to the USS *North Dakota*. Commander Mike Smith leaned over the chart table in the control room of the Virginia-class attack boat and said, loud enough for the entire control crew to hear, "I am going to put an MK 48 torpedo up the ass of the next idiot who wants to go fishing. If they want to go fishing we'll give them something to catch."

❖

In a field under the open sky, Kennedy Russell began to stir. Her first conscious thought was that she was cold. As her mind cleared, her body jerked in shock.

She pushed herself up and tried to shake the sleep from her mind to make sense of where she was. She looked around—it was dark, she was in a field near some woods—and she was naked.

Where was she? Where were her children?

She stood up but was still dizzy and unsure on her feet. Looking around, she saw the glow in the sky of some lights not far off.

She started to walk toward the lights slowly, as the rough ground hurt her feet.

But she quickly dismissed the feeling of pain—she needed to find her children. With that thought, she started to walk faster.

At the same time Kennedy Russell was beginning to walk to find help, a Secret Service agent on duty in the command center called out, "We have a positive hit on Mendham's SPID."

The senior Secret Service agent on duty came over to the screen and asked where the signal was emanating from, then said, "Get Nicols in here now."

Stationed at the largest traffic circle on the island were three Massachusetts state troopers. They had been given one of the few Nantucket police cruisers due to the central nature of the traffic circle, although traffic was negligible because of the curfew.

State Trooper Billy Herbert glanced up in surprise as a figure emerged from the woods. He looked harder to make sense of it. It was a middle-aged woman, in pretty good shape, too, he thought, walking toward him completely naked and calling for help.

He instinctively put his hand on his 9mm and then quickly scanned the surrounding area to make sure this lady wasn't some sort of decoy for someone else sneaking up on him. He saw no one.

Herbert called out to his two partners, and all three troopers stood dumbfounded as the woman approached them.

"My name is Kennedy Russell. My husband is the president of the United States," she said calmly but firmly.

"How's that?" said Herbert.

She said it one more time—slowly and this time with more force. "My name is Kennedy Russell—my husband is the president of the United States." That last part just hung in the air for a second or two.

Every police car in America carries a blanket in its trunk. One of the troopers quickly grabbed the blanket and wrapped it around the first lady. They then helped her into the back of the squad car and shut the door carefully.

The back wheels of the cruiser kicked up a cloud as they sped down Milestone Road toward Tom Nevers. Herbert's partner hit the lights and siren, then got on the radio.

"This is Trooper Williams with a Priority One message for the Secret Service." He repeated the call, and a moment later he got a response.

"Copy. This is the Secret Service Communications Center. Please state your emergency." They were expecting the call, as the SPID was now pinging in real time.

"We have the first lady, repeat, we have the first lady."

"Say again."

Williams replied, "Just clear a path for us. We are headed to the bunker."

The response came back excitedly, "Trooper Williams, Roger that, your path is clear to approach the bunker."

Nicols, who had joined the agents in the command center, radioed ahead to the Marines protecting the perimeter of the bunker and told them to expect a Massachusetts state trooper or Nantucket police cruiser to approach them at a high rate of speed in the next minute. He told them to clear any roadblocks, not to impede them in any way, and to let them through. Nicols then went to update the president.

As Billy Herbert's cruiser approached the turnoff onto Tom Nevers Road, they were traveling at more than one hundred miles per hour. They slowed only a little as they made the slight turn onto Tom Nevers Road.

Half a mile later, Trooper Herbert tapped the brakes harder and turned right onto the road that led to the bunker, where Secret Service agents had their guns drawn and at the ready. Herbert got out of the car and yelled for everyone to put their weapons down. Once all the weapons were down, he opened the back door and out stepped a female figure wrapped in a drab olive blanket.

She turned to the closest Secret Service agent and said, "Take me to the president."

As the Secret Service directed her to the bunker, she paused and turned.

"No, I want them," she said, pointing to Troopers Herbert and Williams.

"Ma'am?" said the Secret Service agent.

"They will bring me to the president."

And with that Herbert and his partner walked the first lady into the presidential bunker, with the Secret Service close behind, MP5s drawn.

She walked right into the president's conference room, where he was on with Jack McMasters and the staff of the Situation Room. He glanced up and said, "I'll call you back," then rushed to embrace her.

They stood hugging in silence. The president said quietly, "Ken, the kids?"

With tears welling up she replied, "I don't know."

At that moment Tate, Spencer, and Nicols reentered the room to begin a debriefing of her ordeal and what she remembered.

Unfortunately her account didn't provide much help. An FBI agent was present during the debriefing, recording everything she said. In addition, the Secret Service was taking samples from her feet and fingernails for forensics.

Back at the NSA, McMahon and her team were informed about the release of FLOTUS.

She immediately voiced the obvious question out loud to her team, "Why did they let her go?"

"Does it make any sense?" added McMahon.

"Why would they would just let her go?" repeated Kristin McMahon, who was with Mannix in the Crisis Room.

"Maybe they released her as a distraction in order to move the kids off the island," one of the analysts commented.

"Possibly, but we haven't picked up anything from the kids' SPIDs," McMahon responded.

"What about a contagion?" asked another.

This was the group's most critical question at the moment. They feared that FLOTUS was released as a carrier of a disease in order to infect the president. Within minutes McMahon was on the phone with Agent Nicols, strongly advising that FLOTUS be immediately put in quarantine.

"A little late for that, I would say," commented Nicols, "as FLOTUS has been in contact with about twenty folks since her release."

"Nevertheless," said McMahon, "you need to take this precaution. Isolate her and have Medical start running tests on her—she's probably asymptomatic for now."

The president was not happy when he was briefed by Nicols about the plan to quarantine his wife, but it made sense. They had to be cautious until they had more information about what had happened to her.

The bunker was equipped with biohazard detectors, which would have gone off if any known biologic antigen had been detected. But the sensors were useless against viral attacks.

The doctors from the Army Field Hospital were now on the line with the CDC reviewing what protocol they would implement on FLOTUS.

There was no Class 4 isolation facility on the island. There was a discussion about helo'ing her to the USS *Theodore Roosevelt* to use their isolation ward or getting her to Boston, but the decision was made to keep her on Nantucket for now.

They did, however, agree to order the Gulfstream jet that had transported some of the Ebola victims from Africa two years prior and get it to Nantucket. It would take several hours to get the plane on the island, but the wheels were already in motion to make that happen.

Doctors took blood, urine, and air samples from FLOTUS, performed spectral analysis on them, and forwarded the results to the CDC for further analysis.

❖

Lieutenant Commander Burduck and his SEAL team were working their way through each of the houses on the Concrete List. A radio call came in to him from Chief Tate, and they discussed the forensics found on the first lady. They both agreed that the forensics suggested that FLOTUS had been held on a ship or a pier, and they discussed the idea of sending a team to town to start searching the docks and boats.

They recommended that the Coast Guard start searching all the boats moored in the harbor. But Chief Tate had some second thoughts. His NYPD instincts were tingling. Something didn't add up. Why would they let her go—she clearly didn't escape—with these clues on her? The terrorists had all the time they needed to check her before they let her go. She was naked . . . surely they would have noticed the tar on her feet.

"No," said Tate. "It's a false-positive. It's a trick. You need to stay on the Concrete List searches."

The SEAL commander said, "I agree with you, but there is no real downside to having the Coast Guard check the boats in the harbor."

And that was the recommendation they brought to Nicols and Spencer.

❖

VP Jack McMasters was on the line with the president. He had spoken with the chief justice as well as the cabinet and had the paperwork in place to invoke the Twenty-Fifth Amendment should the president wish to do so.

"Mr. President, what do you want to do regarding the Twenty-Fifth?" McMasters asked.

The president replied, "Jack, I don't know what is going to happen these next few days and I need to focus completely on getting my family back safely. If anything else happens in the world, I won't have the bandwidth to deal with it."

"I completely understand, Mr. President," he said, but then added, "Andy, I can handle everything in Washington. You focus on Nantucket. If things devolve, of course, we can revisit the Twenty-Fifth, but for now, sir, let's not execute it."

"Thanks for that assurance, Jack. Okay, for now let's hold on the Twenty-Fifth." And he hung up.

Despite his fear and anger, the president knew McMasters was right.

Chapter Twelve

Saturday Evening

Fifty miles off Nantucket was the SS *Milbridge Major*, which flew a Panamanian flag for the Turkish firm Karkont Ege Ticaret of Istanbul. It measured twenty-eight thousand tons, was three hundred feet long, and had two seventy-ton cranes. It was what they referred to in the shipping business as "a floating piece of shit."

The *Milbridge*'s crew was made up of sixteen individuals with Middle Eastern backgrounds. The captain was an Islamic Turk from Antalya. He had been recruited by the sheik's people fifteen years ago.

Over that time he had been the master of numerous ships that transported contraband for the sheik via several of his shell companies.

The captain, a stern disciplinarian who was not very well liked by his crew, barked at them, "Prepare to launch the Zodiacs."

The *Milbridge* had been steaming at twelve knots but was now slowing to a stop so the three Zodiacs could be lowered.

The rigid hulled inflatable boats (RHIB) were equipped with twin 135-horsepower Mercury outboard engines capable of propelling the small boats at more than sixty miles per hour.

As the three Zodiacs were lowered to the water just off Sconset, two crew members climbed into each skiff.

That left ten men on the *Milbridge*, but there wasn't much to do on the freighter besides stay on course and carry out the next phase of their mission.

In addition to the powerful outboard engines, each Zodiac was equipped with a small electric engine that was ultraquiet and capable of propelling the Zodiac at ten knots without emitting virtually any acoustic signature. The time was a little before 10 p.m. on Saturday.

❖

Dale Carmichael had returned to his apartment in Beijing and was communicating nonstop with the CIA when his iPhone started to buzz, signaling an incoming text.

It was from Amy Lu. "Nantucket, I told you," it said.

He replied, "Should we meet?"

"No, I am still out of town."

"Anything else you can tell me?"

"We think they will try to escape by sea," was her response.

Carmichael texted back, "How do you know that?"

"We have some embedded assets. I believe their information is good."

"Thanks, let me know when you are back in BJ."

Carmichael then got on his secure line and shared Lu's information with CIA headquarters in Langley, Virginia.

Carmichael said, "Clearly, the Chinese have a source of information regarding the Nantucket operation that we do not. When I asked them where they got their intel, they told me they had some embedded assets."

❖

At the NSA Kevin Mannix and his team were living on pizza and energy drinks.

They had worked and reworked their list of Nantucket targets based on building permits and concrete purchases—the Concrete List. Now they were analyzing the location where FLOTUS was found. The team also had the information about the tar on her feet and dense foam under her fingernails.

The team did what they always did—they split in two—with one team taking the tar-on-the-feet clue and pursuing it while the other team dismissed the clues as misinformation. Mannix stepped out of the room for a break.

Often during brainstorming sessions, it was important for him to remove himself from the discussion or even go to another room so as not to influence the outcome. But another thing was bothering him: Oasis LLC.

After his bathroom break he went to his desk rather than back to the Crisis Room. He needed some uninterrupted time to think things through.

Mannix sat at his desk executing relational database joins, trying to find a key match. The item he kept digging for was Oasis LLC. He had a hunch it was critical to finding the Russell kids, but he didn't have the link yet. Then he got a hit. It was thin, but it was something.

His Palantir software had detected a return address on a FedEx package to a Manhattan office address that was the listed owner of a house in Sconset. He took that data and continued to work it. After about thirty minutes of data mining, Mannix had what he thought was a link that connected Oasis LLC via a Manhattan front company that had purchased a house in Sconset eighteen months ago. And that house was on the Concrete List. It was a house on Hedge Row Road not far from the president's Low Beach Road house. Bingo.

He jumped up and ran into the Crisis Room. "Everyone stop what you are doing. Everyone stop now," he ordered.

"I need you to do a blind join on a Manhattan business named Garavuso Galleries and see if you can tie it back to our investigation." He didn't want to give the team too much data so as to lead them to his conclusion.

"Come on, guys, now," he said, and then he sat there impatiently with his leg going a mile a minute from nerves as he watched his team crunch the data.

❖

It was 10:35 p.m. when McMasters entered the Sit Room. He motioned for everyone to stay seated; then he sat down. "Okay, what do you have?"

John Standard, the chairman of the Joint Chiefs and a Marine four-star general, stood and approached the flat-screen. "Sir, we have assembled a list of targets and have broken them into three classes in terms of impact and collateral damage."

Group A included three locations—one in Yemen, one in Iraq, and the other in Burkina Faso.

Group B included a city in Syria—the entire city. Also in group B was a building on the island of Margarita (Isla Margarita) off Venezuela.

Group C was the most controversial because it included an apartment in Berlin, a row house outside of London, and an apartment in St. Petersburg.

McMasters asked, "How soon can we hit all of them? I want to take them all out simultaneously."

General Standard hit the button and advanced three slides. The fourth slide showed how all targets could be hit within seventy-two hours. "We will need to inform the Brits, of course—and we should inform the Germans and Russians too," he said.

McMasters sat and considered the comment. "Yes, on informing the Brits. Actually we should ask the Brits if they want to take out the target themselves. No, on notifying the Germans and Russians. They should have known they had terrorists in their cities and dealt with it themselves—fuck 'em. Now, how do we hit the Berlin and St. Petersburg locations without it coming back to bite us?"

The chief of naval operations, or CNO, Brad Johnson, spoke. "Mr. Vice President, we can hit the Russian location with cruise missiles from one of our subs in the Baltic. We have two boats there now and they can be in position within twelve hours. We can hit the Berlin target from either the North Sea or the Baltic."

"I don't want any of this coming back to us—no serial numbers, no anything," said McMasters.

Again Admiral Johnson spoke up. "Mr. Vice President, we started scrubbing our cruise missiles a few years ago. There are no traceable numbers or symbols on any of our Tomahawks or Harpoons now, neither the conventional nor the specials."

"Tell me about the Syrian city," McMasters said next.

General Standard responded, "It is Al Hwaiz, on the Mediterranean coast. It is an easy target for us to hit. Population is about eight thousand and it has been a hotbed for Al Qaeda for years. The problem is up to one-third of the population are noncoms."

"Shit," said McMasters. "We can't take it out with that many friendlies. What are our alternatives?"

General Standard looked around the room and surveyed the group, then said, "Torchlight."

McMasters knew what that meant. *Torchlight* was a new TOP SECRET laser-based weapon the Department of Defense was now deploying. It was a tightly kept secret and everyone in the Sit Room knew *Torchlight* was to be used only in the most critical situation. And even given the seriousness of this crisis – everyone agreed we weren't at the point where *Torchlight's* use was warranted.

He sat in deep thought for a few minutes. "Alert the Brits. Prepare to attack in twelve hours. I will brief the president."

❖

Mannix's team was huddled in their crisis room when they finally concluded, "Kevin, it's the Hedge Row house."

Mannix held up a yellow pad and turned it over. In big red letters it said "Hedge Row."

"Run it again," he told his team, just to be sure. When the team came back ten minutes later with the same answer, Mannix nodded.

McMahon, who had joined them, said, "Get the director on the line. Start preparing the brief."

Less than twenty minutes later, McMahon and Mannix were on a videoconference link with the Sit Room.

Mannix cleared his throat and hit the button to bring up the first of three slides. It showed a large circle. Mannix began, "This is the data universe we started with—which was basically everything: every terrorist group and name we have in all our databases.

"We then started to crunch the data with our Teradata, Palantir, and Cray computers." As he spoke, dots started to appear in the large circle. "We then focused our searches on Nantucket. We looked at all the title records of all the homes and lots.

"We looked at the purchase and rental records as well. We cross-referenced those records with known terrorist groups as well as groups known to have ties to terrorist organizations.

"We then started to analyze why we weren't getting any SPID signals. We opined that FLOTUS and the children were still on the island because the Secret Service and local police put a freeze on all incoming and outbound travel within minutes of the abduction.

"We then analyzed what would cause a SPID signal not to

be picked up. That led us to think about a concrete bunker of some type.

"We then pulled every building permit since the president started vacationing on Nantucket. We listed every sizable purchase of concrete or building permit for pools, new house builds, new foundation, patios, etcetera. That led us to identify thirty-seven target homes.

"Then we gained access to the FedEx package delivery database. There we did a relational join using the list of thirty-seven addresses of the Nantucket homes where concrete was purchased."

"We found a double-stranded link to a management consulting company that does business with one of our Al Qaeda targeted groups."

That was enough technical talk for McMasters. "Net it out for us, son," he said.

Mannix clicked to the last slide in his presentation.

"Sir, the Hedge Row Road in Sconset, sir." The slide dissolved to show a KH-11 satellite picture of the Hedge Row Road house.

"As you can see, there is no pool. The house is three-quarters of a mile from where the president was staying on Low Beach Road."

McMahon added, "This house on Hedge Row Road was purchased eighteen months ago by a group linked to a known Al Qaeda group. Sir, we believe this is the house where the president's children are being held."

McMasters looked at the head of the NSA. "George?"

"Mr. Vice President, it all fits. We tripled-checked the data and analysis."

The vice president turned to the directors of the FBI and CIA. "Ben, Lisa, do you concur?"

They nodded. Next the vice president looked at the Joint Chiefs. "Anything to add, gentlemen?"

They replied, "No, sir."

The CNO added, "We can use the SEAL team that is already on the island backed up by our agents and the Marines."

After a short pause McMasters said, "Get me the president."

❖

The doctors at the CDC in Atlanta were beginning to get concerned. The blood work from FLOTUS was showing signs of a hybrid strain of the H1N1 avian flu virus. The scientists from Atlanta were on the line with the lead doctor from the Army Field Hospital on the island, and they were discussing the findings and the projected incubation period for the virus.

The best projection was that FLOTUS would start exhibiting signs of the virus in the next twenty-four hours, and she would then be in a contagious phase. But just to be sure, the CDC was recommending that everyone FLOTUS had been in contact with also be put into quarantine.

The list included the Massachusetts state troopers Herbert and Williams, Sterling Spencer, Dan Nicols, Chris Tate, and, of course, POTUS.

Supplies and additional equipment were being airlifted as they spoke, with an ETA on the island of about two hours in order to help set up the needed quarantine areas.

While the quarantine rooms were being arranged, the vice president and the Sit Room team had briefed the president, Spencer, Nicols, Tate, and the SEAL commander on the Hedge Row house analysis.

They agreed with the analysis and instructed Lieutenant Commander Knute Burduck and SEAL Team 2 to prepare a plan to first surveil and then assault the Hedge Row house in order to rescue the Russell children.

In the meantime, the Secret Service had dispatched a team to the town offices to locate the building plans for the Hedge Row house. Next, the neighboring houses were evacuated and night vision and thermal-imaging sensors were installed in the homes closest to the Hedge Row target house.

By making use of the building plans and a low-energy ground sonar, the SEALs were approximating where they thought the underground bunker was located.

The house was now under constant surveillance from a Predator drone that was flying above it with its top secret Alpha2 sensor pod. This sensor pod was capable of determining infrared images to such a detail level as to be able to determine a person's sex and age.

In real time, the plan to assault the Hedge Row house was being reviewed by SEAL Team 2 and at SEAL headquarters, the Naval Special Warfare Center on Coronado Island, and by the Joint Special Operations Command (JSOC), located at Pope Field (Fort Bragg, North Carolina). There was a great deal of concern over the impending operation. Any direct incursion ran the real risk that the terrorists would kill the Russell children.

It was going on 11:30 p.m. and all options for raiding the Hedge Row home were extremely risky. The decision was made not to storm the house. It had been decided to continue to monitor and collect data around the house.

❖

The three Zodiacs launched from the SS *Milbridge Major* were now approaching their planned rendezvous location off Sconset.

The plan was not to actually come ashore but rather to loiter one mile directly off the Summer House beach and wait for the Hijra team and their hostages to arrive. They knew it wouldn't be easy with all of the US military now on alert, but they had a plan and another distraction in the works.

The plan called for the Hedge Row Hijra team to split into two groups. One group would use the ATVs, the ones that had been used to move FLOTUS earlier, to lure the Americans away from the Hedge Row house. This team would be the diversion team. Meanwhile, the other Hijra group was inflating two weather balloons with helium.

In order to fool the infrared sensors that the Secret Service and military were undoubtedly using, the Hijra team had custom coveralls, or squirrel suits. The stealth coveralls had harnesses sewn into them so that the children could each be connected to a Hijra team member, much like a set of tandem parachutists.

Once everyone was wearing the squirrel suits, including Andy and Katie Russell, they would attach to the balloons and simply float away from the Hedge Row house undetected.

The balloons would be maneuvered using small tanks of compressed air.

No heat signature, no motor noise, just the occasional jet of air used as a thruster providing a quiet, yet slow, egress from the Hedge Row house.

It was another elegant and low-cost solution that had every chance of outsmarting the Americans.

In order to cause more mayhem, the SPIDs had been extracted from the children's legs and were to be attached to two hunting dogs.

At the designated time, the dogs would be let out with the SPIDs placed in Velcro wallets that hung from their collars.

The Americans could fly as many F/A-18s as they wanted to over the island, but Al Qaeda was about to elude them with weather balloons that cost less than $200 apiece. It was effective terrorism on a budget.

❖

On the bridge of the USS *Jimmy Carter*, Stu Jackson was plotting a patrol course that would encompass a box pattern that ran from Sankaty Head Light to Tom Nevers and back again, creeping along silently at five knots.

The water was too shallow for the *Carter* to deploy its towed sonar array. Had they been able to do so, they might have been able to detect the approaching Zodiacs, which thirty minutes earlier had turned off their electric engines and were now paddling toward the balloon rendezvous spot.

Balloons and paddleboats were fine, but the SS *Milbridge Major* was a large, noisy vessel. Its benefit was that it was also large enough and noisy enough to mask the Chinese diesel-electric sub that was silently moving in tandem underneath it.

It was up to the USS *Jimmy Carter* and the USS *North Dakota* and its captain, officers, and crew, which had just won the Atlantic Fleet's Arleigh Burke trophy for combat efficiency, to detect the Chinese sub that was now entering their patrol area.

To that end, the USS *North Dakota* was tracking all shipping, large and small, in a one-hundred-mile radius around the island. Positioned east-northeast off Sconset, approximately fifteen miles offshore, it was about ten miles east of the SS *Milbridge Major* and its stealthy Chinese sub, which was acting as its pilot fish.

❖

It was approximately 11:35 p.m., almost three hours since FLOTUS had been picked up, when she started to develop a fever. The medical staff had expected as much and they started an IV drip solution to keep her hydrated. Because her infection was viral, antibiotics would do her no good. For now the treatment consisted of fluids and a lot of vital-signs monitoring. The next seventy-two hours would be critical.

Chapter Thirteen

Late Saturday Night in Sconset
Early Sunday Morning in Dubai

On the other side of the world, in Dubai, the sun had already come up and morning prayers were finished.

This Sunday morning found Lauren La Rue in her office checking her email and the balances in her clients' accounts. Interestingly enough, she was also watching a YouTube video.

For the past two years Al Qaeda had effectively used YouTube as a communication portal. In some mindless and otherwise inane video of a teenager or a family dinner, an encrypted message would be benignly inserted.

Sometimes it was a video of a birthday celebration with hidden signs like the number of candles on the cake or a seemingly random comment that would relay information about a terrorist cell or the status of the planning for an upcoming event.

Another technique for communicating with terrorist cells was via product feedback left on Amazon or by posting an item for sale on eBay or via Instagram or a LinkedIn profile. In the spot where the phone number, product number, or some other figure appeared, the account number where the funds were to be deposited was inserted instead.

This was precisely why the NSA had petabytes of data storage in their data centers—to process, analyze, and, hopefully, detect these messages. It was a daunting task.

Lauren La Rue was watching a YouTube video of a wedding with the bride and groom singing the *Grease* classic "You're the One That I Want." Every time the woman in the video put her right hand on the groom's shoulder, it communicated how many millions of dollars needed to be transferred.

Every time the groom put both his hands on the bride's waist, it communicated in which of several known accounts to deposit the funds. It was clever and extremely hard to decode. This YouTube message told her to deposit US$4 million from the account of Sheik Abdul Er Rahman via Oasis LLC to an account controlled by Garavuso Galleries in Manhattan.

This was the largest single deposit the sheik had ever made directly to a US account. That worried her. The amount was too large and ran a real risk of being detected by one of the US banking authorities—either a commercial bank, the comptroller of the currency, or the US Treasury.

She wasn't considered the best in the business because she made careless moves like this.

Even though it was a Sunday, La Rue sat in front of her Deutsche Bank account screen, ready to initiate the transfers. She mulled over whether or not to call the sheik to discuss this transaction. But knowing the sheik's famously short temper, she instead pressed her right index finger and clicked the mouse, and the money was immediately transferred.

She knew it was nearing the time when she needed to get out of the business. But could she? This wasn't IBM or Citigroup, where you could just retire. Could she actually leave Oasis LLC and live to tell about it? How did she ever get this deep into this maelstrom?

❖

The USS *North Dakota* now had a bearing on the SS *Milbridge Major*. It was bearing 120 degrees at ten miles and moving at six and half knots. It was a single-screw small freighter with a four-bladed prop, with its third blade out of balance, probably from hitting an underwater object during one of its port calls.

The asymmetric nature of the ship's propeller worked to create a unique acoustic signature, but the purposely bent prop also worked to mask any ambient noise that might come from the Chinese diesel-electric boat that was directly under the *Milbridge* at a depth of seventy-five feet.

The USS *North Dakota* had started a tape on the *Milbridge*, a common practice for US attack subs when tracking a target. Its sonar room was now recording and tracking the SS *Milbridge Major* as target Sierra 1. This track would instantly be shared with the USS *Jimmy Carter* via their ANS/BSY1 radar software.

But it wasn't just the US Navy that was recording the ocean off Sconset. The captain of the Chinese submarine was also listening to detect and track all the elements of Carrier Strike Group 12, as well as its attack subs, which he knew traveled with the carrier battle group.

The Chinese sub was sailing under the SS *Milbridge Major*, now twenty-five miles off the coast of Nantucket, which put it thirteen miles outside of the US twelve-mile territorial limit. By international law, he was safe, which comported with their plan.

❖

With most of the principals on Nantucket now being put into isolation, logistics became more challenging. The president, Spencer, Nicols, and even Tate were in their own isolation rooms set up in the bunker.

Massachusetts troopers Herbert and Williams were also in isolation rooms, but their rooms were in the Army Field Hospital.

Lieutenant Dunbar, a SEAL who was an expert in flying drones and operating the Alpha2 package, had set up his command in the presidential bunker close to the isolation rooms so Tate, Nicols, and Spencer, not to mention the president, could at least hear what was going on and maybe actually see some of Dunbar's screens. In addition to Dunbar, Petty Officer Conway, a member of SEAL Team 2, was there to act as a liaison for SEAL Team 2 and the Secret Service.

In front of Dunbar were seven screens that monitored the readouts from the Alpha2 pod on the Predator drone circling above the Hedge Row house. One screen showed an aerial view of the house. Another displayed the infrared signatures coming from the home. The next screen had the night vision shot coming from the Secret Service cameras in a house directly across the street.

The next screen had a live shot from the camera on Lieutenant Commander Burduck's helmet. Screen five had an active track of all air traffic within 250 miles of ACK, screen six the same but for all sea vessels within one hundred miles of Nantucket. The seventh screen was the Russell children's SPID monitor.

At 11:53:30, the SPID screen lit up like a Christmas tree. The SPIDs were moving fast and away from the Hedge Row house. In addition, the Predator screen now alerted with a heat signature from what looked like two ATV's moving away from the house at about forty-five miles per hour on a west-north-west heading,

Petty Officer Conway toggled his radio on his left shoulder: "Kingpin Control to Kingpin1, come in 1."

"Roger, Control. Kingpin1," replied Burduck.

"Are you seeing what we're seeing?"

"Copy, Control," came Burduck's reply.

"We have movement out of the back of the house—four tracks—two mechanized tracks heading at forty-five miles per hour on a west-north-west heading—must be a vehicle of some sort, like a dirt bike or ATV," said Conway.

"We also have two tracks on the SPIDs for Minecraft and Missy headed in different directions," Conway informed him.

"Kingpin is moving in on the target," said Lieutenant Commander Burduck. "Alert Marine Det to intercept motorized tracks."

Chief Tate was looking at the screens and muttered, "No, no—something isn't right."

As the Kingpin Team of SEALs approached the Hedge Row house, motion detectors started to register, which in turn triggered incendiary devices throughout the home. In a matter of seconds, pyro devices went off in a synchronized manner.

Within seconds the entire Hedge Row house was engulfed in flames, and all the SEAL team could do was stand on the lawn and watch.

As the ATVs approached the brush just north of Russells Way, rockets about five feet in height popped up from the ground. Their launchers had been buried only about two inches below the surface the year before.

These rockets spoke to the preplanning involved in the attack. They had been transported to the island the previous year and installed—or really buried in brush where few people would venture.

Simple car batteries would ignite the solid rocket fuel, which lifted the rockets off on their five-mile mission. Part of the Amina team's duties the previous week was to go out on ATVs, check the status of the rockets, and install new Exide dry-cell automobile batteries in each of the ten missile launchers.

The missiles were triggered by a Hijra team member as the ATV passed. The operator entered a code into a radiofrequency device, which fired the rockets.

Of the ten rockets, only eight leapt into the August night.

❖

On board the two Aegis-class cruisers of Carrier Strike Group 12, the USS *Normandy* and the USS *Vicksburg*, the Combat Information Centers, or CICs, had detected the missile launch and were now alerting the ships in the Carrier Strike Group.

The USS *Normandy* was tasked as the Red Crown watch stander responsible for monitoring all airspace against an attack on the carrier group which used the call sign Rough Rider. As a result, it was the *Normandy* that detected and first issued the radio call about the missile launch: "This is Red Crown on guard, vampire, vampire, vampire.

"We have detected a launch from the island. We are actively tracking six, no, seven vampires. Recommend Rough Rider to go to battle stations missile."

In addition to the Aegis cruisers, the Predator drone operator in the bunker also detected heat blooms from the rockets. The Predator drone relayed real-time data to the Aegis cruisers in the group, providing coordinates of the launch sites.

A split second later came the second radio call: "This is Red Crown on guard—we are tracking eight rockets on various headings, speed accelerating past three hundred knots, altitude six hundred feet and climbing. We do not know if they are vampires. They maybe MANPADS." Vampire is the term for anti-ship missiles. Given the events of the day, the operator was correct in not taking any chances that the rockets weren't vampires. The term MANPADS was short for Man-portable air-defense systems (MANPADS or MPADS) which are shoulder-launched missiles not unlike the US Stinger missile.

MANPADS are typically used to shoot down low-flying air-craft, helicopters or drones.

On board the USS *Theodore Roosevelt*, CO Tom Fraser was where he always was when at sea—on the bridge. When he heard the call, he turned to the boatswain's mate and officer of the deck and issued the command, "Sound general quarters."

With that, the boatswain's mate hit the 1MC button, sounded several short notes from his pipe, and announced, "General quarters, general quarters, man your battle stations, up and forward starboard side, down and aft port side. General quarters, general quarters."

It was almost midnight, but it took only a few seconds for the USS *Theodore Roosevelt* to transition from a quiet ship to a mad rush of activity, with sailors and officers all rushing toward their general quarters stations for a possible missile attack.

Fraser picked up his phone and pushed the button for the CDC, asking, "Are there any vampires inbound, Rough Rider?"

The reply came back, "Negative, sir, Rough Rider has no inbound vampires."

"What about the group?" Fraser asked next.

"Negative on that, sir—all missiles are tracking land targets, sir."

All ships of Carrier Strike Group 12 went to general quarters, increased to flank speed, and manned all weapons, ready to repel any potential incoming missile threat as well as targeting the silos that had just launched the missiles.

The missile launch was also detected by NORAD in Colorado Springs, two thousand miles away, call sign Giant Killer. Giant Killer was in the process of scrambling their alert F-15s out of Otis on Cape Cod.

Giant Killer was issuing orders: "This is Huntress placing Panta45 and 46 on battle stations, repeat, battle stations. Time 4:53:41 Greenwich Mean Time. Authenticate Hotel Romeo, all parties acknowledge with initials, Command Post."

Panta45 and Panta46, call signs made famous by the 9/11 attacks, were two F-15Cs out of Otis.

"Giant Killer, Huntress acknowledges. Tango Juliet confirms call sign. Panta, Papa Alfa November Tango Alfa, 45, 46. Juliet Papa. All parties are cleared to drop."

Immediately responding to that order, two F-15Cs from Otis Air National Guard Base were now scrambling and would be airborne in two minutes.

Once airborne, the F-15Cs would go to afterburner and be over Nantucket in less than two minutes. But the F-15Cs would be in range to fire their missiles in only one minute. The F-15C Eagles were armed with AIM-120 AMRAAM advanced medium-range air-to-air missiles, along with AIM-9X Block II Sidewinder heat-seeker missiles plus an internal 20mm M61 Vulcan Gatling gun.

Each Eagle could engage multiple vampire enemy missiles. The problem was that these particular missiles had very short flight paths. Their mission was basically to go up and immediately come down and hit a target on Nantucket.

The AMRAAM missile employed an active transmit-receive radar guidance system that was a fire-and-forget missile. When an AMRAAM missile was fired, the pilot used the call Fox Three.

Within three minutes of being scrambled, Panta45 issued a Fox Three call as it launched its AMRAAMs at the missiles. Panta45 launched four AMRAAMs—his entire complement.

Next Panta46 was also making its Fox Three calls.

With the AMRAAMs tracking, the F-15s shot down four of the eight inbound missiles. That left four missiles still in the air and bearing down on targets on Nantucket. Two of the rockets went off course and landed harmlessly in the waters off Pimnys Point at the edge of the harbor. But the remaining two rockets hit pay dirt. The first missile hit the Dreamland Theater on Water Street in the heart of town.

The real target had been the Steamship Authority Terminal, but the homing devices on the crude Russian-made missiles were inaccurate.

In many ways hitting the Dreamland would impart a bigger emotional blow to the legacy of the island. The theater had been a part of Nantucket's cultural history for more than 184 years. When it was originally constructed in 1832, as a Quaker meetinghouse, the building hosted open meetings in support of the abolition of slavery.

The Dreamland subsequently housed a factory that produced straw hats, and then later it was a roller-skating rink. For the last sixty years it had been the island's only movie theater, but now it was ablaze.

The second missles also detonated in town, not far from the Dreamland Theater. It hit the only Catholic church on the island, St. Mary, Our Lady of the Isle, which was located on Federal Street only about four blocks from the Dreamland.

The church, another landmark on Nantucket, was only a block from the Hub. The missile hit near the narthex, and flames from the church fire spread to Murray's Liquor Store on the adjacent Main Street.

The pastor, Monsignor George V. Fogarty of the Fall River Diocese, was slightly injured from the blast but not enough to stop him from helping the Nantucket Fire Department battle the fire. The damage to the church was significant but confined mostly to the narthex.

As the church was constructed predominantly of wood, some dating back to 1896, it was something of a miracle that the fire did not engulf the entire structure.

In what some would later call a sign of divine intervention, the two stained-glass windows honoring Monsignor Lester C. Hull, the church's former pastor, and Albert F. "Bud" Egan, a parish benefactor, both survived the attack.

The damage to the Catholic church, the liquor store, and the Dreamland would impact the quality of life on the island for the near future. But for New Englanders, especially Nantucketers, it would take more than this attack to put them on their heels.

❖

Through their plastic walls, Nicols was talking with Tate and Spencer. "The kids' SPIDs are decoys. We think they have been placed on animals."

Tate nodded.

Spencer asked, "Does that mean the children are on the ATVs?"

Nicols replied, "That is our belief."

Tate spoke up. "Let's not sell out on the ATVs." He was suggesting they not put all their resources on the ATVs.

"The m.o. of this crew has been diversions, distractions, and decoys. Everything they do is a counteraction," said Tate using the police term "crew" rather than the military term "team."

But he was right. Nothing was what it seemed, and every response had to be verified and questioned.

❖

The Hijra ATV team had abandoned their ATVs and put on squirrel suits to hide from the sensors on the Predators. The four members of the Hijra ATV team were now progressing on foot through the backwoods near the airport.

They crossed over Milestone Road and covered the mile and half in just a little over twelve minutes. They entered the newer development of Tetawkimmo, which was just north of the airport.

The four Hijra members entered a house on Tawpawshaw Road called Way Off Broadway, where they removed their squirrel suits. This house was rented for the Hijra team from the Windwalker agency, but not by Oasis LLC. Oddly enough, however, the Tawpawshaw house was on the Concrete List due to the large pool in its backyard.

In support of the Marines, the SEALs were now leaving the Hedge Row house in pursuit of the ATVs, which they soon found abandoned. The SEALs began their search for the Hijra team members, who they believed were now on foot.

In addition, the Secret Service was still tracking the Russell children's SPIDs. Using the Predator drone and its Alpha2 sensor package, they determined that the SPIDs were on animals.

They still wanted to capture the animals to see what clues they could get from the SPIDs, but this was now a lower priority. The current belief was that the Russell children had departed the Hedge Row house on the ATVs without their SPIDs.

The Hijra balloon team, which consisted of two members, including the Hijra team leader, Karim Hamady, and the president's children launched five minutes before the Hedge Row Road house exploded and was now drifting on their way to rendezvous with the Zodiacs. The three Zodiacs had spread out about a quarter of a mile apart in order to increase their chances of connecting with the balloons.

At the designated time of 11:57 p.m. the three Zodiacs turned on their spotlights, which were pointed upward. Because of the orange color of the lights, they could be seen for only about two hundred yards or so.

By now the balloon team had traveled what they assumed was the mile from the beach. Their altimeters read two hundred feet so they started to ease the relief valves on each balloon to gradually lose altitude. They descended until they reached one hundred feet and then shut the relief valves.

Karim and the other balloon pilot both had a light, which was basically an LED flashlight. As a backup they also had strobe lights, but those were to be used only if they couldn't find the Zodiacs.

One of the crew members of Zodiac 3 cried out that he had spotted the balloons. They were due south about 150 yards.

They blinked their orange lights as previously agreed to attract the balloon pilots. With their compressed air it would be a lot easier for the balloons to come north by 150 yards than for the Zodiacs to go south to them.

It is easy to think the Zodiacs could cover the 150 yards with their combined 270-horsepower outboard engines or by using their smaller but quieter electric engines, but they were forbidden to use their engines at this point in the mission unless it was an emergency.

The three Zodiacs started to paddle due south as they continued to blink their orange lights to attract the balloon pilots, who hadn't seen them yet.

In fact, the balloons were drifting away from them, not toward them.

The Zodiac commander yelled to his crew to row faster to close the gap with the balloons, while they kept the balloons in sight using night vision binoculars.

The wind was faster than the Zodiac teams could row, with the result being that the gap was now at 200 yards. In another five minutes the gap would be more than half a mile.

❖

Kevin Mannix was being brought up to speed on the recent developments. The thought was to keep the NSA team current on the situation so they could continue to provide valuable input.

Mannix and his team were tired, as it was going on midnight and they had been working the crisis situation nonstop for eighteen hours.

But that's what the job required, and his team was made up of mostly young people under thirty, so their age, plus the quantities of Mountain Dew, Monster, and Red Bull they were consuming, would keep them going easily for at least another twenty-four hours. That plus the adrenaline surge that comes from working on a crisis situation meant they would be fine.

As a matter of fact, had anyone suggested that they go home or go for a rest period, they would have resisted.

They were on point for the NSA and they planned to keep it that way. That notwithstanding, the NSA had protocols in place that would stage other, fresh team members and get them up to speed so there would be constant coverage and continual support from the NSA's Fort Meade headquarters.

Mannix and the team were absorbing the latest information. The escape of the Hijra team from the Hedge Row house, the errant SPIDs, the missile launches, and now the abandoned ATVs: Did it add up?

Smart people who had some separation from the stress and emotion of the on-site situation often could bring clearer thinking than the on-site teams. The NSA team was sure that something was being missed. It didn't make sense given such a well-thought-out plan that the terrorists would just get on ATVs and run for it. The SPID diversion was clever, but not that clever.

The terrorists had to know that with thermal imagining it would quickly be determined that the SPID signals were not coming from the Russell children.

Debate was under way about the idea that the Hijra team was on their way to finding another safe house. It was plausible but not very sophisticated. Mannix agreed and again split his team in two to come up with alternative ideas. They had thirty minutes.

Chapter Fourteen

Flashback and Very Late Saturday Night

It was now midnight and FLOTUS's temperature was 101 and climbing. The Army doctors and the CDC scientists were certain that FLOTUS had contracted a virus.

Also, a thorough examination by Army nurses had identified a mark above her left hip that they agreed was from a needle. The location was an additional concern because it was close to FLOTUS's liver.

Kennedy Russell drifted in and out of consciousness. She thought back to before Andrew was president. When he was a little-known congressman from Brooklyn and he and Kennedy with their young children first came to Nantucket as a family.

With no Secret Service detail and simply shielded by anonymity, they created memories, just like so many other families.

They enjoyed going to the Rope Walk restaurant in town at the head of Straight Wharf. It was one of their favorite places. She recalled a night at the Rope Walk when Katie was four and Andrew was six.

The kids still talked about it because it was the Fourth of July and there were fireworks off Jetties Beach. One of the nice things about the Rope Walk, in addition to a staff who were very welcoming to families, was how the dining room doors could be opened during the summer. This provided refreshing breezes and a proximity to the wharf, which was filled with a variety of yachts, sport fishermen, and the occasional Gar Wood wooden speedboat.

Once the fireworks had ended, all the boats in the harbor started to blow their horns and whistles. At first it frightened Katie, who was exhausted. But the kids still remembered it and it became one of those wonderful memories that are made when families go on vacation.

Unfortunately, the Rope Walk was gone now, replaced by a new place called Cru—very hip and catering to a younger crowd.

Those were the memories that were running through Kennedy Russell's mind as she drifted in and out of consciousness.

❖

Thirty minutes had passed and Kevin Mannix had reassembled his team in Crisis Room 1. The first readout was that they thought it highly unlikely that the children had left with the ATV team and that the missile launches were a cover to allow the children to leave via another means.

The second team concurred with that assessment, but they went further. One of the analysts on the team was Alex Zucker, an extremely bright but somewhat obnoxious analyst.

It was Kevin Mannix who agreed to take Zucker after he wore out his welcome with two other NSA teams. Yes, he was a pain in the ass, and some of the things he said were out of line, but he was also the smartest person on the team, so they put up with his occasional theatrical outbursts.

Zucker addressed the room. "You people have been relying on infrared technology, which is so 1980-ish. We all know that a squirrel suit can dramatically mask any sort of infrared reading. Yet you keep asking about infrared readings.

"*Wake up*. Of course there were no infrared readings on Minecraft and Missy, because it is very likely they were wearing squirrel suits," he yelled. After exhaling loudly, he grumbled, "Why do I have to put up with Luddites?"

Zucker went on, "Get me the data files from the Alpha2 sensors and I will run those files through my acoustic algorithms, where we will have a much better chance of picking up something than with whatever obsolete technology you're using."

Mannix rolled his eyes but instructed his team to contact the SEAL drone operator and get Zucker the data files.

❖

Commander Burduck called Nicols. "We have just reached the abandoned ATVs. No one is in the immediate area."

Nicols responded, "Copy, we are sending a team to secure the area."

"Also, there are two rockets that did not launch. We will need a munitions team to disarm them." The SEALs easily found the rockets, as they had lifted from the ground and sat poised on their launching rails.

"We will coordinate getting resources on-site for that as well," answered Nicols.

"My team is going to conduct a search in the area for the ATV drivers. Recommend we get the Marines to set up a perimeter."

Nicols came back, "Roger, Commander, we will notify the Marines."

With that, Nicols briefed the Marine colonel on the latest developments.

It was pitch-dark now, which would hamper the SEALs' ability to pick up any trail of the ATV drivers. Of course the SEALs had night vision goggles to assist them, but the process was slow. When they did finally pick up something, it was in the direction away from the airport, toward the Tetawkimmo neighborhood.

❖

In the meantime, a medical evacuation Gulfstream III landed at ACK a little after midnight.

The Army doctors and the CDC scientists had decided that the best course of treatment was to get FLOTUS off ACK and to Emory University Hospital, located outside of Atlanta and near the CDC.

Because of the isolation chambers in which they were both enclosed, Andrew Russell spoke in low, soft tones to his wife, whom they had just awakened via a phone.

"Ken," said the president, "how are you feeling?"

"Okay," she said weakly. "Andy, any word on the children?"

"We'll get them back—I promise."

Kennedy Russell just nodded. "Andy, do whatever it takes to get them back."

"We will," said the president.

The first lady then said they were ready to take her to the airport for her trip to Emory.

Before she hung up she added tearfully, "Andy, bring our babies home safe."

She was exhausted and sick, and now she was going to be in Atlanta, away from her husband and not knowing where or when she would next see her children. Added to that was the stress of not knowing what the bastards had injected into her body.

Unable to fight sleep any longer, she closed her eyes and drifted off, praying that her husband would find their children soon.

❖

The irascible Alex Zucker had received the Alpha2 data files and was now running them against his acoustic algorithms, which he had developed while at MIT. Once the base model was created, he started using fractals and fluid dynamic models he had created from tests conducted on the International Space Station from experiments that he had proposed to NASA three years earlier.

With his analysis complete, he reentered Crisis Room 1, bobbing his head like the Know-it-All he was, indicating to all present that he was sure his hypotheses were correct.

He began, "At MIT I came up with a theory that all fluid dynamics created discernable patterns created from the disruption of accoustics."

"Oh my God, Alex, no lectures, not tonight," interrupted Mannix.

Zucker nodded and restarted. "We can detect the movement of objects from disruptions in sounds detected by ultrahigh-frequency acoustics. My algorithms should be able to detect acoustic footprints from air and fluid dynamics.

"We could detect the passing of a submarine or the movement of a person through a dark room by monitoring to ultrahigh-frequency acoustics. Cool, right?"

He continued, "Look at my analysis of the Hedge Row house taken from the Alpha2 sensor data. This is a few minutes before the house was set ablaze and right before the SPIDs starting pinging." Zucker put up two slides side by side on the high-definition screens.

"The slide on the left," he said, "was taken five minutes before the SPIDs were detected. The slide on the right was taken ninety seconds after the SPIDs went off.

"When looked at with ultrahigh-frequency acoustics, we can detect a slight disruption in the airflow between the two slides."

He then hit the enter key on his laptop and stepped through a time series of the following two minutes, second by second, using the Alpha2 sensor data from the Predator drone.

He had automated the slide show so you could see the movement of something through the air. It was like one of those old movie booklets where you flicked the pages quickly and saw the impression of an animated movie.

It was amazing, and the people in the room were mesmerized.

"Run it again," said McMahon, who had reentered the room.

As Zucker did, you could clearly discern the acoustic pattern showing the disruption of the air as two isolated objects moved due east from the Hedge Row house out toward the beach.

"Again," said McMahon.

The acoustic analysis wasn't perfect, and the data could be interpreted in other ways. As a result, Mannix challenged his team for contrarian arguments showing why Zucker was wrong.

But no one could come up with any viable alternative views.

Without leaving the room, McMahon picked up the handset. "This is Kristin McMahon for Director Riordan. I need to speak to him at once."

She then glanced at Zucker and mouthed the words, "Well done." A second later McMahon was speaking with Riordan.

Riordan had been in the Sit Room but left to focus on what McMahon was telling him. She took him through the analysis.

George Riordan asked, "Kristin is your team prepared to brief the Sit Room?"

"Yes," she said.

Riordan reentered the Sit Room and interrupted the conversation, saying, "My NSA team has come up with something I think you are all going to want to see immediately."

"What is it?" the VP asked.

Riordan replied, "Mr. Vice President, the NSA's done an analysis that strongly suggests the Russell children may have left the island by air. By a balloon or a hang glider or something like that."

That quieted the entire room.

After letting the words sink in for a moment, the vice president said, "Bridge in your team, George."

When the videoconferencing link was established, George Riordan introduced McMahon, Mannix, and Zucker. Zucker presented his analysis and then answered each question succinctly, only once mouthing off when the chairman of the Joint Chiefs asked him how sure he was with his analysis.

Zucker responded, "General, how sure are you your Marines can do push-ups?"

Riordan winced and interceded before the chairman had time to rip into Zucker, by saying, "Kristin, run the analysis again, please."

After the second time, McMasters spoke up, saying, "We need to recall the SEALs. We need to have them put to sea. George, have your team prepare to brief the president in five minutes."

As they worked on arranging the conference with the president, McMasters had a minute to think about people like Zucker and the US leadership in innovation and technology.

McMasters reflected, *While some may hurt us, like this terrorist group did today, with people like Zucker, no one can ever defeat the United States of America.*

Riordan and the entire Sit Room listened again as McMahon, Mannix, and Zucker briefed President Russell and his chief of staff, Chief Tate, Admiral Jacobsen, and Agent Nicols.

President Russell asked for comments from his team on Nantucket.

Nicols spoke first. "Sir, we still need to catch the ATV terrorists, and we know they are out there."

"No doubt," said President Russell. He turned to Tate. "Chris, what do you think?"

"Mr. President, I'm a New York City cop—acoustic analysis is not my area. I will say that I agree that the ATVs and rockets were very likely yet another diversion. The thought that the children may have left the island really takes this into the admiral and SEALs' domain. However, as a poker player, at this point I wouldn't put all my chips on this lead.

"We need to follow up on all of them—and we need to be particularly careful that in the rush to accept this scenario we don't miss something else equally if not more important."

President Russell let Tate's words sink in.

"You're right, Chris. Work with Sterl and the Secret Service to ensure we are not missing something—anything."

Next President Russell turned to Admiral Jacobsen. "Brian, if they have left the island, the tactical situation has shifted to the Navy."

As the president said that, he noticed the look on Nicols' face. "Don't worry, Dan, the Secret Service is still responsible for finding my children, but if they are at sea we need to rely on the Navy to find them. When the time comes to avenge the loss of our agents, your team will be taking the shots."

Agent Nicols simply said, "Thank you, sir."

Jacobsen had been speaking on a headset with CNO Johnson, who was in the Sit Room. Jacobsen took off his headset and answered the president. "Sir, if your children are at sea, the Navy will locate them. Then it will be up to the SEALs to board whatever vessel they are on and rescue them. I think that much is clear."

The president was tired, stressed, and worried about his wife and children, not to mention the impact of the attack on the entire country and whether or not there were other attacks coming. He finally lost his temper.

"Brian, there hasn't been a whole hell of a lot that has been clear today." Everyone in the room remained quiet and understood that this was not only the president speaking but also a husband and a father. He paused for a second, rubbed his temples, and added, "Brian, sorry, I'm just fried. Admiral, you've got your Big Stick. Use it, find my children, and bring them home."

"Copy, sir," said Jacobsen.

The president was beginning to feel some tightness in his throat, which was also worrying him, and he needed to get some rest. But until his children were found there would be no rest.

❖

Hijra team was now in the Tetawkimmo Way Off Broadway house. Like Hedge Row, it was a large, recently built custom house.

There were only four members of the Hijra team remaining on the island. Karim, their team leader, and another team member had left on the balloons with the children.

The members of the Hijra team, just like the other team members, had been recruited and brainwashed against the West well prior to the planning of this mission. Once they'd been vetted, their training began. The recruits were considered elite fighters and as a result their training was much more comprehensive than that for the typical Al Qaeda fighter. These men of the Hijra, Amina, and Kiswa teams were good students and became effective commandos.

That said, they weren't Navy SEALs, Army Rangers, Green Berets, or US Marines. And there were about to find that out the hard way.

As the team settled into the Way Off Broadway house, one of the members commented, "These Americans. Look how they live."

They had only recently seen Sub-Zero refrigerators, Viking stoves, and Thos. Moser furniture.

He added, "These are the trappings of a decadent and godless society and further justifies that what we are doing is right in the eyes of Allah."

None of them had ever lived in a home that remotely approached the luxury of these homes.

As matter of fact, the entire island of Nantucket portrayed a quality of life that none of them had ever experienced. Of course, with their twisted outlook, they had only disdain for America, and especially for the wealthy Americans who owned these homes.

To show his displeasure, the Hijra team member used the barrel of his AK-47 to shatter a bowl on the kitchen island. He then kicked the door of the Sub-Zero refrigerator.

One of the other men yelled at him, "Satyam, stop making noise and breaking things. We need to move to the basement as the plan dictates."

The team leader made a valid point. All of the teams up to this point had exercised extremely good discipline and kept to their plan and its schedule. As misguided and wrong minded as these terrorists were, it was clear they were acting on the deep convictions they held about their religion and way of life.

It was clear from Satyam's behavior that the team's anxiety level was increasing. They knew it was just a matter of time before they were discovered, and they all knew that would lead to their demise.

One of the members had brought a prayer rug with him. He placed it on the floor of the game room in the basement and bowed to Mecca while the others ate whatever food was available in the house and checked their weapons for the inevitable firefight to come.

Chapter Fifteen

Early Sunday Morning

Lieutenant Commander Burduck ordered, "Cast off," as the SDV left Sconset Beach and prepared to rendezvous with the USS *Jimmy Carter*. Burduck had left the task of finding the ATV Hijra team to the US Marines and the Secret Service. Lieutenant Commander Burduck and SEAL Team 2 were now tasked with finding and rescuing the Russell kids.

More accurately, the mission to locate and rescue the Russell children was now the primary responsibility of the US Navy.

That was precisely the point Admiral Jacobsen made on a conference call with the commanders of his surface and sub-surface force.

"Gentlemen," he began, "we have a Nimitz-class carrier, two Aegis cruisers, three Arleigh Burkes, and two subs—all deployed in the theater of operation where we believe the Russell children to be. We are going to prosecute every air, surface, or subsurface contact and get the Russell children back safely to their parents. *And we are going to do it now. Do you read me?"*

In spite of all this firepower and technology, everyone knew that when the children were found, it would be up to the SEALs to rescue them, and no one underestimated the challenge that represented.

The XO of the USS *Jimmy Carter* was in radio communication with Navy SEAL Lieutenant Tom Mahoney, and they worked to maneuver the SDV back on board the *Carter*.

Twenty minutes later, with the SDV secure, Captain Stu Jackson was more than ready to get under way. Jackson called out, "Make your depth 150 feet, all ahead full, steer course 187 degrees."

The diving officer acknowledged, "Aye, aye, sir, I have the dive. Five degrees down bubble, making my depth 150 feet, all ahead full, my heading is 187 true." As the sub started to descend, the crew of the USS *Jimmy Carter* jumped into action. They were ready to finally join in the pursuit of the enemy. Game on.

❖

Just as the Virginia- and Seawolf-class submarines were the pride of the US Navy's silent services, the People's Liberation Army Navy (PLAN) new Type 041 Yuan-class submarines were the pride of the Chinese Navy. The Yuan 041 was China's lead class of diesel-electric attack submarine. Displacing four thousand tons, the Type 041 was equipped with six torpedo tubes in the bow, which carried the Yu-6 wire-guided torpedoes.

The Chinese Yu-6 torpedoes were similar to the US Navy's MK 48 wire-guided torpedoes.

The Yuan's main propulsion system was based on diesel-electric engines, but it was thought that the Type 041 might be the first Chinese conventionally powered attack submarine (SSK) equipped with the Stirling air-independent propulsion (AIP) system, one about which not much was known.

Diesel-electric boats were so quiet they challenged the best US subs, but this new air system could be a game changer.

The new Type 041 was influenced by the design of the very capable Russian-made Kilo attack submarines. Like the US subs, the 041 Yuans featured rubber antisonar coating, which provided a reduction in the acoustic signature.

The Pentagon rated the 041 Yuan subs on par with the Virginia-class subs, the main difference being the source of power.

This, of course, was a huge difference since it meant the Yuans were conventionally powered and did not have nuclear reactors. As such their range was limited to eight thousand miles at sixteen knots. Because of that, their main theater of operation was the South China Sea and the Indian Ocean. If they wished to venture farther they needed to be refueled.

On board the Type 041 Chinese sub Yuan, Captain Liu was keeping station forty feet below and about sixty feet behind the SS *Milbridge Major*. Both were cruising at ten knots about twenty-five miles off Nantucket on a west-southwest course.

At the same time, the balloons were in the process of connecting with the Zodiacs. The two Hijra balloon "pilots" were passing the unconscious children to the Zodiac crews.

It was a little after 1 a.m. when the Zodiac crews finished securing the two Hijra team members and their precious cargo of the Russell children. The Zodiac crews then set sea anchors and started to paddle to the agreed coordinates in order to rendezvous with the *Milbridge*.

At their course and speed, they projected rendezvous with the *Milbridge* by 3:15 a.m.

Karim, who had assumed command of the Zodiacs, told the crew members, "The children will soon wake up. When they do, make sure they take water and eat."

It had been seventeen hours since they had been kidnapped, and they had been unconscious for most of that time. Karim threatened the crew that if anything happened to the children, they would pay with their lives.

❖

McMasters was on the phone with the British prime minister, James King.

"Mr. Prime Minister, as you can appreciate, we are working very hard on a rapidly developing situation."

King replied, "Mr. Vice President, what assistance can Great Britain provide?"

McMasters brought up the Finsbury Park cell outside of London to the British PM.

King responded, "I will have our MI6 unit look into this Finsbury Park business as a top priority. If we can confirm your information, you have my personal assurance that British Special Forces will move on the cell ASAP."

McMasters was well aware of the long history between the two countries. He knew the Brits would take pride in doing their part in assisting the US as it dealt with the attack on the president and his family. Second, they would be extremely motivated to ensure that any link back to the UK and this kidnapping would be dealt with in an expedited manner.

King added, "Jack, if we can provide any assistance, either by our intelligence or military, please do not hesitate to let me know."

McMasters replied, "No, Mr. Prime Minister, we can handle it. It's our fight and our president. But it is always gratifying to know we can count on your full support. If you can look into the Finsbury Park cell, that would be very helpful."

King closed with, "Consider it done. Good luck, Mr. Vice President. Alastair will call Director Collins on the Finsbury business once we have an update. Please tell President Russell that we stand ready to help in any way we can. Also, I am keeping his family in my thoughts and intentions. " And with that he hung up.

McMaster's next call was to the French president. He knew when the world was on edge, communication with the top international leaders was key.

McMasters explained that President Russell had no band-width for calls to world leaders—he needed to get his children back and take care of his wife's health.

❖

Lauren La Rue was concerned about the cash transfers she had just made. She had stayed safe by *always* exercising cau-tion, and now these transfers were so blatantly risky that they had her greatly concerned.

Had Sheik Abdul Er Rahman just slipped up? She'd never known him to do so before. Was there some emergency that required the immediate movement of such transfers? Had the sheik done this on purpose in order to set up La Rue?

La Rue had a plan in place when the time came for her to leave the sheik's employ.

The plan involved access to cash in several denominations of US dollars, euros, and British sterling; forged passports; and an es-cape route. The plan had to be prepared well in advance, because once the situation arose where she needed it, there would be very little time to think about it—she would just have time to act.

She was sitting at her desk looking at the screens of the various cash-management systems. All the money wires had been made, with several of the transfers originating from Oasis accounts going directly to US-based accounts. This was mad-ness, she thought.

Just then the phone at her desk rang. She looked at the caller ID display and saw it was one of the numbers that Sheik Abdul Er Rahman used. She paused but didn't pick up. She would let the call go to voice mail.

She watched to see if the message light came on, but it did not come on. Next her cell rang. Again she recognized the number as one of the sheik's. She still didn't pick up. It was possible that she wasn't at her desk to take the sheik's call, but to not pick up her cell would raise concerns, especially given the circumstances.

Every fiber in her being was telling her something was wrong—very wrong.

Just then, her iPhone buzzed as she received another in the series of mysterious WhatsApp text messages she had been getting over the last couple of weeks. She wasn't sure if they were sent by the sheik's security chief, Kaizad Shehzad, as a test or from an intelligence organization from some country trying to gain access to her.

What she did know for sure was that she didn't trust Kaizad, and with good reason, knowing some of the "assignments" he performed on behalf of the sheik.

Prior to this the texts had been puzzling but benign. But this one was alarming, "Leave now. Text 052 343 8998 when you have a new phone."

And that was enough for La Rue. She jotted down the number, gathered her handbag and iPhone, and left her office immediately. As is the custom in the Middle East, Sunday was a workday, and as a result the office was staffed like any other workday. She looked around to see if anyone was paying undue attention as she left.

As she exited the elevator and walked across the lobby, she had already decided she would not take her car. She would leave it in the building's underground garage, as she assumed it was being tracked. As she left the building and started to walk across the plaza, she began looking for a "drop."

Then she saw what she was looking for—a moped messenger had just pulled up. As the messenger dismounted the moped and made his way to the lobby of her building, La Rue approached the moped, flipped open the rear saddlebag, dropped her iPhone into it, and kept walking.

She hoped that no harm would come to the messenger, but that wasn't her concern. Her safety was her top priority.

Next she hailed a cab and took it to the Ibn Battuta Mall on the other side of town. The car ride gave her a few more minutes to go over her plan. Once at the mall, she purchased three prepaid SIM cards from a kiosk, paying cash for them. She then went into an electronics store and purchased two smartphones—both without SIM cards.

She then inserted one of the prepaid SIMs into one of her newly purchased smartphones. She now had a new phone that would be untraceable as long as she didn't call any number that would raise a red flag.

She texted 052 343 8998, "Who is this?"

The reply came back to use La Rue's Skype ID. La Rue opened Skype on her phone. Instantly she received a Skype message, "Lauren, I am a friend. You are in danger. Do not go home and do not go to the American embassy in Dubai. They are both compromised."

A second later a second message appeared, "Go to Jassa Beach in Muscat, Oman and look for a boat named *Al Raisa* that will take you to India. Go now."

She took the SIM card out of her phone and threw it out as she passed a trash bin. While not an intelligence agent, La Rue was well versed in the tradecraft.

She left the mall and hailed another cab, which took her to a storage locker facility. She got out of the cab and asked the driver to wait. She then entered the storage building and unlocked locker 153.

In the locker was a backpack that had three passports: Saudi, Jordanian, and Egyptian. There was also cash— 100,000 EUR, $100,000 USD and £100,000 GBP—and a change of clothes.

In the backpack was an unlocked iPhone, in which she placed one of her newly purchased prepaid SIM cards. She knew the iPhone from the locker was clean.

She located her small form-factor 9mm Glock G43 with three extra six-bullet magazines. She threw all of it into the backpack, leaving her handbag in the locker. She then made her way back to her cab.

Her next stop was a beauty salon—not her regular salon, but one on this side of town. She needed a new look, she needed to have her nails "undone," and she needed to take off all her makeup.

She needed to "un-Americanize" her look and do it quickly. An hour later she emerged with her long hair now cut short into something resembling a pixie haircut.

Next she went to a public restroom and changed into the clothes she had gotten from her storage locker. It was a working outfit and not the $3,000 Chanel pantsuit she had been wearing.

Her mini-transformation was now complete. Her nails lacked polish, she wore no makeup, she had a different haircut, and her clothing would not stand out from that of any other Arab woman.

What she couldn't change was her perfect smile and white teeth and her pierced ears—even without earrings the holes and tweezed eyebrows would give her away as a Westerner. A close inspection by a trained eye would reveal her as a woman of means and not a local. And all of the members of the sheik's UAE-based security team had trained eyes.

❖

Sheik Abdul Er Rahman didn't talk to many people. He had a small circle of trusted associates to whom he spoke. This afternoon as he sat in his opulent office in Riyadh he called over one of his most trusted aides and spoke very softly into his ear.

The aide nodded and left the room. The sheik knew of the operation under way on Nantucket, and now he would start cleaning up any loose ends that could possibly lead back to him. The first loose end that needed to be cleaned up was Lauren La Rue.

He knew Lauren was smart and she would be difficult to find if she ran. He had wondered if the bank transfers were enough to make her suspicious, and his hunch was confirmed when neither of his calls to her had been returned. It had been more than an hour since he'd left a message without a response, and that never happened.

That was all he needed to confirm that La Rue was on the run. He said as much to his aide—who then quickly left the sheik's office to put the necessary actions in motion.

Just as La Rue had her escape preplanned, the sheik had a termination plan in place for her. The sheik didn't just single out La Rue. He had plans for all of his associates. He even had termination plans in place for his wives.

The only ones he didn't have termination plans for were his five children—his three sons and two daughters. They would be spared no matter what happened.

La Rue wasn't trained as a spy or a field agent. But she was a very smart woman both in how she handled her work life and in how she dealt with her personal life. That was why he had hired her, so he knew he was up against a cunning adversary.

And he now realized that he had inadvertently given her a head start. That was regrettable and would make the task of finding and killing her more difficult. With a smart woman like La Rue, who had an hour head start and an escape plan in place, he gave his security team only fifty-fifty odds that she would be dead by the time the sun set in Dubai today.

He was not overly concerned, though. It was just a matter of time before she was found. How hard it was to find her would factor into the manner of her death. If they found her in the first forty-eight hours, she would die quickly and with the minimum of pain.

Anything beyond that and the sheik would become angry, and his anger would translate proportionately into how much more painful her demise would be.

❖

The SS *Milbridge Major* was just now coming to the location where the plan called for them to rendezvous with the three Zodiacs. It was just a little after 3 a.m. and the bridge crew, using night vision binoculars, had all three Zodiacs in sight.

The plan called for them to pick up the Zodiacs without stopping. The seas were calm and there was little roll, so the captain had to alter his course only slightly, allowing him to come up on the Zodiacs and place them in the lee of the *Milbridge*'s hull, which would make the Zodiac transfers even less risky.

The ship's crew fired shot lines to the Zodiacs in order to pull them to the pilot ladder.

Karim yelled to the crewman on the pilot ladder, "Take the children first."

The crew member grabbed Andrew first and pulled him to the ladder, using both of his arms to make sure he didn't slip.

Next came Katie, who was so light they just picked her up and carried her up the ladder all the way to the deck.

Karim followed, and once on board he went directly to the bridge. "Captain, your Zodiac crews performed well."

The captain of the *Milbridge*, who carried himself with a cold demeanor, was a career seaman who had never advanced beyond commanding ships the likes of the *Milbridge*. He just nodded.

Karim pressed the one-sided conversation, "Is everything all set with our 'friends'?"

The captain nodded again and replied, "Everything is proceeding as planned."

Karim then left the bridge to make sure the children were being given some food and water.

The crew attached metal cables to the Zodiacs and winched them aboard. Once on the deck they would be stowed in freight containers so anyone curious about the *Milbridge* wouldn't see them on the deck.

❖

The 2nd Marines were tasked with finding the members of the Hijra team still on Nantucket. This was the team of ATV riders and rocket launchers. The Secret Service were already securing the rocket sites and examining the launchers as well as the abandoned ATVs.

Working with the Marines, the Secret Service had identified an area where they expected the Hijra members were hiding. It was an area the shape of a rectangle defined by the airport on the south, Pout Pond Road to the north, Nobadeer Farm Road to the west, and Russells Way to the east.

The Marines further broke the area down into nine sectors and assigned a squad of eight Marines to search each sector.

In addition, another squad of Marines was assigned the task of tracking down and capturing what were believed to be two animals that now had the childrens' SPIDs attached to them. The SPIDs were showing up in the village of Sconset, leading to the assumption that the dogs were probably looking for something to eat.

The search for the Hijra team members was going to be methodical and would require a house-to-house search. The main challenge was the fact it was 3:30 a.m. and most residents would be asleep. The idea of a squad of camouflaged Marines waking people up in the middle of the night would be not only frightening but also potentially dangerous, as a random homeowner might mistake them for an intruder and start shooting.

Squad C of the 2nd Marines was assigned to Tetawkimmo. Most of these houses were large and would take some time to inspect. In the case where the home was occupied, once it was ascertained that the people in the home weren't terrorists, the Marines would need to size up the family to ensure they weren't being held against their wills by Hijra members who might be hidden somewhere in these large houses. The homes that were vacant were more challenging and took even longer to search.

The Marines were plotting the progress using a variant of Google Maps to mark each property that had been cleared.

As the squads advanced, everyone knew the noose was tightening, and with it so was the anxiety level. All nine squads were working from south to north in the search area, with another squad patrolling along Pout Pond Road to cut off any potential escape routes.

To the west, on Proprietors Way, the Massachusetts state troopers who were working in cooperation with the US Marines had set up roadblocks and were confident that no one from the Tetawkimmo neighborhood could get past them. The time was 3:45 a.m.

❖

At Emory University Hospital, where FLOTUS had recently arrived, her temperature was now 102 and still climbing, and her respiration was growing labored.

Her vital signs were relayed to the scientists at the CDC, who were now processing the blood and urine samples they had just taken.

In addition to the samples from FLOTUS, they also had samples from the two Massachusetts state troopers who found FLOTUS, POTUS, his chief of staff, Chris Tate, and Secret Service Agent Dan Nicols.

The doctors had determined the virus FLOTUS had con-tracted was a weaponized variant of the H1N1 virus. This particular virus kills through creating an overreaction by the body's immune system. Just like the Spanish flu of 1918, this variant relied on the victim's immune system to carry the at-tack to the respiratory system.

The virus could be transmitted via the air, by touch, and/or by the transfer of bodily fluids.

The doctors and scientists knew they were racing time, as most hypervirulent viruses usually either killed their hosts or burned themselves out within seventy-two hours. Right now they estimated they were at T plus fourteen hours.

No one at the CDC doubted they could engineer a cure for this virus in the next thirty days or so. But the bigger ques-tion was whether they could find an antidote in the next twen-ty-four to thirty-six hours in order to save FLOTUS.

❖

It was noon in Dubai and Lauren La Rue had been on the run for about two hours when the first lead on her where-abouts came in to the sheik. The sheik had ordered his cyber-team to start searching video feeds from La Rue's UAE office building and the surrounding area. They had eventually spot-ted a woman who looked like La Rue buying a smartphone in the mall in Dubai.

The sheik, who had connections with the Ministries of Tech-nology in all the Gulf states including the UAE, had his cyber-team work with the local mobile network operators to pull the list of every new prepaid SIM activated in the last two hours.

In the entire city, during the last two hours the three larg-est cell phone carriers had activated three thousand SIM cards.

By examining the sales records from the shop, they were able to discern the model of smartphone La Rue had purchased, which dramatically reduced the sample set to only eleven phones. Of the eleven Samsung Galaxy S7s that were purchased during that time frame, nine had prepaid SIMs. Now the team started to track those phones by their numbers.

It would only be a matter of time before they discovered which of these phones was La Rue's. They expected she would buy several prepaid SIMs, so they would need to track all new activations on Samsung Galaxy S7s in Dubai for the rest of the day. It would be hard, as the Samsung S7 was the second most popular smartphone in the country, after the iPhone.

La Rue had known this, and her choice of the Samsung S7 was not a random decision. As a result it was going to take longer to track La Rue. That plus the fact that her Samsung S7 was now in a storage locker in Dubai and she was using the iPhone from her escape bag gave the momentary advantage to La Rue.

So far La Rue had succeeded in avoiding capture, but it had been only two hours and she still needed to leave the city and the country.

She had three options to get to Oman: first, rent a car and drive herself to Muscat. But she knew the sheik would have all rental car companies under surveillance, so that option was not viable.

Her second option was to go to one of the private airports and charter a plane to take her to Muscat. But the sheik's men would certainly be monitoring all private plane departures. There were no trains from Dubai to Muscat.

That left her third option: to go by land via a truck or taxi to Oman. She quickly eliminated the taxi option, knowing the sheik would soon text all the taxis, notifying them that La Rue was wanted and offering a large reward.

That left the truck option, which was also risky. First she had to find a trucker willing to take her to Muscat. That wouldn't be that hard. But she also needed to find a driver who would keep his mouth shut.

No doubt the sheik would notify truckers about her and offer an award, but La Rue was going to be offering cash to take her to Oman, and she was confident that cash in hand would be a strong incentive for the right truck driver.

With her new haircut and attractive figure, it would not be hard to find a trucker willing to give her a ride. But she knew her attractiveness could also cause her trouble. Knowing Middle Eastern men, she worried about being sexually harassed by whichever trucker she found.

Psychologically, she could convince herself she would be able to endure whatever was necessary in order to survive. It was purely a survival instinct. And she knew that any of the travel options would be a hundred times better than what would happen to her if the sheik caught her—maybe a thousand times better.

By now the sheik would have all escape routes covered, so she needed to move fast and smart. She took three different cabs on her way to the Samaher truck stop, where she hoped to find a truck headed to Muscat via the border city of Al Ain. Even if the sheik had notified the cab drivers about her, La Rue was confident her new look and clothing plus the head scarf she was now wearing made recognizing her much harder.

Hopefully she could find a trucker who was a married man or at least a man of principles so the ride wouldn't be too bad.

It was only a hundred-mile drive from Dubai to the border crossing between the UAE and Oman at the town of Al Ain, so the drive would take only two hours or less once they started.

She had cash to give the driver so he could bribe the border agents, which wasn't unusual at all. At the Samaher truck stop she looked for clean trucks that also exhibited some sort of religious artifact hanging from the mirror. That was how La Rue hoped to find a trustworthy driver. It wasn't a great plan, but it was the best she could come up with.

She approached a truck that met her requirements and after a short conversation made the arrangements. It would cost her US$20,000, which was many times more than the annual salary of the typical UAE trucker. The trucker was eager to get going, knowing that time was not on their side.

As she climbed into the cab of the truck she experienced a moment of despair. How had she ever gotten into this situation? But she knew the answer: In Dubai she lived the good life, and she was paid exorbitantly for her expertise—much more than her equivalents were making in New York or London.

That plus the fact that she was an adrenaline junkie. She was driven by the need to take chances, and working with someone like the sheik provided the ultimate rush.

❖

It was 3:55 a.m. on board the USS *Jimmy Carter*, and the CO, XO, and SEAL commander were meeting to discuss their next steps when priority flash traffic was received.

The incoming message was a series of high-definition photos with write-ups from the NSA on each of the vessels thought to be the top suspects to be holding the Russell kids. In all there were three fishing boats, a yacht, and the SS *Milbridge Major*.

The fishing boat the *Gayle B*, which had been at sea for several days, and was owned by well-known Nantucket fishing couple Bill and Ruth Count, was eliminated, as was another fishing boat, the *West Wind*, a fifty-eight-foot Bertram, where sensors confirmed only six men were on board.

The third vessel was another fishing boat—the green-hulled *Donna Marie*, a sea scalloper, also well-known on the island, with a crew of two in addition to the captain on board—again no children, so it, too, was eliminated.

The yacht was *The Brown-Eyed Girl* out of Nantucket, a T48 Flybridge Hinckley boat registered to island resident Ted

Schnell. Thermal sensors detected four people on her, two males and two females, but the size of the images again indicated only adults, so this was not the boat with the Russell kids on it.

The final photo and write-up was for the SS *Milbridge Major*, the Panamanian-flagged Turkish freighter. Thermal imaging showed about twenty people on board. The imaging was not conclusive due to the sensors having trouble penetrating the decks of the freighter, but there was, in the analyst's judgment, "a strong possibility" there could be two younger people on board. The next document sent by the NSA showed the ports of call for the *Milbridge* for the last twelve months, which included Yemen and Saudi Arabia.

A Turkish freighter twenty-five miles off Nantucket at the same time the president's family was kidnapped was their number one target now. Bingo.

The XO asked the SEAL commander, "How should we approach the freighter?"

He said, "XO, I recommend we board the freighter while it is under way via grappling lines. Also we should go with only a squad of eight, not the entire SEAL team."

The XO, Tom Walsh, asked, "What if we get a Coast Guard cutter to stop them on a random safety inspection?"

CO Jackson was quick to dismiss that idea. "Tom, we don't have time to get a Coast Guard cutter on station. And I have no interest in having the *Carter* try and stop them and risk them ramming us."

The SEAL commander added, "A parachute jump onto the ship would be good, but again we really don't have the time to get that in place. We would need to surface immediately and rendezvous with a helo, and then board a C-130 for the jump. We just don't have the time before sunup."

The best option was Commander Burduck's first. The *Carter* would get the SEALs as close as possible to the *Mil-*

bridge and the SEAL squad would board the freighter using grappling lines.

The *Carter* was just twelve miles from the *Milbridge*, its target already in range of the *Carter*'s photo-optic mast, which had replaced the periscope on modern subs. They would be in position to deliver the SEAL team to board the *Milbridge* by 4:18 a.m. That would give them a little over an hour before sunrise to find and rescue the Russell children.

Lieutenant Commander Burduck went to brief his SEAL Team and start to assemble their equipment.

There would be no need to use the SDV on this mission. The *Carter* would surface so just the sail would be visible. Then SEALs would exit via take an inflatable to approach the *Milbridge*.

The *Milbridge* had increased speed after picking up the Zodiacs and was now steaming at ten knots. The *Carter* would need to maneuver upwind and about a quarter of a mile ahead of the *Milbridge*.

An E-2 Hawkeye from the USS *Theodore Roosevelt*, with no navigation lights on, was orbiting twenty miles away from the *Milbridge* at an altitude of twenty-five thousand feet. It had the *Milbridge* under full surveillance. In addition, a Predator would be on station in ten minutes, with its ability to send data back to the Sit Room and other commands.

The USS *Jimmy Carter*, at 453 feet long, was more than a hundred feet longer than the *Milbridge*, and with a draft of thirty-six feet it needed at least fifty feet of water to remain submerged.

A check of the depth chart where the *Milbridge* was sailing showed a depth of 105 feet, which was tight. There was also the Rose and Crown shoal, not far away from where the *Carter* was planning to rendezvous with the *Milbridge*.

Jackson didn't want to be the US Navy captain who ran his sub aground while attempting to rescue the Russell children, and he told his bridge crew as much.

The dive officer and navigator were huddled over the charts as the officer of the deck looked on. The only sound was the murmur of their voices as they discussed the plan for approaching the *Milbridge* and keeping the *Carter* off the shoal.

Captain Jackson assumed the *Milbridge*, if it had the children on board, would start to head away from Nantucket in order to have more room to maneuver. A south-southeast course would put them on track to enter the busy New York Harbor shipping lanes, where an old freighter would draw less scrutiny.

With that in mind, the *Carter* would maneuver to put itself between the *Milbridge* and the island. That would make it darker and help the SEALs with their mission to board the *Milbridge* unnoticed.

It was going to be a difficult mission, but the SEALs were used to getting the tough assignments. They often joked that the easy jobs went to the Army Rangers.

Then the SEALs caught a break.

The NSA sent a data package that included a real-time 3-D model of the *Milbridge* that the NSA had just produced. Unknown to everyone other than Jackson and the SEALs, there was a top secret room on the *Carter*. During its last overhaul the *Carter* was equipped with a virtual reality studio.

It was only a ten-foot-by-eight-foot room, but it was equipped with the latest in virtual reality, or VR, technology. In it, once the 3-D model of their target was loaded, the SEALs would don VR goggles and be able simulate the phases of their mission.

Two of the SEAL petty officers were already putting the VR goggles on in order to become familiar with the deck layout of the *Milbridge*.

Where the VR technology wouldn't provide any benefit was in dealing with the fact that under the SS *Milbridge Major*, undetected by the US Navy, was the Chinese Yuan 041 diesel-electric attack submarine.

Neither the USS *Jimmy Carter* nor the USS *North Dakota* had detected the Chinese sub on sonar. Nor were they looking for an enemy sub in the area around Nantucket. That was exactly the point Admiral Jacobsen had cautioned about when he said, "Keep a lookout for surface and *subsurface* contacts."

Right now the US subs were focused to the point of tunnel vision on the *Milbridge* and hadn't caught a hint of the Chinese Yuan submarine lurking just below.

Book II

Chapter Sixteen

Very Early Sunday Morning

The tactical situation was now well in hand, with the Marines hunting down the known remaining members of the Hijra team on Nantucket and the SEALs getting ready to board the SS *Milbridge Major*. The time was 4:11 a.m.

McMahon and Mannix had just about completed their team rotation. Most of Crisis Team 1 had been replaced with fresh members.

Unlike the US submarine commanders, McMahon was challenging her team to avoid myopia. She asked everyone, "What else is happening in the world? Are we overlooking something?"

McMahon's lead analyst responded, "The threat board is clear. The secretary of the treasury has already suspended trading for Monday." He was referring to some of the circuit breakers, or triggers, that were put in place post 9/11 to protect the global capital markets from panic.

In addition, Vice President McMasters was calling the president of Russia and the prime minister of Israel to make sure the other countries did not escalate their defense posture to a dangerous level.

The heads of State, the CIA, and the NSA would also, of course, be talking to their counterparts both in Russia and in

China, as well as with US allies in the UK, France, Germany, and Israel.

From this data a consensus would be established that would determine the current threat assessment. That threat assessment was then represented on the screens available to the Joint Chiefs as well as the heads of the US intelligence communities. Kristin McMahon's screen reflected that the US current DEFense CONdition was at level 3.

Depending on what was going on in the world, the DEFCON would be raised or lowered to reflect the combat readiness of the US. The current system defined five DEFCON levels:

> DEFCON 5—Normal peacetime readiness
> DEFCON 4—Normal, increased intelligence and strengthened security measures
> DEFCON 3—Increase in force readiness to above normal readiness
> DEFCON 2—Further increase in force readiness, but less than maximum readiness
> DEFCON 1—Maximum force readiness, preparation for war

When the first report of the attacks on ACK came in, the defense apparatus of the United States automatically moved from DEFCON 5 to DEFCON 4. Once it was known that the president's children had been kidnapped, the condition was increased to DEFCON 3.

Vice President McMasters was considering the current DEFCON level. In the Sit Room McMasters asked the chairman of the Joint Chiefs, "John, what if we move to DEFCON 2?"

General Standard answered, "Of course, that is an option we can take. But, Mr. Vice President, at this point I would advise against doing so as it would surely draw a similar response from all the world's powers, along with our allies in NATO."

Every major nation would move to a matching heightened alert status, with the ensuing risk that comes from having all the world's most powerful navies, air forces, and armies on heightened alert.

General Standard added, "Mr. Vice President, with everyone at a DEFCON 2, all we need is for two planes to touch wingtips or for two ships to collide and we could find ourselves in a situation which could escalate very quickly."

General Standard was correct and McMasters knew it.

In addition, the US was readying retaliatory strikes on Yemen, Syria, Burkina Faso, Germany, and Russia, with the Brits already planning to take out the identified cell in North London.

The DEFCON remained at 3.

❖

McMahon received a text from Lieutenant Commander Mike Bartlett.

He asked, "How are you holding up?"

She texted back, "Fine. We are pretty focused, as you might guess."

Bartlett added, "I understand. I am thinking of you."

McMahon simply replied with an "xoxoxo."

His final text to her was, "The world is focused on Nantucket, what's next? Are we missing something?"

It was that last phrase that stuck in her head. A minute later she went to the whiteboard in Crisis Room 1 and wrote in large letters, "WHAT'S NEXT?"

Then under it she wrote in equally big letters, "WHO'S BEHIND THIS?"

McMahon and her team shared the belief that Al Qaeda was behind the kidnapping of the Russell children and had infected the first lady and released her so she could then infect the president and other senior officials.

But McMahon continued to challenge her team. "Could Al Qaeda alone pull this off? Were others involved in the attack? And are other attacks imminent?"

It was the newer members, who had just rotated in, who wanted to examine if there were any corollary actions coming from any of the hot spots in the Middle East, North Korea, China, or Russia.

The team started to check the databases for any recent activity or reports from agents stationed in these locations.

At first, the team dismissed the idea that either Russia or China could be involved in the attack. The sheer thought that a superpower could be involved in kidnapping the president's family was beyond the pale and clearly ran the real risk of starting World War III.

One of McMahon's analysts spoke up. "Certainly Russia or China's governments wouldn't be involved in the attack, but what about a renegade faction from either one's government or military?"

❖

It was just after 4 a.m. when Squad C of the 2nd Marines, consisting of six men and two women, approached the Way Off Broadway house in the Tetawkimmo neighborhood.

The standard operating procedure, or SOP, for their incursion would be the same as it had been for the other four houses they had checked so far. With their night vision goggles on, two Marines would circle around back. Four would then approach the house from the front, also with the goggles on, and one Marine each would be positioned on either side of the house to guard the flanks. There were no lights on in the house as they approached, and it appeared the home was vacant.

The SOP for a vacant house required the Marines to either open the front door by force or jimmy the window nearest the door.

Most of these homes had alarm systems, but with the networks down the Marines didn't have to worry about them. The decision on this house was to jimmy the window on the front porch to the right of the main entrance door.

The members of the Hijra team hiding in the basement of the Way Off Broadway home immediately detected the sounds as the Marines entered the house. As the Marines made their way across the foyer to the kitchen, the weight of their equipment made the longleaf pine floors creak.

The terrorist leader whispered to the team, "There is movement upstairs. Check your weapons."

One of the Hijra team members started to repeat in a low voice, "I pray to Allah in the Heavens above, I pray to Allah so that I have no fear."

As the Marines entered the home, they began their room-to-room search upstairs.

Out back near the pool the two Marines kept their M4s ready as they listened for updates from the incursion team via their earpieces.

With the bedrooms upstairs cleared and the main floor with its master suite also cleared, they prepared to search the basement.

The Hijra team leader quietly ordered, "Satyam, you and Bunda go behind the pool table. Mahmood, over there." He pointed to the entrance to the media room.

It didn't take long. Step by step the first Marine started down the basement stairs.

When the first Marine was on the last step, a second Marine was already halfway down the staircase behind him.

As the first Marine entered the basement, two things happened. First, all the basement lights came on, which had the effect of blinding both Marines, who were wearing their night vision goggles. Then a split second later shots were fired from the Hijra AK-47s.

In that instant history was made on Nantucket. It would be the first Marine fatality ever to take place on the island.

Unable to see but hearing the report of gunfire, the second Marine started to fire his M4. He took rounds to his legs and abdomen, falling on top of the lead Marine.

The radios started to light up with chatter. "Shots fired, shots fired."

Immediately the third Marine at the top of the stairs dropped a flashbang down the stairs. A nanosecond later it exploded, filling the basement with noise and smoke.

The four Marines outside looked around for another entrance to the basement. There were some small basement windows, and two Marines ran up and stuck their rifle barrels through them, breaking the glass. They had to hold off on firing until they knew their fellow Marines were clear. The flashbangs also made it impossible for them to see through the smoke.

The other two Marines, also outside, on either side of the house, quickly ran to the front door to aid the other members of the squad.

As they did, one radioed to the platoon CO, "Shots fired, shots fired. We are at Tapa-something Road."

The Marine platoon CO, back at Sconset, hearing the call and looking at the map, quickly identified the house correctly as being on Tawpawshaw Road.

He radioed C Squad, "Confirm shots fired on Tawpawshaw Road."

"Copy, shots fired," came the reply.

The CO then said, "Charlie squad, calvary on the way your posit."

The CO broadcast to all 2nd Marines, "Tango One, Tango One, shots fired at 4 Middle Tawpawshaw Road, Charlie squad on prem, repeat, friendlies on prem. Posit lat 41.2737 long −70.0600."

Next the Marine CO issued a scramble order for the two Marine CH-53E Super Stallion helicopters stationed at ACK Airport. "Vulcan512 and 513—scramble, scramble, scramble—posit 41.2737 dash −70.0600, repeat, 41.2737 dash −70.0600."

Having heard the scramble call, the Army Apache helos at ACK were also spinning up.

In addition, the other squads in C Company were abandoning their searches and heading double-time to the Way Off Broadway house.

Easy squad was the first to arrive on scene, followed by Bravo and Delta squads.

With four squads on site, the Marine major decided to gas the terrorists out. They were counting on the enemy not having gas masks. And they were right.

The Marines started throwing a strong derivative of tear gas into the house via the basement windows. Then Marines wearing gas masks quickly went down the stairs to extract their fallen squad members.

As they entered the basement they fired on full automatic, filling the room with gunfire.

As the two wounded Marines were carried out of the house, Vulcan512 and 513 arrived and hovered just above the house.

Mudder 1, the call sign for the on-site Marine major, called to the helos, "We need a priority medivac."

"Copy, Mudder, Vulcan512 will put down in the circle just north of you—prepare for extraction. Vulcan513 will orbit to provide cover," replied the Super Stallion pilots.

"We are putting down," the pilot said to his copilot and the waist gunners, who were on their two door mounted .50 BMG GAU-15/A machine guns just itching to let loose. The other crew member, the cargo master, was already lowering the ramp.

As the helo's wheels set down, four Marines carried each of the wounded Marines onto the ramp. No one knew yet that one of the Marines was KIA.

The CH53E's wheels didn't even compress before the cargo master radioed to the pilots, "Packages on board, rotate, rotate."

Vulcan512's main engines revved as the huge Super Stallion lifted off.

Immediately they made a radio call, "Vulcan512 inbound Sconset with medical priorities—repeat, 512 inbound with medical priorities."

The medical staff at the field hospital at the Sconset Coast Guard station once again came to life.

At the Tawpawshaw house the tear gas had done its job and incapacitated the Hijra team, but not before one of the Hijra team members, the team leader, took his own life with a shot to the head.

The Marines zip cuffed the remaining three Hijra terrorists. They were being roughly handled as they waited for Vulcan513 to land and evacuate them to the CIA interrogation center at the Coast Guard station.

The Hijra prisoners were still blind as a result of the gas used by the Marines. Mudder 1 said to his troops, "Twenty-four hours from now they'll have wished we had shot 'em."

❖

The Marine CO, a full-bird colonel, entered the presidential bunker and informed Agent Nicols, Chief Tate, Chief of Staff Spencer, and the president that they had captured the ATV Hijra team.

The Marine colonel went on to say, "At this point we believe we have captured all the ATV terrorists, sir."

The president asked, "These captured terrorists—these are the ones who kidnapped my family and killed the Secret Service agents?"

The Marine colonel replied, "Right now we believe that is

the case, sir. They appear to be the team that came from the Hedge Row house and left on the ATVs."

He added, "And, Mr. President, we have a Marine KIA and one seriously wounded from the operation."

The president nodded, then turned to Nicols. "Dan, I want them interrogated immediately."

The Marine bird colonel then spoke with Secret Service Agent Nicols and the NYPD chief to discuss the possibility that there could still be other terrorists at large on the island.

After some more discussion the Marines decided to continue to search the identified area until every house had been checked twice.

In addition, one of the Predator drones was still on station and streaming data from the target area back to the NSA.

It was not yet 4:30 a.m., so none of the island residents would be out yet. Even the most dedicated runners would know better than to go out running in the dark on this Sunday morning. And if they didn't know better, one of the Mudders of the 2nd Marines would quickly educate them.

Chapter Seventeen

Still Very Early Sunday Morning in Sconset

La Rue had made her way to the truck stop outside of Dubai. There she had found a driver willing to drive her to Al Ain via highway E66. They would get off the main highway as they got closer to their destination.

She gave the driver $10,000 up front with the agreement that she would give him the other $10,000 on arrival. There was no mention by the driver of any sexual favors—yet. In the meantime she worried about the driver overpowering her and stealing her bag with the rest of her US cash, British sterling, and euros. As a result she kept her hand in her bag and wrapped around her Glock, ready to fire in an instant.

As the truck started to leave the truck stop, the driver received a text message that had been broadcast to all drivers, warning them of an American woman trying to escape from Dubai. In addition, it offered an award of US$5,000.

The text, which had a photo included, stated that the woman was an enemy of the state and anyone trying to help her escape would be imprisoned.

The driver passed his phone over to La Rue, who was seated beside him in the cab, still with her hand on the Glock in her bag.

As she read the text she knew she was at the man's mercy.

He said to her, "You seem to be a lady who is in a lot of trouble. Let's get to Muscat quickly."

She replied, "Salaam Alaikum." They drove on in silence.

❖

Captain Mike Smith of the USS *North Dakota* Virginia-class attack submarine was tracking the SS *Milbridge Major* as target Sierra 1.

The *North Dakota* had cleared Tuckernuck Island and was at 150 feet depth on a due-east heading at eighteen knots. The *North Dakota* was eight miles from the *Milbridge*.

If Smith wanted to, he could take the *Milbridge* out right now with two MK 48 torpedoes—hell, he could take it out with one, and he was already well within range to do so.

It would be like shooting fish in a barrel. Smith was in contact with Stu Jackson on the *Carter*, who was approaching the *Milbridge* from the north. The *Carter* could take out the *Milbridge* too if it wanted—it was even closer, at about six miles. But none of the US subs had any interest in sinking the SS *Milbridge Major*—they first needed to rescue the Russell children, and that would be the work of the SEALs on the *Carter*. Of course, the *North Dakota* had a role to play in the mission as well.

The tactical plot was for the *North Dakota* to approach the *Milbridge* from the south and the *Carter* to approach from the north. Both would be on station fifty yards off the *Milbridge* in exactly twenty-one minutes, when they would put their plan into action.

The time would be 4:22 a.m., which would leave less than an hour until sunup. The *Milbridge Major* was on a south-southwesterly course moving at ten knots and was slowing according to the sonar on the *North Dakota*. The *North*

Dakota would approach windward on the *Milbridge*'s port side, which was the Atlantic Ocean side.

The *Carter* would approach in the opposite direction and shoot the gap between the island and the *Milbridge Major*. This approach would require more difficult maneuvering from the *Carter* but would be deftly handled, given the sophistication of the *Carter*'s electronics and navigation; they could park the *Carter* under center ice at Madison Square Garden if they wanted to.

The *Carter* would be off the *Milbridge*'s starboard beam as close as the navigator could place them. That would put them in the lee of the island and would make for the easiest approach for the SEALs to get on board the *Milbridge*.

The radar on the *Milbridge Major* showed only surface contacts, so they had no clue about the US subs that were stalking them.

The sonar operator on the USS *North Dakota* then called out, "Sierra 1 aspect change—she's slowing—now four knots, sir."

The *Milbridge Major* was slowing to the point where within minutes it would be stopped about ten miles off the coast, at Tom Nevers, which is where the ACK airport was located. Ten miles put it inside of US territorial waters.

The *Milbridge* was stopping just where the seabed dropped off to about 250 feet of depth, which was welcome news for the navigators and dive officers of both the USS *North Dakota* and the USS *Jimmy Carter*.

It was also welcome but not unexpected news for the captain of the Chinese type 041 Yuan diesel-electric sub, which was now directly under the *Milbridge Major* and was also slowing to a stop, still undetected by either US submarine.

❖

Kennedy Russell was finally in a deep sleep in a hospital bed at Emory, which was good because both physically and mentally she needed rest. Her vital signs showed an increase in respiratory rate as her body worked full time to fight off the virus that infected her.

The disease was causing the airways of her lungs to narrow, making it difficult to exhale. The virus was destroying the alveoli, where oxygen and carbon dioxide are exchanged, which gradually starved the body of oxygen.

Eventually, if the condition wasn't reversed, she would not be able to take in enough oxygen to sustain herself. Her lungs were filling with fluid that would ultimately kill her.

Doctors had her in an oxygen tent to allow her to breathe pure oxygen. The doctors knew that the virus was a variant of H1N1, and they had several therapeutic vaccines for H1N1. But what they needed here was an enzyme that would attach itself to the cells of this particular virus and not attack the antibodies that her body was generating to fight the disease.

With a few days of lab work they would no doubt have an antidote, but they needed it sooner than that. The real race here was with time.

As they treated FLOTUS, the staff provided updates to the Secret Service, which were passed on to POTUS every hour.

It wasn't just the doctors at the CDC and at Emory who were working on FLOTUS's health. The CIA was pressing all its contacts, as were the British and Israelis, in order to identify the lab that had produced the virus. This lab would require special equipment and expertise that was possessed by only a few people in the world.

Also, interrogations were just commencing on the newly captured Hijra team terrorists on Nantucket. The Ruku team members, the drone team captured in Madaket, had already been through several water boarding sessions. Many of the techniques normally used for interrogations, such as sleep deprivation or stress positions, would just take too long in this case.

The decision to use "special" enhanced techniques was made at the director level of the NSA and CIA and approved by Vice President McMasters.

The focus now was on interrogating the Hijra team members who had actually carried out the kidnapping and had just been caught at the Way Off Broadway house.

The three remaining Hijra team members were brought into the ex-officer's residence at Coast Guard station Sconset. Some of them would not leave there alive.

In addition to the interrogations going on in Sconset, CIA field operatives around the world were urgently reaching out to all their contacts to obtain added information on the location of the lab and the doctor who created the virus that had infected FLOTUS.

Field data was beginning to come into the CIA that confirmed the identified cell locations—the ones in Finsbury Park in London, St. Petersburg, Berlin, Venezuela, and the Syrian city of Al Hwaiz. Those locations were going to be hit within forty-eight hours, but all agents were trying to first obtain whatever intel they could before the strikes.

Chapter Eighteen

Going on 4 a.m. Sunday in Sconset

The NSA Was About to Catch a Break

All the data pointing to Oasis LLC led McMahon's team at the NSA headquarters in Maryland to agree with the CIA that capturing Lauren La Rue was now a US intelligence priority.

They believed La Rue was still in Dubai. The CIA knew all too well that the UAE secret police would rather kill her than allow her to fall into the hands of the Americans. Therefore, Grey Wolfe, one of the CIA's top secret teams in Dubai, now had capturing La Rue as their top priority. They were working this assignment with a deep-cover CIA agent, Aziz Mahmood, based in Dubai .

Sheik Abdul Er Rahman continued to get updates on the progress, if one could call it that, on his men's search to capture La Rue. Her bank accounts had been frozen, but that was just a formality. As smart as La Rue was, he knew she had an escape bag filled with cash.

The sheik knew she would be running, and that meant only a few avenues of escape for her. It would be by air, by sea, or perhaps overland by truck. There were no trains in UAE to speak of.

The sheik's security team was also picking up known friends of La Rue's to ensure they weren't involved in hiding her or her escape.

So La Rue now had the sheik's people and his private secret police force, as well as the CIA's Grey Wolfe team, all looking for her. It was impressive that she had not been caught yet.

The truck ride from Dubai to Al Ain was only about an hour and a half. From there it would be another hour or so to her final destination of the capital of Oman, the city of Muscat.

As the truck approached the border of UAE and Oman, the driver knew he would need to stop at the checkpoint and show his papers. The norm was for the driver to hand over his passport with an American $5 bill inserted in the back pages—it was a bribe, but more accurately it was a toll. Everyone knew this was the system, and as long as everyone paid, it worked just fine.

Every truck in the Middle East had a secret compartment, if not more, used for smuggling contraband. On the truck in which La Rue was riding, the secret compartment was located in the trailer, which was accessible only via the cab.

The hidden compartment was about the size of a casket and was entered by shimmying into it via a folding false floor. Once the contraband was inside, the false floor would spring back into place.

In order for the border agents to find this compartment, they would have to unload the entire trailer, something that was rarely done, which was exactly what the driver was counting on.

It was hot in the trailer and even hotter in the secret compartment, which wasn't meant to hold a person for long. As La Rue lay hidden, she knew she would have to lie still in order to lower her respiration rate, exerting as little energy as possible.

She could feel the truck start to slow down as it approached the checkpoint. After what seemed like forever, the truck started moving again.

As agreed, she would wait twelve minutes after the truck started moving before she made her way back into the cab of the truck.

While La Rue lay in the confined space, her thoughts drifted back to growing up in Iowa.

Her father was her hero, and he always quoted Mark Twain to her.

How many times did she hear him say, "Lauren, the secret of getting ahead is getting started." That was one of his favorites.

When she entered college at the University of Wisconsin his use of quotes became more meaningful, as she now better understood them. He once said to her, "Forgiveness is the fragrance that the violet sheds on the heel that has crushed it."

La Rue cried out for her father—*Daddy, I'm sorry, can you forgive me?* After a few more minutes in the dark that allowed her further reflection on her life, her watch timer went off.

La Rue was relieved as she exited the box and reentered the cab.

Now it was only about an hour or so until they reached Muscat. Her relief was short-lived, however, as she retook her seat to the right of the driver. Once she was settled, the driver turned to her and slowly pointed his finger to her and then to his crotch.

She knew what the driver meant. La Rue shook her head no. The driver again mimed the overture to her. La Rue then reached into her bag and took out $1,000 and handed it to the driver. The driver pocketed the money without another gesture.

La Rue had dodged another bullet. She hoped that this was all she would have to pay before they reached their destination. La Rue was relieved she had enough cash to buy her way out of these sorts of situations. As they drove on, La Rue clutched the Glock in her bag.

❖

The bond between the US and the UK was strong and steeped in history. The two countries had stood together even in cases where one of the parties (the UK) was not convinced about the other country's policy, such as the US's decision to invade Iraq.

For that reason as well as others, Sunday morning UK time found Special Forces surrounding a row house in Finsbury Park just north of London.

US and UK intelligence units had identified a link between the team that attacked the American president's family on Nantucket and the occupants of a home in Finsbury Park.

The target home was in the middle of a string of row houses along Beatrice Road. MI6 had determined that there were six male occupants in the home.

Using fiber-optic cameras and flashbangs, the Special Forces team rushed the home. In the aftermath, three of the suspected terrorists were killed, and two were wounded, one critically, and one seriously. One survived without any material wounds at all.

❖

McMasters, with the president's approval, had put steps in motion to attack the group A identified targets in Yemen, Iraq, and Burkina Faso in Africa. The plan called for US submarines to launch the improved version of the Tomahawk Land Attack Missile—Conventional (TLAM-C), capable of traveling at speeds just under six hundred miles per hour with a range of nine hundred nautical miles.

The US submarines in place to launch these attacks were Los Angeles–class attack subs. The Los Angeles–class submarines, or 688 boats as they were called, after the number of the first boat of the class, the USS *Los Angeles*, were legends in the submarine community. The last twenty-two boats of the class, were referred to as Improved 688s or 688i boats. These boats had a variety of enhancements over the base 688 boats, including the addition of twelve vertical launching system (VLS) tubes specifically designed for launching Tomahawks.

First up was the USS *Santa Fe* (SSN-763), which was patrolling in the Gulf of Aden off the Arabian Sea. The *Santa Fe* target package was to launch six TLAM-Cs against the city of Dhamar in Yemen.

The *Santa Fe* was now at battle stations missile, hovering at launch depth approximately two hundred miles off the coast of Yemen. The CO gave the command, and at thirty-second intervals each of the six TLAM-Cs leapt skyward.

In approximately twenty minutes the six TLAM-Cs would slam into a building in downtown Dhamar, taking out the suspected Al Qaeda terrorist cell. Only one TLAM was really needed to do the job. The other five were for redundancy and insurance.

One target down, six to go, thought McMasters as he and the Joint Chiefs as well as the directors of the NSA, CIA, and FBI, along with their senior staffs, all watched the destruction captured from a KH-11 Key Hole spy satellite that was broadcasting live images back to the Sit Room at the White House.

Next up was Iraq and the beehive of terrorist activity known as the city of Shiraz. The US kept at least one attack boat in the Persian Gulf at all times.

Today that duty fell to the USS *Tucson* (SSN-770). The *Tucson* launched twelve missiles, but these, called TLAM-Es, were of an upgraded variety.

The TLAM-Es had enhanced guidance and warheads, and the *Tucson's* were targeted at two locations in the city of Shiraz.

The first target was a nondescript two-story building, which soon was nothing more than a crater.

The next target was a vacation home of a wealthy Iraqi businessman with close ties to Al Qaeda. The house would not remain standing much longer, as six TLAM-Es were now in the air.

The message the US was sending to Al Qaeda was clear and unmistakable: You attack our president and his family, and we will attack your families.

The scene now shifted to Africa and the Burkina Faso target. The USS *Springfield* (SSN-761), also an improved 688 boat, was loitering silently off the Gulf of Guinea.

The target here was a home in the town of Zabré. Due to a lack of clarity on this target, only four TLAM-Cs were launched.

In a matter of minutes, twenty-two TLAMs had been launched by three US attack submarines. The group A targets were now nothing more than burning holes in the ground.

That left the group B and C targets—all but the UK Finsbury Park location, which the Brits had already hit.

Vice President McMasters, to whom President Russell had delegated the details of taking out the approved target list, discussed with the Sit Room officials the group B targets: a terrorist house in the city of Porlamar on the Isla of Margarita and the Syrian city of Al Hwaiz.

Where McMasters was having second thoughts was with the two group C targets: the apartment in St. Petersburg and the one in Berlin. McMasters had been mulling over the idea of hitting both targets without informing the Russians or Germans. He had moved off the notion of launching TLAMs at either site.

A Grey Wolfe team could do a "Q&Q hit," a "Quick and Quiet," but the decision to take military action on Russian and German soil was something McMasters no longer supported.

McMasters rightly worried that if he brought the Russians and the Germans in on the operation they might not take out the targets with alacrity and might thereby allow the cells to escape.

On the other hand, once each of those governments was informed of the link to the Russell family attack, it would be in their best interest to hit those targets hard and fast—just like the Brits had in Finsbury Park.

The US had a tremendous amount on its plate right now with the Russell family crisis and the attacks the US had just executed. Everyone in the Sit Room was in agreement that there was no need for added problems with the Germans and the Russians.

In support of that point, McMasters placed calls to the president of Russia and the German chancellor, informing them of the nexus between the Nantucket kidnapping of President Russell's children and the cell locations in their countries. Both leaders, as expected, agreed to look into the matter as a top priority and to take the targets out ASAP once their link to the kidnapping was confirmed.

What then followed were calls between the intelligence agencies of the US, Russia, and Germany to share the necessary data. It was during the call with Vasyl Fedorov, the head of the Russian Foreign Intelligence Service, or FIS, that Vasyl brought up the Chinese.

Vasyl shared with NSA head Riordan that Russia believed there was a link between China and the Al Qaeda teams responsible for the Nantucket attacks.

Russian FIS agents believed that Chinese agents had met with Sheik Abdul Er Rahman in Riyadh and that the sheik was the chief architect of the Nantucket operation.

Director Riordan thanked Fedorov with a *do svidaniya* and said they would stay in touch as the situation developed.

After getting off the phone, George Riordan placed a call to McMahon. He asked McMahon and Mannix if they had come across any links between the Nantucket terrorists and China.

McMahon answered, "Director, we haven't come across any direct links between China and the Al Qaeda Nantucket attackers."

She added that they did have what the NSA called a "bank shot," where China was implicated but there were no direct connections.

Riordan rolled his eyes and said, "Kristin, I'm not looking for the six degrees of Kevin Bacon here."

At that point the most senior member of the NSA's China team, who was with Riordan, spoke up. "Director, we have a report from one of our field agents who received a text from a Chinese agent, which said, 'We think they will try to escape by sea.' That is the only direct link we have between China and Nantucket at this point."

There was a pause in the discussion as everyone in the room turned their attention to a flat-screen that had a live image of the SS *Milbridge Major* from a Predator drone that was on station. The video showed that the *Milbridge* had just about come to a complete stop in the water.

McMahon provided a status update. "Sir," she said turning to Riordan, "the *Carter* has a SEAL team on board, which is planning to board the *Milbridge* shortly. So the text from the Chinese about them escaping to the sea appears to be accurate."

"I just had a conversation with the Russian FIS director, Fedorov. He told me they understood Chinese agents had met with Sheik Abdul Er Rahman and they believed the sheik was the architect and the funding source behind the Nantucket attack."

That got everyone in the room typing madly as they searched for known links between China and the sheik and Oasis LLC.

But what wasn't yet clear was any relationship between the Chinese and the Nantucket attack. Riordan debated calling his counterpart at the Ministry of State Security, or MSS, China's CIA equivalent.

He thought it was too early and maybe too bold for that move. But whether he called the MSS director or not, it was now clear that the US needed to learn what involvement, if any, China had in the Nantucket operation. Riordan knew the answer to that question could very well determine whether or not the world went to war.

❖

The president, who was still in his isolation ward, was on with the Sit Room, ready to be given an update.

He began by asking, "What is on the threat board, and what is our defense condition?"

McMasters informed the president that the military readiness had been increased to DEFCON 3.

The president followed up with, "Jack, what about the markets?"

"Mr. President, I have had calls with the secretary of the treasury and the chairman of the Federal Reserve. We are planning to delay or cancel trading on Monday. The Asian and European markets likewise are not planning to open on Monday."

With that, the director of the CIA, Lisa Collins, and George Riordan, the NSA director, took over the briefing.

They briefed the president on Sheik Abdul Er Rahman, La Rue, and Oasis LLC. They added that they had increasing data patterns and intel suggesting that the Chinese either knew about the attack or were even possibly involved in it.

It was that last part that caused the president to interrupt. "What do you mean the Chinese may have been involved?"

Riordan went over what they surmised. "Clearly the Chinese had at least an inkling about the attack. Whether they were involved or not, at this point we don't know."

The president was quick to respond. "George 'inkling'—'we don't know'—what the fuck? Start telling me what you do know, and if we don't know something, then tell me when we will know, for Christ's sake. Jesus!"

Everyone in the room had known that was coming. It was just a question of who was going to be on the receiving end of it.

Russell was known to be a very direct communicator, and Riordan was the fall guy this time.

Riordan paused and then replied, "Yes, Mr. President. We are working on understanding the Chinese involvement. We will let you know as soon as we have any substantive information."

Russell then asked, "What are our friends telling us?"

Collins spoke up. "Mr. President, we have been in communications with the Brits, Germans, Russians, French, and Israelis—right now the only valuable intel has come from the Russians. The Russians have confirmed CIA reports that the Chinese seem to be involved."

Collins winced as she used the word "seem"; she knew that could elicit a similar reaction from the president that Riordan's comment had. But the president was too tired and concerned about his family to cut into his staff for every misspoken word in the briefing.

McMasters then added, "Mr. President, we have made TLAM strikes in Yemen, Iraq, and Burkina Faso. In addition, we have informed the Brits about a suspected Al Qaeda cell north of London that we believe was related to this attack, and the Brits have already taken out the target."

Just then Secret Service Agent Nicols joined the president in the bunker, as did NYPD Chief of Detectives Tate, both of whom had been released from quarantine earlier.

The president asked, "Dan, has the virus spread to anyone else?"

Nicols replied, "Only Massachusetts Trooper Herbert has contracted the virus. His condition is about eight hours less advanced than FLOTUS's."

"Should we evacuate the trooper to Emory?" asked the president.

The president was informed that that was already under way and they expected to have Herbert off the island within the hour.

He moved on and asked, "What other targets are we planning to hit?"

McMasters responded, "Mr. President, we are planning on hitting Venezuela and Syria. Also there are two apartments in Berlin and in St. Petersburg. I have spoken with the Russian president and the German chancellor, and both have given us assurances that those locations would be hit once the intel was validated."

McMasters continued with more details, adding that the Venezuelan attack would be by a Stealth Bomber out of a base in Puerto Rico. The Syrian attack would be by a submarine launching Tomahawks.

The president nodded and then asked, "Lisa, can we use a Grey Wolfe team in Venezuela instead of the Stealth Bomber?"

"Yes, we can, sir. However, it would delay the mission by at least forty-eight hours."

The president mulled it over and then gave his order to cancel the Stealth attack on Venezuela and to go with a Grey Wolfe team.

He was right, and even though he was tired and stressed, his judgment was the sharpest of those in the room, and in this case he made the correct decision.

He then added, "You have a go on the Syrian attack to take them out at the earliest opportunity."

Just before the president signed off, he said, "George, sorry for the outburst before. I know you and the team are doing everything you can."

Riordan replied, "Mr. President, I know I speak for the group when I say it is our collective honor to serve you, especially at this extraordinary moment."

President Russell nodded and cut the video link to the Sit Room.

He then turned his ire on the doctors he had summoned.

"When can I get out of this damn bubble?" he yelled.

The doctors responded, "Mr. President, in a perfect situation we should wait another twenty-four hours."

"If I get out now, what is the risk to the rest of the staff here?"

"Mr. President, the odds are low, but it's possible you could spread the virus and create an epidemic."

"How long?"

"At least another two hours, sir," was the response.

The president then turned to Nicols and Tate. "What about them?"

"Given that we haven't seen any elevation of their vital signs and their exposure was very limited, I made the call that they could be released from quarantine."

Tate and Nicols moved close to the plastic barrier separating them from the president and started to confer with him.

"Mr. President," said Chief Tate, "I'm not an expert where submarines are concerned, but I have my doubts that your children are on the *Milbridge*. The terrorists had to know we would detect the *Milbridge*, especially with the naval assets we had in the area. Surely they would know we would eventually track the children to that freighter. It's a stretch of credibility to have this level of planning, exhibit all this sophistication, and then go dumb on the escape phase. Does it make any sense to you, sir?"

The president considered the argument and then replied, "Two points, detective. The NSA tells me we only learned about the aerial escape by some wizard in the department who invented some kind of breakthrough in acoustic surveillance or something like that.

"So saying we know for sure that my children are off the island is not clear-cut to me. Second, if they are on that freighter, how do we know that they are still alive?"

Tate wanted to address that last point first. "Mr. President, if they wanted to do harm to your children, they didn't need to leave the island to accomplish that. The only reason to undertake a dangerous aerial mission with the children is because they intended to escape."

With conviction Tate added, "Your children are more valuable to them alive than not. Now, do they have a plan to harm them if they come under attack? We don't know, and that is the danger of this SEAL incursion. But my police sense is telling me that something's not right. There has to be an angle that is more advanced than moving the kids to a slow, foreign-flagged ship just a few miles offshore."

That was enough for the president. "Get me Jacobsen on the line now," he demanded.

A minute later President Russell was on video link with COMFLTFORCOM and COMCARGRU-12. "Brian/Mark, what do you think?" asked the president after outlining Tate's points.

"The detective makes sense. We are getting ready to deploy the SEALs on the *Milbridge*, sir. Let's first see what the SEALs find."

The time was 4:20 a.m., and both the *North Dakota* and the *Jimmy Carter* were arriving on station. The tactical plan called for the *Carter* to be closest to shore on a southern heading, which would keep it in the dark.

The *North Dakota* would be on a northern heading on the windward side, or port side, of the *Milbridge*. The plan was just about ready to be put into action.

The *Carter* deployed with the more advanced ARCI Modified AN/BSY-2 combat system, which included a new, larger spherical sonar array in its bow, a wide-aperture array (WAA), and a new towed-array sonar, all improvements over what the USS *North Dakota* carried.

As a result, it was the sonar officer on the *Carter* who first noticed the peculiarity. As the *Milbridge* slowed, the *Carter* sonar operator on the BSY-2 detected a shadow. In submarine parlance, a shadow is a sub that is closely trailing a surface contact.

"Sir, did you see that?" the sonar petty officer asked the sonar officer.

"I don't know, Connors," said the lieutenant. "Whatever it was, it's gone now."

The sonar officer knew why the petty officer had said what he had, because for a split second the BSY-2 had picked up the faintest of signals. Due to the depth and closeness to the shore, the *Carter* had not deployed its towed array.

The question was whether it was really a shadow or whether the BSY-2 had picked up the USS *North Dakota* on the other side of the *Milbridge*. The shadow very well could have been the *Dakota*.

The sonar officer said, "Damn, we could use the towed array right now." The petty officer, wearing his headphones, just nodded, trying to concentrate on the sounds in the ocean around them. They both knew the depth was too shallow to deploy the towed array, which would have given them a better tactical view and a better reading on whether or not the shadow was the *North Dakota*.

The sonar officer mulled over whether or not to alert the captain of the *Carter* about the possible shadow. He knew there was too much on the line; he couldn't take any chances that might compromise the mission to save the Russell children.

"Captain, for a split second Connors and I thought we saw a shadow under Sierra 1, but we don't know if it was a shadow or the *Dakota* on the other side of Sierra 1," said the lieutenant.

Jackson thought it over for a minute and then went to the radio room off the bridge. "Send to *North Dakota*—possible shadow reading from Sierra 1. *Jimmy Carter*." Jackson recalled Admiral Jacobsen's mention of subsurface contacts.

With the message sent to the USS *North Dakota*, Captain Jackson returned to getting ready to launch the SEAL team.

Everyone agreed it would be much easier for the SEAL team to board the *Milbridge* while it was stopped, so there was a real urgency to get the SEALs deployed *now*. With the *Mil-*

bridge stopped, the SEALs had changed their plan. Instead of the *Carter* surfacing and the SEALs taking an inflatable to approach the *Milbridge*, which ran the risk of being spotted, the SEALs would now exit the *Carter* using rebreathers rather than bulky scuba equipment. This change in plans would make it easier and faster for the SEALs to board the freighter and greatly reduced the likelihood of being detected by the *Milbridge's* crew.

Of the eighteen-member SEAL Team 2, just eight would be used on this mission. They would now disembark the *Carter* in two groups via the escape hatch.

It would take only two minutes for the escape hatch to purge after it had filled with water, so the overall process of getting the SEALs into the water would take less than six minutes.

The navigators on the *Carter* had done an expert job bringing the sub alongside the *Milbridge*. The SEALs surfaced just off the starboard beam of the *Milbridge*, less than fifty feet from the hull of the rusted freighter. Once on the surface the SEALs assembled silently and swam toward the *Milbridge* in preparation for boarding it. They would accomplish this the old-fashioned way, via grappling hooks. In order for the SEALs to board the *Milbridge* without being detected, it was agreed that a diversion would be staged in order to distract its crew.

The decision was to go big. The USS *North Dakota* would do an emergency blow fifty feet off the *Milbridge's* port beam. In this maneuver the submarine rapidly empties its ballast tanks by forcing high-pressure air into them. It is a way to get a submarine on the surface fast— so fast, in fact, it is often referred to as "flying," as the bow of the sub launches fifty feet into the air at a forty-five-degree angle.

An emergency blow is a very impressive sight and was sure to attract the attention of the entire crew of the *Milbridge*.

One thing was certain: There would be a great deal of confusion on that freighter—confusion the SEALs would use to their advantage to get aboard.

For insurance, Admiral Jacobsen had two F/A-18s in the air ready to buzz the *Milbridge* if the SEALs needed more cover.

It was now time to execute the emergency blow. The USS *North Dakota* had circled away from the *Milbridge* in order to increase its speed to flank well over thirty-five knots. That would allow the *North Dakota* to achieve the most air as it leapt from the ocean, making an impressive sight against the backdrop of the early morning sky, as it was only about forty-five minutes from sunrise.

Captain Mike Smith issued the order: "Steady on course 010, ahead flank, prepare for emergency surface."

The officer of the deck repeated the order, as did the dive officer.

The chief of the boat, who stood behind the maneuvering console, where two operators controlled the depth and speed of the submarine using what looked like a control yoke from a 747, acknowledged the order.

Captain Mike Smith then gave the command on the 1MC, "Emergency surface, emergency surface."

In the next few seconds the 377-foot sub, weighing almost eight thousand tons, literally jumped out of the water. The maneuver had the intended effect on the crew of the SS *Milbridge Major*, commanding their attention as the giant US Navy sub suddenly appeared off their port beam.

The *Milbridge* crew began yelling and scrambling around, worried that the Navy sub would torpedo or board them. That was when the first grappling hook caught the starboard railing of the *Milbridge*. As anticipated, the entire crew of the *Milbridge* was manning the port rails, looking at the USS *North Dakota* as it settled on the surface.

The downside of the maneuver was that it put so much air and sound into the water that it basically blinded any sub's sonar until the sea settled down.

As a result, the *Carter*'s sonar operator was blinded by the sounds from the *North Dakota*. In a few minutes, when the air and sea started to calm down, the sonar operators on both US subs would be back listening for whatever the sea could tell them.

Not only was the crew of the *Milbridge* taken by surprise, but so was the crew of the Chinese diesel-electric Yuan type 041 submarine.

The Chinese sonar operator took off his headset and yelled to warn everyone as the US submarine started making hull-popping sounds just before it breached the surface. The Yuan's sonar was blinded, as was the *Carter*'s, for several minutes. Almost as an afterthought, the excited Chinese sonar operator reported, "A US Navy submarine has just surfaced off the port quarter of the *Milbridge*, Captain."

"Has he detected us?" came the calmer question from the Chinese captain.

"It is unclear, Captain. The US submarine is stopped dead in the water fifty feet from us.

It was the view of the captain and officers of the Yuan that the US sub had not detected the Chinese sub. And, of course, the Yuan had no idea that the *Carter* was just on the other side of the *Milbridge*. Nor did either US sub have a positive contact on the Yuan—yet.

The Yuan and *Milbridge* were effectively sandwiched between the surfaced USS *North Dakota* and the submerged and still hidden USS *Jimmy Carter*. It was an incredible number of submarines all inhabiting a tiny area of ocean.

As the second grappling hook took hold, the first two SEALs had already made it to the deck from the first line. Once on deck they unsafetied their Belgian-made SCAR-L automatic machine guns and then dropped a third and fourth line over the side. Ninety seconds later, all eight SEALs were on board the *Milbridge* without being detected. Phase 1 of the operation had been successful.

Chapter Nineteen

4:38 a.m. Sunday in Sconset

Attempt to Rescue the Russell Children

President Russell was still in his isolation chamber in the Nantucket bunker, but as yet he had no symptoms. The earlier tightness he felt in his throat turned out to be nothing. He was watching the video feed from the on-station Predator of the SEAL operation, as were the members of the Sit Room.

The president interrupted and asked, "Do we have a live feed from the SEAL team?"

Admiral Brad Johnson answered, "Sir, no, we do not have a feed. We did not want to emit anything that could give the SEALs away, sir. They are EMCON," referring to being radio silence or Emissions Control whereby they would not emit any signals that could be detected.

They all then turned their attention to the video feed from the Predator.

❖

As the truck in which she was riding approached the city of Muscat in Oman, La Rue's anxiety level began to rise again.

She knew this would be the end of the truck phase of her escape. Her next plan was to find the boat whose name had been texted to her: *Al Raisa.*

As the truck pulled into a waiting area on the waterfront of Muscat, La Rue reached into her bag and handed the driver his remaining fee of US$10,000, which brought the total amount she paid to $21,000.

She asked if she could remain in the cab of the truck for a while. The driver just shrugged and left to go get some dinner. From the cab of the truck La Rue surveyed the waterfront. About fifty yards away was the *Al Raisa*, docked among the collection of other vividly painted small boats, mostly family-owned fishing vessels.

She exited the truck and walked over to the stern of the relatively new white thirty-six-foot cruiser named *Al Raisa*. The problem was that no one was around. She called out, but no one was on the boat. She glanced around the dock, trying not to attract too much attention, but there was no one around or even headed toward the *Al Raisa*.

She turned and left, went back to the truck, and got back in the cab. She thought for a while about what her next steps should be.

She decided to send a text using one of her new SIM cards. She sent to 052 343 8998, "I am at the specified location but no one is around."

After a short wait she received a reply: "They will leave at midnight. Stay out of sight until then." Unbeknownst to La Rue, these texts were coming from Chinese MSS agent Amy Lu.

It was going on 1 p.m. and she needed to hide for eleven hours until the *Al Raisa* departed.

La Rue thought about responding to the text to ask where she should go, but she knew that she needed to keep her electronic footprint to a minimum, for surely the sheik's tech people would be looking for her.

La Rue thought for a few minutes. She would have liked to stay in the truck, but she knew the driver would be back soon from his meal, and his plan was to leave immediately. She could offer him more money to stay, but the driver had already taken on as much risk as he was going to. So that was not a viable plan.

A parking garage would be good. She thought about the perfect cover—she could get a van or work truck, sleep in the back until just before 11 p.m., and then make her way to the port.

Putting on her head scarf, she hailed a cab and asked the driver if there were any used car lots in town. After a short discussion, she told him to take her to the closest one. Entering the lot, she was immediately descended upon by the salesperson.

Speaking Arabic, she explained that she wanted to buy a work truck as a surprise gift for her nephew, who was a house painter. There weren't a lot to pick from, and after a little back-and-forth, they arrived at a final price. The salesperson was glad to get the cash and happy to get the truck off the lot.

This sort of transaction—fast and all in cash—wasn't that unusual in the Middle East. La Rue used euros to pay for the truck in order to conserve her US cash in case she needed to pay the *Al Raisa* boat captain later. La Rue knew women were allowed to drive in Muscat so after the transaction was completed, she got in and quickly drove away.

After driving just a couple of blocks she parked the truck and hailed another cab, which took her to a seedier part of town where she went shopping for a pillow, a blanket, and a change of clothes at a street market.

An hour and a half later another cab dropped her off a block from where she had parked the truck. She was wary of the cab drivers, most of whom could not be trusted, so she always made sure to get dropped off a block or two from her desired destination.

She opened the tailgate of the beat-up old Nissan truck, threw her purchases in the back, and got into the truck. She sat for a while reviewing the paper map she'd bought at the market.

Normally she would just use a navigation app on her iPhone, but not today. She was looking for a side street near the docks so that she would be near enough to walk to the dock at 11 p.m.

Wearing her newly purchased baseball cap, she drove slowly around the waterfront checking out several alleys to see if they were suitable for her needs. She selected one and backed the old Nissan into it.

Once parked, she got out, walked around the back, and climbed into the bed of the truck. There she laid out her blanket and pillow, changed into her new clothes, a workingman's outfit, and lay down. Her last task was to take the SIM card and battery out of her iPhone. She checked her watch. It was 4:45 p.m. She now needed to try to catch some sleep, which would be hard given her anxiety level.

She opened her backpack and placed her 9mm Glock next to her pillow so it would be within reach, just in case her plan broke down.

❖

At the CDC Dr. O'Keefe was working on blood samples from FLOTUS she had received from Emory. It was clear this was a variant of swine flu, or H1N1, but it was the subtype of influenza that was creating the concern.

Technically speaking, it was an orthomyxovirus that contained the glycoproteins hemagglutinin and neuraminidase. Hemagglutinin causes red blood cells to clump together and binds the virus to the infected cell. Neuraminidase is a type of glycoside hydrolase enzyme that helps to move the virus particles through the infected cells and assists in spreading the virus from the host cells.

Some strains of virus are endemic to humans. Other strains, like H1N1, are endemic to birds (avian influenza) or pigs (swine influenza). The problem occurs when a swine or avian virus makes the jump to humans. Because the virus is so new, the human immune system hasn't developed a defense against it. These are the cases that usually result in an epidemic and, depending on how virulent they are, sometimes a pandemic.

The World Health Organization (WHO) had tracked the types of H1N1 variants and shared that data with healthcare officials around the world. O'Keefe's job at the CDC, in addition to being an expert on infectious diseases, was to attend WHO conferences, where she would hear lectures by other scientists with a focus on talks by scientists from countries that were on the US's watch list.

O'Keefe's responsibility was to get to know the scientists from these countries, so should any disease from these regions enter the United States, the CDC would have an in-country contact.

She had attended a conference the previous year in Munich where a Pakistani doctor gave a paper on H1N1 subtype 09 and how it was morphing from an avian flu to a swine flu, threatening the livestock of farmers in Pakistan. After his presentation, O'Keefe introduced herself and asked some follow-up questions. From that dialogue she came away with the impression that this doctor was skilled in the art of orthomyxovirus and would be one of only a few people from that region who could theoretically weaponize the H1N1 virus.

As Dr. O'Keefe examined the blood cells taken from the first lady under the electron microscope, she could detect surface viral proteins in the shape of a crook, similar to the swine variant of H1N1.

Maybe it was a coincidence, or maybe she was grasping at straws, but what she was seeing in her electron microscope made her think of the lecture given by the Pakistani scientist in Munich the year before. She reached for her iPhone and scanned her contacts, and there it was—the contact data for a Dr. Muhammed Abdul Wajid, Islamabad, Pakistan.

O'Keefe got up from her workstation, called her counterpart at Emory, and asked to speak with a CIA agent there.

A few moments later O'Keefe was explaining her conclusions to a CIA agent. "The virus that the first lady has contracted closely resembles work done by a Pakistani doctor I met last year in Munich."

Without delay, the CIA agent briefed her boss back at Langley, where they both agreed that they would notify their in-country agents to find this Dr. Wajid in order to ascertain if there was a link to the first lady's virus.

While the CIA began working the lead on Wajid, Dr. O'Keefe conferenced in the Emory doctors and took them through her analysis, which indicated that the first lady was infected with an 09 variant of the H1N1 virus.

The Emory doctors, along with the CDC doctors, discussed the next steps. They all agreed that the teams should start working on several antidotes for the H1N1-09 virus.

❖

Lieutenant Commander Burduck and SEAL Team 2 had quickly made their way to the bridge of the *Milbridge*, where they shot the four occupants with their Belgian made SCAR-L automatic machine guns equipped with silencers.

Most of the remaining crew was still looking at the *North Dakota*, which was settling down on the surface of the ocean.

Using only hand signals, Burduck instructed his team to split into two sections. Burduck would lead a section to search from the bridge forward to the bow.

The other section, led by Lieutenant Tom Mahoney, would move aft along the starboard side, enter the ship's superstructure from the rearmost cabin, then search the stern section. Once both teams were below decks, they would work toward the center of the vessel.

As Lieutenant Commander Burduck's team continued down into the lower decks, it was eerily quiet. There were machine sounds but no voices. Nevertheless, they checked each cabin, looking for the Russell children.

It was Lieutenant Tom Mahoney's team that first came upon it in the section just forward of the engine room. Affixed to the hull was a device made of new high-tech metal.

Mahoney and his team were looking at a stainless steel mating collar. It was clear from the shine of the metal and the newness of the bolts that attached the collar to the *Milbridge* that this was a recent addition.

On the top of the stainless steel collar was a dogged hatch. The men looked at one another as Mahoney got on the radio. "KP2 to 1."

Burduck heard the call, and pulling his mike closer to his lips, he said quietly, "One, go."

"Sir, we are on the lower deck just forward of the engine room. Sir, there appears to be a recently installed escape hatch, over."

Burduck stopped in his tracks as he processed the data. "An escape hatch? Copy."

"That's affirm, sir."

Burduck again pulled the microphone on his headset close to his mouth and called the USS *Jimmy Carter*: "Papa Juliet, this is Kingpin1, come in."

Jackson quickly responded, "Roger, Kingpin1."

"Papa Juliet, we have found what appears to be a recently installed escape hatch on the lower level of the target."

"An escape hatch, copy?"

"Roger, PJ, an escape hatch. And we have found no sign of the packages yet either," added the SEAL team commander.

Jackson repeated out loud, "An escape hatch, no packages?"

The chief of the boat, who was standing near Jackson, exclaimed, "A sub, skipper, there's a sub out there."

Jackson blinked for a moment, then turned to his officer of the deck and barked, "Rig for ultraquiet, man battle stations torpedo, all ahead one-third."

With that the officer of the deck grabbed the 1MC and sounded general quarters.

Red lights came on throughout the ship to indicate they were now at general quarters.

Jackson then said, "Patch me into the *Dakota* now."

Chapter Twenty

5:00 to 6:30 a.m.
Sunday in Sconset

A corpsman was using a utility knife to slice open the quarantine booth that President Russell had occupied for the last six or so stressful hours. As the slice grew larger, POTUS stepped through it, impatient to breathe fresh air.

The president instinctively swung his arms around, appreciating his newfound freedom, then walked quickly into the communication center of his bunker. There he joined Nicols, Tate, and Spencer, who were linked into the Sit Room and watching the Predator feed of the SEAL mission.

The three men stood as the president entered the communication center. "At ease," he said.

McMasters began, "Mr. President, it's good to see you up and about."

"Thank you, Jack. What is the latest with the SEALs?" came Russell's response.

The chief of naval operations replied, "Mr. President, the SEALs are aboard the *Milbridge*. They discovered what they believe to be a recently installed escape hatch on the hull of the freighter.

"They have not found your children. They are continuing their search but they believe your children have been taken off the freighter via submarine. We are scouring the area for the unidentified submarine."

"Submarine?" repeated the president.

"Yes, sir, that is what we believe."

The president turned to the director of the NSA. "George, whose sub is this—do we know?"

"Mr. President, it is likely a Chinese sub."

"George, are you certain?"

"No, sir, we are not certain. I am telling you who we think it is based on our intelligence."

"We need to make sure."

"Yes, sir, we are working on it right now," replied Riordan.

The president asked, "Anything else, gentlemen?"

The CNO spoke up. "Sir, the *Carter* is at battle stations as we speak, as is the *North Dakota*. If this is a Chinese sub, it would be one of their diesel-electric boats, which are very quiet and very capable. But it is conventional, meaning they can't stay down forever, although they can stay down for days."

President Russell looked at Spencer and McMasters. "We should get sec state in on this." He paused, then asked, "Could this be someone framing the Chinese? A stolen sub or some sort of head fake?"

The director of the CIA, Lisa Collins, answered, "It could be. We need to follow all possible scenarios."

The president then asked the chairman of the Joint Chiefs, "John, have the Chinese or anyone else raised their defense posture?"

"Mr. President, the Russians, Chinese, and our NATO allies have all raised their defense posture, but we believe that was only in response to our heighted state of alert."

❖

In the seas off Nantucket, Stu Jackson was on the sub phone with the captain of the *North Dakota* and Admirals Singer and Jacobsen.

Jackson said, "Admiral Jacobsen, we could go active and find this Chinese son of a bitch in a minute."

The admiral replied, "Stu, let's play this game a couple moves ahead. If we go active and find them, then what? We can't torpedo them."

Smith added, "Sir, I could ram them and force them to surface."

Jacobsen admired Smith's moxie but said, "At ease, cowboy. How about we form up on them. Stu, you come in from behind, and Mike, you approach on their port quarter. Then we just shadow them until we get orders from the White House. They'll know we have them and they will either stop or we can force them to surface, or just wait them out. That will be our plan, but we can't execute it until we get clearance from Washington. For now, just get yourselves in position."

❖

On the *Milbridge* Lieutenant Commander Burduck had secured the remaining members of the crew when he received a call from Petty Officer Tad Holland.

"One, this is Four, sir, this entire ship is rigged to blow. I repeat, this entire ship is rigged to blow."

Behind a stack of boxes that were marked as engine parts, Holland had found wires that led to plastic explosives.

Burduck went below decks to see for himself. It took Burduck only a couple of minutes before he was on the SEAL radio.

With a possible enemy sub in the area, Jackson did not want to give away the position of his $3.5 billion Seawolf-class sub. They patched in Admirals Jacobsen and Singer as well as Captain Smith on the *North Dakota*. They all agreed they would not deviate from their tactical plan. Jacobsen told Burduck to prepare to abandon ship immediately.

Jacobsen said to the SEAL commander, "I am going to send you help in a couple of minutes. Jacobsen out."

The challenge was that the USS *Theodore Roosevelt* was forty miles away, as were his Arleigh Burke destroyers. It would take them almost forty-five minutes to get to the SEAL team. Jacobsen could send some helos, but he didn't want to put added sound in the area that could impact the search for the Chinese.

He wasn't worried about the SEALs lasting in the ocean. Hell, they could swim the ten miles to shore. The concern was the *Milbridge* crew.

On the USS *Theodore Roosevelt*, Jacobsen, along with Singer and CO Captain Fraser, entered CDC and told the radar officer to bring up the plot around the *Milbridge*.

Only a few miles away was a radar contact. The admiral tapped his finger on the scope where the contact appeared. "There, who is that?"

The radar operator moved the cursor on the scope onto the radar contact and then zoomed in on it. "Sir, it is a private boat out of Nantucket."

The radar operator looked over his notes from the Predator. "Sir, it's *The Brown-Eyed Girl*, a forty-eight-foot sport fisherman registered to an island resident named Ted Schnell."

Jacobsen turned to Fraser. "Captain, you still have those F/A-18s capping over the *Milbridge*?"

"That's affirm, Admiral, we have two Rhinos up."

"Tom, have the Rhinos buzz this boat. We need to make sure they are awake and their radio is on. Get their attention, Captain."

"Copy, sir," responded Fraser.

A minute later the CDC on the USS *Theodore Roosevelt* was calling, "Rough Rider, Hammer flight."

"Hammer flight, Rough Rider," came the response.

"Hammer flight, Strike, we have tasking from AB to buzz a fishing boat at your four o'clock. Rough Rider 1 wants to make sure they are awake. Your contact is 237 for 11 miles."

"Hammer flight copies, Rough Rider. Just how hard do you want us to buzz them?" asked Hammer 12.

"Hammer flight, Rough Rider 1 says to give them a big bang, copy."

"Strike, a big bang, copy," came the reply.

On that command, the two F/A-18s, which were orbiting at ten thousand feet, pushed over and onto a heading of 237 degrees. They advanced their throttles. It was only a moment later when the boat showed up on the F/A-18s' forward-looking infrared (FLIR) scope. Now they advanced their throttles a notch as they tightened up their two-ship formation.

They passed over *The Brown-Eyed Girl* in excess of four hundred knots at an altitude of two-hundred feet.

The Brown-Eyed Girl was owned by Ted Schnell, a New York investment banker. This weekend, his girlfriend, along with a colleague of his from the bank, Antonio Vargas, and his wife, had joined him for some fishing and relaxation.

The forty-eight-foot Hinckley boat shook from the flyover as the *Knighthawk* F/A-18s conducted their low highspeed flyby.

Schnell and Vargas, who were at the controls of the boat, jumped and looked at one another in shock. Schnell yelled, "What the . . . ?" As the F/A-18s disappeared into the gray morning haze, they heard the radio on *The Brown-Eyed Girl* come alive.

"*Brown-Eyed Girl, Brown-Eyed Girl*, this is the United States Navy hailing you on channel 9. Please ident. *Brown-Eyed Girl, Brown-Eyed Girl*, this is the US Navy hailing you on channel 9, do you copy?"

Schnell reached for the mic of his radio, touched the volume control, pressed the mic button, and responded, "This is *The Brown-Eyed Girl*, over."

"Is this Mr. Schnell?" came a different voice.

"Yes, this is Ted Schnell, over."

"Mr. Schnell, this is Admiral Mark Singer, commander, USS *Theodore Roosevelt* carrier battle group. We would like your assistance."

Schnell looked over at Vargas and shook his head. Tapping the transmit button on his radio, he said, "How can we be of help, Admiral?"

"We need you to provide assistance to a freighter that is five miles off your starboard quarter. The crew and a team of Navy SEALs are in the process of abandoning ship. We need you to make best possible speed and lend assistance. Can you handle that, *Brown-Eyed Girl*, over?" said the admiral.

As Ted was listening to the admiral, he was already advancing the power on his twin Volvo eight-hundred-horsepower diesels. His boat was also equipped with twin Hamilton model HJ364 jets that gave it a top speed of forty knots. He brought up the rpms to warm both engines, then exhaled.

"Roger, *Roosevelt*, we can see the freighter. We will make best possible speed to the freighter."

The admiral added, "Mr. Schnell, once you have recovered the SEALs and crew, the SEAL team commander will assume command of your vessel. The freighter's crew will be detained by the SEALs, do you understand?"

"I understand, Admiral," came back Schnell's reply as he lifted his binoculars to get a better look at the *Milbridge*. With that, he pushed his throttles halfway and swung the wheel so *The Brown-Eyed Girl* was now headed directly to the freighter.

As *The Brown-Eyed Girl* came out of its turn, Schnell pushed his throttles to the stops. The bow of the Hinckley pitched up and the speed quickly accelerated to just over forty miles per hour.

Schnell told Vargas and the women what to expect. They were going to be picking people up out of the water, and so he told them to throw the bumpers over the side and ready the ladder off the stern.

He left out the part about the crew being detained.

"*Roosevelt*, this is *The Brown-Eyed Girl*. We are max speed, I have the freighter in sight. We will be on station in five minutes."

"Copy, *Brown-Eyed Girl*. Call us back on this freq once you have the SEALs and the crew on board. Rough Rider out."

Schnell leaned down to the glove box and opened it up. He reached in and took out a 9mm Sig Sauer pistol he kept on board for protection and tucked it into the waistband of his True Religion shorts.

❖

On board the *Milbridge* it was time to go. Burduck had his men lined up on the starboard, leeward side. The SEALs threw cargo nets over the side along with two life rafts. His men had already unzipped the remaining twelve crew members. Of the twelve *Milbridge* crew, two of them were the members of the Hijra balloon team, which included the overall mission team leader, Karim Hamady.

The men started to climb over the side—first over were four SEALs, next the *Milbridge* crewmen, including the two Al Qaeda balloon terrorists, who were trying to blend in as crew members. Then over went the four remaining SEALs, including Commander Burduck.

As they all hit the water, Burduck yelled to his men to break some fluorescent neon green water flares and to start to swim away from the *Milbridge* with the crew in tow.

As *The Brown-Eyed Girl* was approaching the *Milbridge*, Schnell cranked the wheel to the right and started to line up with a starboard approach.

Just as he was steadying on his new heading, explosions went off on the *Milbridge*.

The explosions were muted and underwater but unmistakable. Geysers of water started to appear all around the hull of the *Milbridge*.

Out of instinct, Schnell juked *The Brown-Eyed Girl* more to starboard to give the *Milbridge* a wider berth. Vargas, who was on the bow as a lookout, yelled to Schnell as he spotted the flares.

Schnell retarded the throttles and made a slow approach to the men, who were now waving to the boat.

Schnell called for his girlfriend, Helen, who was now awake and on deck, to take control of the wheel as they idled up to the first group of men in the water. Schnell and Vargas went to the port side of the boat and threw lines to the SEALs first.

Then Ted yelled to Helen to stop the engines. In a matter of just a minute or two, four SEALs were on board *The Brown-Eyed Girl*. Following procedure, the SEALs searched the ship and then asked if there were any weapons on board.

Ted lifted his shirt and showed them the handle of his Sig.

"Sir," said Lieutenant Tom Mahoney, "we are going to have to take that. We will return it once we are off the ship."

Ted nodded and handed the Sig 9mm to the SEAL, grip first. He wasn't going to argue with a Navy SEAL.

The next group on *The Brown-Eyed Girl* was Lieutenant Commander Burduck and his team. Once the SEALs were on board and their weapons checked, they started hauling the twelve crew members out of the life rafts.

Vargas, who could always be counted on for humor, observed to Schnell and the SEALs, "We're gonna need a bigger boat."

As the SEALs pulled the rail-thin crew members onto the sport fisherman, Burduck's men zipped them again and sat them along the stern of the boat.

The *Milbridge* was sinking, going down by the stern with a slight roll to starboard. It wouldn't be long before it slipped under the waves and joined the other wrecks around the island of Nantucket.

Schnell, who was back at the controls of *The Brown-Eyed Girl*, asked, "Where to, Commander?" Burduck consulted the chart along with Schnell and saw they were about fifteen miles off Sconset. He responded, "Best possible speed to the Brant Point Coast Guard Station."

Schnell again pushed the throttles to the stops as *The Brown-Eyed Girl* responded.

Burduck got on his SEAL radio and made contact with the USS *Theodore Roosevelt* and Admiral Jacobsen.

"Mr. Schnell," yelled Lieutenant Commander Burduck, "the admiral would like to speak to you."

Ted turned the helm over to one of the SEALs and stepped down the four steps into the cabin.

Burduck turned to Schnell and handed him his SEAL comm unit. "You will be speaking with Admiral Jacobsen, commander of the Atlantic Fleet, a four-star admiral."

Ted nodded.

"Mr. Schnell, this is Admiral Jacobsen. "I know you spoke earlier to Admiral Singer, but I wanted to personally thank you for your assistance this morning."

Ted pressed the transmit button on the SEAL radio and replied, "We were happy to help, Admiral. I'm just glad we were in the area."

"Mr. Schnell, I have to ask that you and your passengers keep everything that happened confidential, do you understand? We are in the middle of an active military operation and it is vital that no information leave your ship. Is that clear?" ordered the admiral.

"I understand completely, Admiral," answered Schnell.

"Well done, *Brown-Eyed Girl*. Jacobsen out," replied the admiral, and then he was gone.

Lieutenant Commander Burduck called the Brant Point Coast Guard Station and had them tell the Secret Service to be ready to pick up their prisoners.

The CIA and Secret Service would want to interrogate the prisoners right away to learn more about the whereabouts of the Russell children.

Burduck then decided, *Why waste the thirty minutes it will take to get to the Coast Guard station? Why not start the interrogation now?*

The president's children were missing and they needed answers. Burduck told his SEALs to get some line and get ready to begin interrogating the prisoners.

Burduck looked over the twelve prisoners. He selected Karim Hamady first for interrogation. Burduck chose him because he had the hardest look of the group.

He went over to Hamady and demanded, "Where are the kids?"

The terrorist just shrugged and said, "No English." It was a reply in similar tone to the one he'd given the Secret Service agent who confronted him in the Sconset Market on Friday.

But that just made Burduck madder. "Tie 'em up," he yelled.

On command, two members of the SEALs tied a rope around the wrists of Karim Hamady. They also tied a rope around his waist.

"Over," yelled Burduck, but before they threw the prisoner overboard, he told Schnell to cut back on the throttles so they would be going about twenty-five knots. And with that the two SEALs pushed the terrorist over the side of *The Brown-Eyed Girl*.

Schnell could see his girlfriend was about to object, but he shook his head at her and mouthed the word "Don't."

After the prisoner had spent about two minutes trailing *The Brown-Eyed Girl* and bobbing up and down in the surf, Burduck yelled to his men, "Pull him up."

As they dragged in the waterlogged terrorist, he retched over the back of *The Brown-Eyed Girl*.

Burduck yelled, "Where are the children?"

Again Hamady just shrugged.

"Don't you fucking shrug at me again—I swear to God I'll put a bullet in your head," yelled Burduck. He then put his hand on his holster but did not take his weapon out. Hamady didn't flinch.

Burduck told his team to grab another of the seated crew. This time they chose the crew member who had struggled the most while in the water.

It was clear this crew member did not know how to swim. The SEALs took the rope from the first crew member and started to put it around the neck of the second crew member.

They then moved the visibly frightened crew member to the side of *The Brown-Eyed Girl*, getting ready to push him overboard, when he suddenly yelled, "On the sub, on the sub."

"Sub, what sub?" Burduck screamed.

"Chinese sub, Chinese sub," said the frightened crew member.

Burduck immediately went down into the cabin and got on the radio, but before he did he nodded to Schnell to open up the throttles again.

Burduck reported in to Admiral Jacobsen, who quickly shared the information with the US subs and relayed the intel to the Sit Room.

As *The Brown-Eyed Girl* entered the harbor, it was met by a Coast Guard Rescue Boat with its blue lights flashing and was escorted to the Brant Point Coast Guard Station dock.

As they tied up, the SEALs kept the twelve zipped crew members under covered as they handed them over to the Secret Service agents who were waiting for them.

Karim Hamady, who had personally delivered the Russell children to the *Milbridge*, was satisfied with the progress of the mission.

Even though Hamady had been captured and faced an ugly future at the hands of the Americans, he had completed his objective. The Russell children were now on the Chinese submarine for the next phase of the mission.

As agreed with the sheik, the Chinese submarine would escape undetected by the Americans and deliver the Russell children to the sheik in KSA. Once in Saudi Arabia, the children would be used to create propaganda videos. But the real use of the Russell children was as a bargaining chip. The sheik would return the Russell children only if the Americans freed every prisoner held in Guantanamo. The sheik knew this would be a win-win scenario for the Islamic Front. Either President Russell would capitulate and free all the prisoners, showing the world the US did negotiate with terrorists, or the sheik would kill his children, streaming it live on the web. It was a vicious plan, and its execution had been perfect so far.

The Secret Service, with MP5s drawn, quickly moved the *Milbridge*'s crew onto a school bus they had obtained from Nantucket High School.

The SEAL squad was now joined by the rest of SEAL Team 2, who had traveled from Sconset to town to be there when the squad arrived at the Brant Point Coast Guard Station dock.

Before they left, Burduck pointed out Karim Hamady to the Secret Service. "That one, he's a hard case. I think he is their leader. Make sure you interrogate him first."

Once on board the bus, Karim Hamady just smiled at Burduck through the bus window.

Burduck walked up to the window where Hamady was sitting and mouthed to him, "Enjoy the rest of your stay on Nantucket, you son of a bitch."

Lieutenant Commander Burduck gathered his team near the Brandt Point dock, where he told them they had two more things they had to do. They needed to conduct a mission debrief, which was protocol, but before that they needed to find a place for breakfast.

The SEALs made their way to Black-Eyed Susan's on

India Street, where over breakfast Burduck would debrief with his team.

He only hoped the kitchen of Black-Eyed Susan's was prepared for eighteen hungry SEALs.

❖

Chinese MSS agent Amy Lu texted Carmichael with the message, "We need to talk."

Carmichael responded, "Sure, where and when?"

"Get a prepaid phone and text me with the new number."

That got Carmichael's attention. He had known Lu for two years, and this was the first time she'd asked him to get a new cell phone in order to communicate with her. He responded with, "Will do and will text you once I have it."

Carmichael then left his apartment and stopped at the Chinese version of a convenience store, where he purchased three prepaid SIM cards.

One SIM was for a data-only plan, and the other two had both voice and data plans. He then walked a few blocks into an electronics store and bought a XiaoMi Redmi 3 4G smartphone. He then inserted the first SIM card into the Chinese smartphone and texted Lu from it.

A second later he got a response with a new number for him to use. Carmichael took out the second SIM, inserted it into the XiaoMi phone, and texted the number Lu had just sent him.

With anonymous communications now established, they began their conversation using the data-only SIM which allowed for messaging via the data channel instead of the SMS channel.

It was much harder to trace a WhatsApp conversation than a typical SMS conversation. About halfway through their dialogue they both switched SIMs again and this time used Skype instant messaging rather than WhatsApp. They were both skilled in the art of evading electronic detection.

Amy Lu texted Carmichael, "I have information about the Russell children."

His reply was brief: "What information?"

Lu responded, "The man behind the operation is Sheik Abdul Er Rahman of KSA."

"How certain are you on this?"

"One hundred percent."

"Do you have a sub off Nantucket?" asked Carmichael.

"I will meet you at our regular spot in an hour," responded Lu.

Which meant the park near Carmichael's apartment.

❖

The sonar operators on both US Navy subs picked up the explosions on the *Milbridge*. The sinking of the *Milbridge* put a lot of sound into the water and again effectively blinded the subs so it would be minutes before they would be able to detect a deadly quiet diesel-electric enemy submarine, with or without the US Navy's towed arrays.

On board the Chinese Navy Yuan type 041 submarine, the captain was monitoring the sinking of the *Milbridge*, which had occurred as planned.

Simultaneous with the explosions that ripped the *Milbridge*'s keel out, the Yuan had launched its version of a Deep Submergence Rescue Vehicle, or DSRV. It was similar to the US Navy's DSRV; however, the Chinese DSRV wasn't transporting a SEAL team. Instead it had on board three Chinese sailors plus the precious cargo of the Russell children.

The DSRV was now a minute away from docking with a second Chinese Yuan-class submarine that had been on station for a week, sitting on the ocean floor waiting for this transfer to happen.

The Russell children were being moved to the Chinese submarine *Deagal* under the cover of the sinking of the *Milbridge*.

With the transfer complete, the two Chinese subs would start their preplanned maneuver. The Yuan would come off the bottom and start to make headway quietly but not silently, with the goal that the American subs would detect him and follow him. The Yuan would be the bait.

The *Deagal* would remain on the ocean bottom a little longer, until the Yuan had cleared the area, taking with him the US subs.

Then, as quietly as possible, the *Deagal* would sneak away in the opposite direction to begin the next phase of their mission, now with the Russell children on board.

The captain of the Yuan gave the order for the sub to lift off the bottom and to start moving at three knots on electric power only.

❖

Clearly, with all the intel now pointing to China being involved in the Nantucket attacks, it was time for Secretary of State Mark Holloway to get involved.

From the Sit Room a call went out summoning Holloway who was already standing by.

Holloway was a lifelong diplomat and had served three administrations as a senior State Department diplomat before assuming the lead position of secretary of state for the Russell administration.

A graduate of Fordham and Georgetown, he was Jesuit trained through and through. He was pensive and slow to rile, a trait President Russell and Vice President McMasters appreciated, as they both possessed more animated personalities.

Mark Holloway entered the Sit Room shortly after being called.

"Mark," started President Russell via the video link from Nantucket, "we believe the Chinese are somehow involved in the Nantucket operation. What could be their motives for such an act?"

Holloway put his elbows on the table, folded his hands, and rested his chin in his fingers.

"Mr. President, it is hard to imagine any scenario where China would take part in an outright offensive operation against us. Especially one that is as deeply personal as this. They know it would risk starting a shooting war with us.

"I think only two scenarios make sense: It could be a rogue faction of the Chinese military or a political faction attempting to destabilize the current Chinese government. Or the government is involved and they plan to act as a white knight, coming to our rescue in order to exact some goodwill or cooperation from us."

President Russell opened the topic for debate and commentary from everyone on the call.

McMasters said, "Mr. President, any involvement in a hostile operation on US soil, especially one against your family, is unconscionable. It would be the work of a madman, and China's president, Wei Zhang, is no madman. I think we need to regard this as the work of a rogue group."

President Russell said, "Let's go around the room with CIA, NSA, FBI, and the Joint Chiefs."

Lisa Collins, the director of the CIA, spoke: "Mr. President, we are gathering intelligence from the field that confirms China is involved. In addition, the Russian FIS has sent word to us that they, too, believe China is involved. But all this could be a *Hunt for Red October* scenario."

George Riordan, director of the NSA, added, "I agree with Lisa. We have two reports of China's involvement in the operation."

Ben Marrone, director of the FBI, went next. "Sir, our interrogations of the captured Al Qaeda fighters on Nantucket have not revealed a link to China. However, we are just beginning our interrogation of the crew of the *Milbridge*, where the SEAL commander has told us they admitted to rendezvousing with a Chinese sub.

"Plus we have the photos of the collar on the hull of the *Milbridge*, which certainly supports the point."

The president asked the CNO about the latest intel from the Navy. That was the cue for the CNO, Admiral Brad Johnson, to join the conversation.

"Mr. President, the *Milbridge* just sank from explosives set by the crew. We have two subs in the area where the *Milbridge* went down.

"Both are looking for an enemy sub. We are looking specifically for a Chinese diesel-electric boat, but as of now we have not detected one.

"We could go active with our sonar to find it. The question is, if we do go active and detect them, what next?"

The president asked out loud, "Should we go active?"

The CNO replied, "Let's play out the scenario if we go active. First, we would no doubt locate the sub, but they would know we have them. We know they have your children onboard. With that knowledge, they know we will not shoot. So what would they do—fire at us? Doubtful. Would they surface and just hand over your children to us? If they don't surface and don't surrender your children, what then? Do we just tail them?

"Sir, we could ram them, forcing them to surface, where we could use the SEALs to board the sub, but the risks are very great. Or we could—"

"Enough," said the president. "Brad, we don't need ten options. We need one well-thought-out plan."

Mark Holloway commented, "Mr. President, we should approach the Chinese through diplomatic channels. We need to establish a dialogue with them to ascertain what they are willing to say officially on the matter."

"Mark, call the Chinese, but don't bring up their involvement directly. I don't want to force their hand until we know what is going on. Just reach out to them—tell them you are reaching out to each member of the Security Council.

"Lisa, connect with the Brits, Russians, and Israelis again to see if they have any new data on the Chinese involvement."

"General, raise our defense condition to DEFCON 2—that will send the message to the world that my, or rather our, patience is running out."

"Gentlemen, Lisa, I am going to talk to my wife now. Her first question is going to be: Where are our children?

"I want answers."

❖

La Rue had settled down in the makeshift bed of her newly purchased and beat-up Nissan pickup truck and was resting.

The cap over the bed of the pickup had dark plastic opaque windows that were old and dirty, and as a result no one could see inside.

She lay down on the pillows and blankets and tried to get some rest while the many details of her escape filled her mind.

When the time came, she would exit the back of the Nissan and walk under the cover of darkness like any other crew hand reporting to work.

The plan was sound; the old pickup was good cover. Now it was just the waiting, the hardest part of all.

Chapter Twenty-One

6:30 to 7:30 a.m. Sunday

Kristin McMahon and Kevin Mannix, now back from a thirty-minute mandatory rest period, were conferring with George Riordan.

Director Riordan wanted the team to brainstorm on what motivation the Chinese would have to get involved in the Nantucket operation, plus find more data supporting or debunking China's involvement.

Leaving the Oasis LLC work behind for the moment, the team started up a new thread of Palantir brainstorming AI software to build a journey map around China's possible involvement in the Attack on ACK, which was what the NSA team was now unofficially calling it.

The Palantir software worked based on an inputted subject-matter premise, covering basic questions like "Why would the Chinese attack the US? What are current hot topics between the US and China? What would China have to gain from participating in an attack on the US?"

From there the AI software, running on the NSA's Cray supercomputers and interfacing with the NSA's Palantir software, would pull together every tagged piece of data it could find that involved subject-matter-premise questions and start to build a supposition matrix.

Within the hour, Crisis Team 2 could start to manipulate the Palantir matrix using the graphic user interface to make connections to other events occurring in the world—political, economic, or even social—that would either support or break down the subject-matter premise.

The Palantir software was nothing short of a breakthrough in the intelligence community and was a closely guarded secret. But some of Crisis Team 2 was old-school, and they didn't need to wait for a software matrix to be built to start their analysis. On the Crisis Room whiteboards one of the analysts wrote, "China kidnaps the president's children—Why?"

Below it they started doing a brainstorming exercise where they threw out ideas: (1) to start a war; (2) to frame someone else; (3) they didn't expect to get caught; (4) they wanted to look like heroes; (5) they wanted to use the kids as negotiating chips; (6) the attack was the work of a rogue group; (7) if not China, who else had the assets to pull this off—meaning who had advanced subs?

What the AI software was going to identify that none of this whiteboard work had picked up on was the connection with the Spratly Islands issue—and the fact that the Spratly Islands issue was timely and important to China.

❖

President Russell was on the phone with his wife. She was doing better and Dr. O'Keefe's team was preparing to administer several therapeutic vaccines based on the 09 variant of the H1N1 virus.

The first lady's condition was still not stable; she was still running a high fever and felt weak and nauseous. But, of course, her main concern was the children.

"Andy," she said tearfully, "the children, where are they? They must be so frightened. You know Andrew will try to put on a brave face for Katie, but he will be scared too." She was in agony.

The president explained about the sinking of the *Milbridge* and the general consensus that the children were on a Chinese sub somewhere off Nantucket. He told her the Chinese would never hurt the kids or risk World War III.

"Andy," she said, "you're the most powerful man in the world. I don't care what you have to do—just get our babies back." Her words stuck with him. He told her he loved her and rang off.

❖

On board the two US subs, all ears were focused on trying to find the Yuan. None of the US subs had gone active as per the president's order.

The *Jimmy Carter* was the first to pick up the Yuan. The *Carter*'s sonar operator yelled out, "Sir, I have a broadband contact, range two miles, bearing 025 degrees, barely making headway, starting track Sierra 2."

Jackson then ordered, "Comms, let the *Dakota* know we are on him." The *Carter*'s sonar operator smiled as he heard the captain's order.

On board the US Navy subs, the BSY-2 sonar sets were in network mode so each of the subs could share the data from the *Carter*'s Sierra 2 track, which was the Chinese Yuan. And as everyone with a technical background knew, having multiple plot points allowed for a more accurate track.

The Yuan's course was now due east of Nantucket, headed for the blue water of the Atlantic. Unbeknownst to the Americans, the *Deagal* slowly and ultraquietly was on a westerly course, staying very close to the Nantucket shore as it shadowed the island.

❖

By now it was 7 a.m. and a new day on the island, but things were nowhere close to normal. Cell and landline service was still down, as per the Secret Service.

The ferry service and airports were closed but had plans to start operating at 9 a.m. The fires were now all out, but the damage was substantial. That included the missile hits on the Dreamland Theater in town and St. Mary, Our Lady of the Isle.

Today there were no drones flying over the island, no missile attacks, and no fires. But the Massachusetts State Police, along with the military, had a very strong presence on the island, augmented by the SEALs, who were just finishing a massive breakfast at Black-Eyed Susan's in town.

In a nice touch, Lieutenant Commander Burduck had invited Ted Schnell and his guests on *The Brown-Eyed Girl* to join the SEALs for breakfast.

The local police were broadcasting over the radio and providing updates to their website about when normal phone service as well as ferry and airport services would be restored.

In addition, in every neighborhood there were still police roadblocks, which were acting more like information centers.

None of the residents of Nantucket knew many of the details regarding the attack, the condition of the first lady, or even that the children had been kidnapped.

The Secret Service, along with the FBI, had put an embargo on any information regarding the president. That is not to say the news organizations on the island weren't trying hard to ferret out any details they could gather.

All around the island Nantucketers exhibited steady nerves and stout hearts after the attack that had occurred on their bucolic island.

The famous New England resilience was on display this morning, as many of the merchants of Nantucket were open and operating just like they would be on any other Sunday in August. That included the Juice Bar and the Fog Island Cafe, which had put out tables on the sidewalk to offer a Sunday brunch alfresco, the Hub, the Club Car, the Tavern, and Arno's. All of the businesses saw it as their civic duty to open and to go on with business as usual. And it wasn't just in town.

In Sconset the Sconset Market, Sconset Café, the Claudette's Sandwich Shop were all open. The Sconset Market had remained open all night to support the firefighters and the military. The Summer House and the Chanticleer both had put out buffets for any of the first responders or military—all free of charge.

In a time of need, it is important that the community come together—this was true in Manhattan after 9/11, in Boston after the marathon bombing, in Paris, and now, added to that list, on the beautiful island of Nantucket.

❖

"Sir, Sierra 2 is approaching the deepwater fathom line." Mike Smith went over to the chart and saw the Yuan would be entering deeper water momentarily as she proceeded to the continental shelf. Smith turned to his XO.

"What do you think, Tom? If he tries to run, how about we put an ADCAP up his tail?" said the captain using the other name for the Navy's advanced MK-48 torpedo.

The XO nodded but knew the captain wasn't serious.

"You know what let's screw with this son of a bitch." The captain called, "Load firing solutions in torpedoes one and three. Open outer torpedo doors."

On board the *Carter*, Jackson received the news that the *North Dakota* was opening its torpedo doors.

"What the ...?" let out the *Carter* CO without thinking.

"Get me the *Dakota*," yelled Jackson. Jackson was the senior of the two sub captains, which put him in command of the submarine group.

"Papa Kilo, Papa Kilo, this is Papa Juliet, come in," called the radioman on the bridge of the *Carter*.

Smith already had the mike in his hand, expecting the call. "Roger, Papa Juliet, Papa Kilo, over."

Jackson grabbed the mike from the radioman. "Mike, what are you doing?"

"If we can't shoot this son of a bitch, let's at least give him something to think about," was Smith's response.

Just then the sonar man on the *Carter* called out, "Con, Sonar, aspect change on Sierra 2, she's slowing."

Jackson yelled, "Quick stop."

"Aye, sir, all stop."

Immediately, all three submarines off the coast of Nantucket came to a halt, one with his outer torpedo tube doors open, ready to take out the Chinese sub.

As all attention was focused on the Yuan stopping, the *Deagal* was rounding Madaket point when its crew started to hear a scraping sound on the sub's hull. The captain immediately ordered all stop, but the sound short had already occurred, which meant the sub had given its position away by creating a discernable sound.

"Conn, Sonar. I am picking up ambient noise on the BSY-2, starting track Sierra 3," called the sonar operator on the USS *North Dakota.*

The captain entered the sonar room and called, "What do you have?"

"Sir, we picked up a sound short just west of us. It's gone now but it sounded like a grinding noise."

"Could it be a fishing boat pulling up a net or some lobster pots?" queried the captain.

"Not unless as soon as they realized they were making noise they immediately went quiet. That doesn't make sense for a fishing boat. It's a sub, sir."

Smith agreed.

"What is the position of the contact?" They looked on the chart and determined it originated toward the western tip of the island.

Smith had a hunch about what this meant, plus the *Carter* didn't need his help tracking the Yuan, which was now stopped.

"Papa Juliet, this is Papa Kilo. We are breaking off pursuit of Sierra 2. We are initiating a track on Sierra 3 off the western tip of the island and wish to investigate, copy."

"Papa Juliet copies. Agreed. Let us know if you require assistance. Out," replied Jackson to Smith.

"Helm, come about to course 300, ahead two-thirds. Pilot, watch the sounding. Close outer torpedo doors," called Smith.

The order was echoed by the officer of the deck and the pilot as the *North Dakota* started a sweeping turn to starboard.

The chief of the boat added, "Sir, the ship is now at ultraquiet."

Smith just nodded, as he was deep in thought. Another sub—could it be?

Meanwhile, Captain Jackson on the *Carter* was informing Admiral Jacobsen about the new Sierra 3 track the *Dakota* had just picked up.

On the *Deagal* the officers and crew were assessing their situation. Using high-definition cameras attached at various points on the hull, they could now see they had run into an old fishing net.

The best possible scenario would be to back up the way they had come and let the net slip off the hull. The problem was sometimes that made things worse. It could also be noisy and attract unwanted attention.

The captain conferred with his second-in-command, not a common procedure in the Chinese Navy, indicating the seriousness of the situation and their mission.

They mutually decided they would try the backing maneuver. He then gave the command, "All back, dead slow, one boat length," to see if the net would come loose. If that didn't work, they would send out divers to cut the netting off the sub using underwater torches, although that would make a detectable sound.

Using just their batteries and turning very few rpms on the single-shaft propeller, the *Deagal* moved backward dead slow. Just as quickly as the net grabbed on to the sub, it slipped off with minimum sound due to the dead slow speed. The captain and first officer wiped the perspiration off their foreheads as they called, "All stop."

The Chinese sub then resumed backing away from the hazard of the net and ever so slowly turned west until they lay in ninety-four feet of water two miles off the westernmost tip of Tuckernuck Island.

Tuckernuck Island (latitude: 41°18' N, longitude: 70°15' W) is a private island off the western tip of Nantucket, just off Madaket. The island has an area of about nine hundred acres.

There are about thirty-five houses on the island, and the population hovers around fifty, which doubles in the summer months. The island has no paved roads or public utilities. Electricity is generated by gas-powered generators, solar panels, and mini wind turbines.

The island has some cars, but most of the motorized transportation is provided by electric golf carts. There is a rarely used and not always well-maintained grass airstrip. It is a perfect place to hide something—or someone.

Chapter Twenty-Two

11 a.m. Sunday

In total silence the Deagal surfaced two miles off the western end of Tuckernuck Island. No one would see the sub in spite of the fact that it was now broad daylight.

The captain surfaced enough for only the sail and a sliver of the hull to emerge from the water, what submariners call "a wet deck." His men deployed a Zodiac rigid boat.

Once the Zodiac was secured, two tiny figures made their way onto the black hull of the Chinese sub, escorted by three Chinese sailors. It was Andrew Russell holding the hand of his frightened ten-year-old sister, Katie.

He said to her, "It will be all right, Katie." But Katie was shaking almost uncontrollably. The sailors gently helped both of the children onto the Zodiac. Once on board, the crew of three started the engine and set a course for the North Pond on the westernmost tip of Tuckernuck Island.

They would circle into the pond so their approach would not encounter any strong surf.

❖

It was now 11 p.m. in Muscat, and Lauren La Rue was ready to leave the old Nissan pickup truck and make her way to the *Al Raisa*, tied up near the pier, and eventually to her freedom.

She had visualized how she would walk to the boat over and over in her head during the hours she waited so that the actual walk to the boat would feel very familiar.

She opened the tailgate of the pickup and pushed herself out of the truck.

The cool night air felt good after being locked up in the truck for so long. She stretched quickly and silently, then surveyed the alley and the parking lot that lay between the alley and the pier.

With her backpack over her shoulder, she started to walk toward the boat. It was the walk of a tired fisherman who was slightly intoxicated, if not totally drunk.

She continued walking without turning her head too abruptly, avoiding any sign she was surveying the area around her.

She was only about ten yards from the pier when a black SUV suddenly came out of the darkness and stopped just in front of her. The doors opened and three men dressed in black got out and grabbed her. They quickly put a pillowcase over her head and threw her into the backseat of the SUV, then sped off.

No words were spoken. It all happened in less than ten seconds.

Watching from another alley near the Muscat waterfront was the CIA's deep-cover agent, Aziz Mahmood. He had found La Rue and was monitoring her to ensure that she was picked up by the Americans. But Mahmood knew the people who had just snatched La Rue weren't the US Grey Wolfe team. Mahmood's first thought was that the sheik's people had gotten La Rue.

If the sheik had gotten La Rue, her life would end soon, and what was left of it would be filled with agony.

❖

Amy Lu was sitting on a bench in the corner of the small park in central Beijing waiting for Carmichael.

He approached her from behind, walked around the bench, and then sat down next to her.

"What do you have for me?" he asked, dispensing with any pleasantries.

"Dale," she began, "what I am about to say to you is top secret. Very few people in my government have this information."

Carmichael just listened.

"We infiltrated the Islamic Front's organization. We did so to protect the president and his family. A few minutes ago we snatched La—" Suddenly a shot rang out, hitting Lu in the chest. She slumped to the side, killed instantly.

Carmichael pulled out his sidearm, which was strictly forbidden in China, and looked for where the shot originated. It had come from a high-powered rifle, which meant the range could have been up to a mile away.

He glanced back down at Lu, at her lifeless body. He bent down, put his hand over her face, and closed her eyes. Then he quickly left.

The sheik had people everywhere, and they had suspected for some time that Lu had infiltrated his organization and had been funneling information to the Americans.

❖

The Chinese Zodiac had just cleared the Point of Tuckernuck Island and was now headed into North Pond and its calmer waters. The Chinese crew member steering the Zodiac saw a good landing spot and gunned the engine, allowing him to make better time without jostling his precious cargo too much.

Soon the throttles on the boat retarded and the motors quickly cycled down.

The rubber boat glided smoothly as it made landfall and the pontoons slid onto the sandy bottom of the pond. Once they had stopped, two of the crew members jumped out of the Zodiac and pulled it a few feet farther onto the shore. With the Zodiac now secured, the friendlier of the crew members reached his arm out to help first Katie and then Andrew onto the sand.

In practiced English, he said to them, "The Chinese people return you safely. Please go now to your parents."

Next the crew member took out an official-looking envelope and, giving it to Andrew, said, "To give please to the president."

Andrew accepted the letter and put it in the back pocket of his pants.

With no more talk, the crew members pushed the Zodiac off the sand, turned it around, jumped into the rigid boat, and gunned its engines. And just like that they were gone.

Andrew and Katie looked at each other. "Where are we?" asked Katie.

"I think we're on Nantucket but on the other side of the island, out near Eel Point," Andrew said. "Let's start walking and we'll stop at the first house we see."

They began walking over the sand and soon came to a trail, which they followed. They could see a house about a quarter of a mile away.

Ron Orden had inherited his house on Tuckernuck from his uncle. Ron spent the summers on Tuckernuck and the winters as a ski instructor in Winter Park, Colorado. He led a stress-free life centered on his love of nature and the great outdoors.

It was late morning on Sunday and Orden was in his kitchen starting to make a sandwich when he heard the sound of footsteps on the front porch.

Next he heard a knocking on the front screen door and a young voice saying tentatively, "Hello?"

"Coming." When he got to the front door he saw two children. One was a boy about twelve, tall and lean, still wearing the pajamas from the morning when he was abducted. They now were dirty and stained.

Next to him was a young girl wearing a nightgown. Her hair was matted and they both looked tired and drawn.

The boy spoke. "Hello, my name is Andrew Russell and this is my sister, Katie. Can you help us get back to our parents? We are staying in Sconset."

Orden did not recognize them or have any clue they were the children of the president. He swung open the screen door and replied in a friendly tone, "Sure, I can help you. Come on in. I was just making lunch. Are you hungry?"

Katie looked at Andrew. They hadn't eaten in some time.

"How about some potato chips?" asked Orden. The two children followed Ron into the kitchen, where he passed them the bag of potato chips, which they both started to devour.

"What are you doing out here? How did you get on Tuckernuck?" asked Ron.

Katie answered, "We were on the Chinese submarine and they dropped us off here, so now we need to get home to our parents. Our father is the president of the United States."

Ron dropped his fork as the last line sunk in.

"You're the children of the president? President Russell is your father, the president of the United States?"

Andrew answered, "Yes, our father is President Russell and our mother is Mrs. Russell. We are staying in Sconset. Can you help us get back there?"

Orden grabbed his vest with his sunglasses and keys and said, "Okay, then, let's get you back to your parents. You said they are in Sconset, right?"

They nodded.

"Bring the potato chips if you want," he told them as he opened the back door and made his way to his golf cart.

He jumped in the driver's seat, turned on the golf cart, and said, "Go ahead, get in."

Cell phones were still down, but that really didn't matter, as coverage on Tuckernuck was spotty at best, especially on the western end of Tuckernuck, where Orden lived.

As he drove he thought about stopping at a neighbor's house to use their satellite phone but decided the children were his responsibility and it was up to him to deliver the kids safely to their parents. He wasn't going to delegate this job to anyone.

The ride was a little less than two miles to the lagoon where everyone on Tuckernuck kept their boats.

They bounced over the sand road with Ron looking back occasionally and smiling as he asked, "You both doing okay?" Still eating the potato chips, they both just nodded.

Ron didn't pass anyone on the trail, which wasn't unusual for Tuckernuck. He finally brought the golf cart to a stop at the area the village inhabitants all used as a parking lot.

That's when Andy exclaimed, "A boat? I thought we were on Nantucket!"

"No," replied Ron. "You are on Tuckernuck Island, right next to Nantucket. It will only be about a two-mile ride to Madaket."

He saw that both kids looked worried.

"Have you guys ever gone on the seal cruise?" That helped bring a spark of excitement to their eyes, especially Katie's.

"Yes," she said with the most energy he had seen from her so far. "We've gone on the seal cruise, the whale watch, *and* the ice cream cruise."

"Perfect," said Ron. "The seal cruise comes out to Tuckernuck. All the seals live on the north side of the island. So you have seen Tuckernuck from the seal cruise boat. Now we're just going to go back the way you came."

Ron pointed. "Over there, that's Nantucket. It will take us about five minutes to get there," he said. "And there," he added, pointing again, "is my boat. We'll have you in Sconset in a jiffy." He was working hard to put the children at ease.

All three jumped into Ron's boat, a twenty-eight-foot Grady-White Model 285 equipped with two three-hundred-horse-power Yamaha outboard engines.

He turned the key to the on position, pumped the primer, and then pushed the start key.

After letting the engines warm for a couple of minutes, he nudged the throttles forward as he cleared the lagoon.

Once out of the lagoon, he advanced the throttles to the stops.

He headed to Jackson Point and into the inlet, all the while keeping the Grady-White at top speed. He sped past Nantucket Outfitters and then up the inlet at top speed exceeding the posted 5 mph speed limit.

As Madaket Marine came into view, he pulled back hard on the throttles and started blowing his horn in short bursts.

He went right for the main dock at Madaket Marine, on his left, and threw his bumpers over the side. He put the engines in reverse and brought the boat to a stop as the bumpers made contact with the wharf.

Turning off the engines, he threw a line to a person who looked like he worked at Madaket Marine. The young guy grabbed the line and yelled, "Dude, what's the hurry?"

Ron yelled to him, "We have an emergency. I need a car." The man made the line fast and quickened his pace as Ron threw him the stern line.

"I have a pickup in the parking lot."

Ron asked, "Are there any police nearby?"

"There are some Mass. state troopers up on Madaket Road."

Ron helped first Katie onto the dock and then Andrew.

"Where's the truck?" Ron said. The man pointed up to the parking lot.

"Come on, let's go." He gathered the kids and they all started to jog toward the truck.

"What's the emergency?"

Ron replied, "We need to get these kids to Sconset ASAP." With that, they all jumped into the Ford pickup, four across the front seat with no seat belts, no motorcade, no Secret Service detail—just an old sky-blue Ford F-150 pickup.

As the truck headed up onto Madaket Road the young man pointed. "See, up ahead there's a roadblock with the state troopers."

Ron said, "Okay, stop when we get there and I'll get out."

As the Ford pickup approached the roadblock, the state trooper waved his hand to the driver to slow down, which he did.

Ron jumped out, which prompted an immediate reaction from the state trooper, who instinctively put his right hand on his revolver and said to Ron sternly, "Sir, please get back in the vehicle, *now*."

Ron yelled to the trooper, "We have an emergency." Instinctively Ron put his hands up to show he wasn't carrying anything. By now all four Massachusetts state troopers were closing in on Ron, two from each side.

"Stand where you are, sir. What is the nature of your emergency?" demanded the first trooper.

Ron said calmly, "My name is Ron Orden. I live over on Tuckernuck. A half hour ago two children knocked on my door. They said they were dropped off by a Chinese submarine. The children's names are Andrew and Katie Russell—*Russell*. They are the children of the president."

As he listened to Orden's words, the driver of the pickup was as dumbfounded as the state troopers.

With their hands on their holsters two of the troopers made their way to the driver's side of the pickup and told the driver to put his hands on the wheel.

The other two troopers approached Orden from either side with the lead trooper saying, "Say again?"

Andrew then got out of the passenger side of the pickup, where the door was still ajar.

He called out, "Ron's right, my name is Andrew Russell. My sister and I need to get back to Sconset."

For a moment, time seemed to stop, with everyone looking at one another, trying to figure out what had just happened.

Then in the blink of an eye, the lead trooper regained his composure and said, "Okay, everyone in my cruiser now." He grabbed the kids and put them in the back with one trooper on either side of them.

The trooper then motioned to Orden to get in the front with him as he jumped into the cruiser and started it while hitting the lights and siren, all seemingly in a single motion.

He floored the accelerator on the Ford Crown Vic police cruiser, causing the back of the cruiser to fishtail as it gained speed. The remaining trooper got into his cruiser to follow them with the pick-up truck driver joining him.

The troopers knew they needed to follow protocol to enter Sconset. With or without lights flashing, the military and Secret Service were in no mood for troopers acting like cowboys.

Massachusetts Trooper Thomas Meyer got on the radio. "10-0, 10-0 emergency, 10-0."

The 10-0 radio code meant "Emergency, clear the air." The Nantucket police radio, which was now being run by the Massachusetts State Police, came back with, "Roger on your 10-0. Please identify yourself and state your emergency."

As Trooper Meyer passed the Nantucket Airport on Milestone Road going almost one hundred miles per hour, he replied, "This is Trooper Meyer, badge number 1528, I am headed eastbound on Milestone Road. We have the Russell children on board.

"I repeat, we have the Russell children in our cruiser. They are in good shape. I repeat, they are in good shape. I am headed to Sconset—clear the way."

The police band started to crackle with radio calls. The Secret Service told Meyers to take a right onto Tom Nevers Road, which would bring him to the presidential bunker.

He replied, "10-4, copy. Alert the president we will be there shortly."

As the Crown Vic made the turn onto Tom Nevers Road, two more police cars joined up. Now there were four cars all speeding to the bunker.

❖

President Russell had just finished a call with Holloway and McMasters when Nicols burst in. "Mr. President, Mr. President, we have them—your children—we have them."

"Say again."

Nicols took a breath and said more slowly, "Mr. President, your children, we have them. They say Andy and Katie are fine, no injuries. They'll be here in a minute."

The president slumped in his chair for a second, letting the tension and stress from the last two days drain from him. He closed his eyes for three seconds, exhaled, and thanked God. Then he opened his eyes and said, "Get the first lady on the line."

❖

As the black SUV traveled away from the Muscat waterfront, La Rue didn't know if she was going to be shot or tortured.

With the hood over her head and duct tape around her mouth, she was at her captors' mercy.

There was no talking in the SUV. She could tell they had accelerated, and she could feel the curves of the road as they drove. After a few minutes the SUV came to a halt and she was escorted out of the vehicle.

She was pushed and steered to a flight of stairs, and at the top someone held her head down as she entered what she sensed was the cabin of a jet. From there she was seated and belted into a chair as the engines revved for the plane's takeoff run.

In a matter of minutes the plane was airborne. Only then was the hood removed. She realized she had not been taken by the sheik's security people but instead she was in the company of the Chinese. She had no idea what was in store for her.

She identified herself as a US citizen and then asked who they were and where they were headed.

The senior Chinese MSS agent sitting in one of the four facing seats began to speak in perfect English. "Miss La Rue, what can you tell us about Sheik Abdul Er Rahman and his involvement in the Nantucket operation?"

La Rue knew to hold out was futile.

Her survival instincts, which had always served her well, kicked in, as she decided her best chance of survival was to cooperate fully. She started telling them about the sheik, although she was a good enough negotiator to hold back some information for later—if it was necessary.

As it turned out, the only useful information La Rue knew about the Nantucket operation was the plans for the drone attacks and the iPad network disruption. She knew nothing about the plan to kidnap the president's family. As a matter of fact, when she was interrogated about it she replied vehemently, "Do you think I'm crazy? Do you think I would participate in a plan to kidnap the US president's family? Our goal was to disrupt the island and create havoc. There was no talk of outright violence." None, as it turned out, that she knew about.

Her level of cooperation would weigh heavily on how the MSS treated her.

❖

As soon as the police cruisers pulled up to the presidential bunker, the kids jumped out of the car and ran to the waiting arms of their father. He hugged both at the same time.

It only took a second for Katie to ask, "Where's Mommy?"

The president put them down and said, "Mommy is not here but she is fine. We are going to go inside and talk to her on the video."

"But where is she?" asked Katie.

"Mommy's in Atlanta. She has the flu and they wanted her to see some doctors there," said her father. "Let's go inside and talk to her."

As they entered the bunker, the medical staff descended upon the children to take their vital signs and to make sure they, too, weren't infected with the H1N1 virus. Their blood would be drawn after they had talked to their mother.

As they entered the communication room of the bunker, Kennedy Russell was already up on the monitor.

She beamed when the images of her son and daughter reached her screen.

"How are you? You had us so worried," she said through her tears.

Andy spoke up first, rather nonchalantly, "We're fine."

But there was nothing nonchalant in Katie's voice. "Mommy, where are you? Why aren't you here? Are you sick?"

"No, no, I am fine. I'm in Atlanta just as a precaution. The doctors are running some tests. But I am either going to leave here and fly up to you—or maybe you can come down here."

Katie immediately responded, "When?"

The medical staff needed to spend some time with the children, so the president said, "Okay, for now, let's let Mommy rest and you two will go with this nice doctor for a checkup. By the way, when was the last time you had something to eat?" the president asked.

Andrew said, "We had some potato chips on Ron's boat."

The president asked, "Ron who?"

Andrew replied, "Ron. Ron from the other island. Who got us back to Nantucket on his boat."

As he left the room, the president made a note to have his staff get a list of all the people who had helped his family during this difficult ordeal.

Just then Andrew ran back to him and said, "Dad, I was supposed to give this to you." He handed over the envelope the sailor had given him.

"What's this?"

"The sailor from the Chinese submarine told me to give this to you," he said. And then Andrew left to go with the doctors. The Secret Service agents quickly took the letter from the president to check it for any foreign substance such as Anthrax. In a few minutes, once convinced the letter was clean, they handed it back to the president.

Chapter Twenty-Three

Midday Sunday

The president sat down and opened the letter:

Dear Mr. President,

A year ago we became aware of a plot by Al Qaeda to target your family. During that year our agents worked to infiltrate the group responsible for this attack. The group was led by Sheik Abdul Er Rahm of Riyadh, KSA, the leader of the Islamic Front.

Working closely with the sheik, we eventually gained his confidence and convinced him that China also looked upon the US as an enemy. Our feigned hatred for the US allowed us to participate in the Nantucket operation. China sent two submarines into US territorial waters off Nantucket to support the operation.

Our plan was always to ensure that your family would not be harmed, but in order to achieve that we first needed to secure them from the terrorists. Our Special Forces were responsible for the sinking of the SS *Milbridge Major*, where your children were being held.

We apologize for not informing you earlier of this plot, but we felt the only way we could guarantee the safety of your family was to keep this information tightly held and confidential.

I believe had the US detected a plan to kidnap members of my family, you would, no doubt, have done the same thing. I share this information with you as a sign of our good faith and as a basis for our going-forward relations.

It is our fervent desire to establish a positive relationship with the United States and for our relationship to grow over time.

We believe our actions were those of an ally and a friend, and were acts of courage and honor. I am very pleased to know your family is now safe.

Sincerely,

Wei Zhang

President of the People's Republic of China

The president got on the line with the Sit Room. "Gentlemen, my children are safe and are now in the bunker with me. My son handed me a rather extraordinary letter from the president of China, Wei Zhang. General Standard, stand down our troops and resume a DEFCON 5 posture immediately.

"George, have your people pull everything we have on Sheik Abdul Er Rahman of the Islamic Front in Riyadh—he's our man and the one responsible for this attack.

"Admiral Johnson, get word to our subs and the *Roosevelt* strike group that there are two Chinese subs off Nantucket. They are to be given safe passage."

The president then turned to his chief of staff, who had entered the room. "Sterl, schedule an address to the nation for tonight. It's about time we tell everyone what has been going on. I will give it from Atlanta.

"Dan, tell the local police they can resume landline and cell service and reopen the Nantucket airport and harbor."

The president added, "Gentlemen, Lisa, you have served our nation, my family, and me well during this very difficult time, and I am grateful. We need to review our intelligence and security protocols. We owe it to future presidents to never allow this to happen again—and I owe it to my wife.

"We are the most powerful nation on the face of the planet. Yes, we live in a free society, but we can never again let a handful of zealots stage an attack the likes of what we just experienced.

"If not for the intervention of China, whose motivation we need to understand, things could have turned out much worse.

"Sterl, ready my plane. I want to be wheels up on the way to Atlanta within the hour."

The president broke the conference line and went to check on his children.

❖

On board the USS *North Dakota*, the sonar man was calling, "Change in aspect on Sierra 3, sir, he is turning."

Just then the communications officer came onto the bridge, "Sir, we have flash priority traffic." He handed the message to the captain. Captain Smith reread the message just to be sure.

Smith passed the message to his XO, saying, "You are not going to believe this."

Captain Smith then grabbed the 1MC and addressed his crew, "Secure from ultraquiet, prepare to surface, prepare to surface."

Simultaneously on board the USS *Jimmy Carter* Captain Jackson ordered, "Secure from general quarters. Prepare to surface." Again an expert crew automatically responded to their leader's commands.

Within minutes of receiving the flash traffic, both US submarines were now cruising at one-third speed on the surface and had secured from any offensive posture.

Captain Jackson had one order yet to complete. He called to his communications officer, "Put this out on all channels unencrypted: To submarines operating off Nantucket, I have a message from the president of the United States: You will be given safe passage through our waters. May you have fair winds and following seas. With deepest gratitude Andrew Russell."

There was no response, but a minute later the sonar on the US subs detected hull-popping sounds as the two Chinese Yuan-class diesel-electric subs also surfaced.

As the subs rode on the surface, their captains posted limited watches and allowed off-duty crew to get some fresh air. It was a good start to a new détente between the United States and China.

On board the USS *Theodore Roosevelt* carrier battle group, Admirals Jacobson and Singer also received the message and initiated the stand-down order for all ships in the battle group.

Chapter Twenty-Four

The Aftermath

President Russell and the children took off for Atlanta that afternoon. They took the C-32 to Otis Air National Guard Base on Cape Cod, where they changed planes to VC-25A, the 747 version of Air Force One.

On their two-and-a-half-hour flight to Atlanta, Sterling Spencer worked with the White House communications staff on the president's address to the nation, to be given from Emory.

President Russell had asked for the bios of the four agents who had been killed in the attacks as well as his cook and the dead US Marine.

His staff provided bios on each of the agents, then left the president alone in his office on Air Force One as he made the difficult calls.

As with any terrorist attack and the planned address to the nation, the discussion was around how much detail to share with the American people.

After a rapid series of discussions between the intelligence agencies of the US and China, it was agreed that no mention of China's involvement would be made public. This was for several reasons, but mostly so as not to alert the Islamic Front that they had been played by China.

The public version of what had happened was that Navy SEALs rescued the Russell children from a Turkish ship with a crew made up of Al Qaeda terrorists off Nantucket.

Furthermore, both China and the US wanted to keep the sheik in the dark about the whereabouts of La Rue. By now the sheik would suspect that La Rue was being held by either the US or China, but which country was to be a closely held secret. In point of fact, the Chinese had agreed to transfer La Rue to the CIA once they were finished with her.

The Chinese were also investigating the murder of their MSS agent Amy Lu. All indications were that it was the work of the sheik, but nothing had been confirmed yet.

Meanwhile, the staff on Air Force One kept a very close watch on the Russell children, knowing full well that in a matter of hours they would have a remedy far better than any medicine or counseling they could provide.

The doctors felt FLOTUS would require at least another forty-eight hours in quarantine. With that in mind, the hospital arranged for accommodations for POTUS and his family, with the Secret Service managing the heightened security requirements that would need to be put in place.

The Secret Service was anxious to get the first family back to the White House and its state-of-the-art security systems. There was a discussion about possibly moving the first lady, but for now her medical treatment needs took priority over the security concerns.

The combined team of doctors and staff were running tests on the first lady's blood to create various antidotes for the 09 strain of the H1N1 virus. They still hadn't isolated the remedy that would cure the first lady, but they were getting closer.

The remaining challenge was to keep FLOTUS strong enough so the virus did not get the upper hand and cause her lungs to start to lose function.

What they could still use was information from the Pakistani doctor, Dr. Muhammed Abdul Wajid.

The trail on Dr. Wajid was helped enormously by the information the Chinese MSS team was obtaining from the interrogation of Lauren La Rue.

"What can you tell us about a Dr. Muhammed Abdul Wajid?" the lead Chinese MSS team member asked La Rue.

"What do you want to know about him?"

"Everything."

"He is one of my clients. I know his bank accounts, his family and business associates," said La Rue.

"What about addresses?"

"Yes, of course I have them. My phone address book, please."
The Chinese agents handed La Rue her address book, from
which she quickly gave them Dr. Wajid's home address in Islamabad as well as his vacation place in Karachi.

One of the members of the Chinese MSS team took the
data and entered it into his laptop. Within minutes the MSS
agent was sending the data to his contact in Fairfax, Virginia,
at the CIA headquarters.

The Chinese MSS team then stopped the interrogation and
allowed La Rue to rest.

❖

As Air Force One flew toward Atlanta and Emory University
Hospital, the president had a few minutes to reflect on the events
of the past two days. He checked to see that his children were
okay. He then went into his office and stretched out on his couch.

Like Maslow, his first thoughts were of survival and protection. He thought, *This can never happen again. Not to my
family, not to any other first family.*

He owed that to his wife. He also was concerned that Kennedy, who had already been exhibiting signs of strain from the

security worries that went along with being the first family, would now be even more protective of the children and less supportive of public events, let alone wanting to campaign for a second term. And who could blame her?

Starting tomorrow morning the president would begin reviewing the presidential and first family security plans. It was clear there would be no public events for his wife or children for a long, long time.

As the president started to drift off, his thoughts turned to payback. Sheik Er Rahman and his associates were going to pay a high price for their actions. The question was, how would he exact revenge against those who had perpetrated this crime on his family? But that would have to wait, as the president was now asleep, his first sound sleep of the last two days.

Air Force One was just touching down at Hartsfield-Jackson Atlanta International Airport, with the motorcade standing by for the fifteen-mile drive to Emory University Hospital, when the president awakened, refreshed.

Knowing how eager the president and his children were to see the first lady, the motorcade wasted no time at the airport. They covered the fifteen-mile trip in barely ten minutes.

The Secret Service ushered the Russells up to the floor where Mrs. Russell was, and the president's chief of staff made sure there were no cameras to interfere with the intimacy of the moment.

Kennedy Russell was sitting up in her hospital bed with an IV in her left arm shrouded by a clear plastic tent the staff had erected for her. The children entered the room on her right, and she lit up like the sun. Even though they couldn't touch it was still a heartwarming scene.

As the president followed his children, he spoke the line he always said when he entered a room where she was: "Please, don't get up." Even now he thought it was funny.

❖

Two hours later at 9 p.m. eastern time, the president approached a lectern bearing the Seal of the President of the United States.

The president began, "My fellow Americans. . ."

❖

The CIA located Dr. Wajid, who fully cooperated in identifying the strain of H1N1 that FLOTUS and Trooper Herbert had contracted.

Using the Wajid information, Dr. O'Keefe had the antidote manufactured within a few hours.

Wajid was subsequently flown out of Pakistan. His whereabouts today are unknown.

❖

Order was being restored on Nantucket with the resumption of both wireless and landline communications.

That plus the reopening of the harbor and airport were major steps in restoring order and a normalcy to everyday life.

Now all the networks were broadcasting nonstop the details of the Attack on ACK, as it was being promoted by all the cable networks.

❖

The first family left Emory Tuesday morning, taking the time to thank each member of the staff for their care of the first lady.

The president and his family flew back to the White House immediately after her release.

❖

As another demonstration of goodwill, the Chinese had turned over Ms. Lauren La Rue to the CIA, but not before fully debriefing her on the sheik, his operations, and his associates. La Rue had provided a gold mine of information to the Chinese and would now do likewise to the Americans. There was talk of making her an employee of the NSA focusing on counterterrorism and banking.

Book III

Chapter Twenty-Five

The Ten Weeks After the Attack on ACK

Operation Warlord

With life returning to normal in the White House, the president started working on a plan that he kept secret from many of his closest advisers, including his wife.

Under doctor's orders, the president had cleared a five-hour block of time every week for the next ten weeks on either a Friday or Saturday so he could relax and play golf.

When the appointed time came every week, Marine One would take off from the south lawn of the White House, but instead of heading to Congressional Country Club or the course at Fort Belvoir, Marine One turned south.

An hour later, Marine One touched down at Naval Air Station Patuxent River, Maryland, better known as NAS Pax River.

There the president was met by Lieutenant Commander Mike Bartlett, of VX 23, the *Salty Dogs*. VX-23 was one of the Navy's elite Air Test and Evaluation squadrons. In the aviation community there are a few assignments that are highly coveted – the Blues, TOPGUN and Test pilots were some of the most prized billets. And Bartlett had the good fortune to be a test pilot for VX-23 the *Salty Dogs*.

Once at Pax River the president would enter a locker room in Hangar 2 and gear up along with Lieutenant Commander Bartlett. With a contingent of Secret Service agents surrounding the hangar, the president would take refresher courses on the F/A-18F as well as spending time in the flight simulator. Once he was deemed ready he would be allowed back into the cockpit.

The president was flying again, with his goal to requalify on the F/A-18F Super Hornet.

The president knew from his days as a naval aviator that in order to fly a fighter jet, you needed to not only master the switchology of the cockpit but also develop the muscle memory needed to fly high-performance jets successfully and safely.

During the first three weeks of his training, the president flew numerous hours in a flight simulator as he familiarized himself with the systems of the F/A-18Fs.

When week four came, POTUS got back into the cockpit, with Lieutenant Commander Bartlett monitoring from the rear seat. It was only a few weeks before the president got his touch back.

He wasn't pulling 7.5-G turns anymore, but he had a good feel for the stick and thought he could keep up with the other members of VX-23.

He was developing a respect and fondness for the new Block III Super Hornet.

The president's decision to requalify on the Super Hornet was a tightly held secret known only to his chief of staff, the members of VX-23, his Secret Service detail, and a very few members of the Navy brass.

No one else knew about it, not the directors of the CIA, FBI, or NSA—or even his wife, Kennedy.

The president had retired from the Navy as an O-5 commander with 476 carrier-arrested landings to his credit, as well as four deployments, but now he was a nugget all over again.

"Nugget" is the term given to a new member of a squadron and an aviator who has yet to make his first deployment on an aircraft carrier.

Every naval aviator is given a call sign early in his or her career. When Andrew Russell fleeted up, he was given the call sign Rudy. It was a reference to the movie by the same name and his time at the academy, where, based on a dare, he tried out for the football team as a walk-on (he didn't make the team but was on the practice squad).

Unlike the US Air Force, where a pilot's call sign was usually something like Viper, Stinger, or Stick, Navy call signs were supposed to be clever and carry a meaning specific to the pilot and his personality.

As a naval aviator, Andrew Russell was known as Rudy. But now that he was POTUS, requalifying on the F/A-18, his VX-23 squadron mates had taken to using Rusty as his call sign. The president chuckled when he first heard it, and the name stuck.

❖

The NSA director, George Riordan, was on the president's schedule this morning, about five weeks after the Nantucket ordeal, along with Sterling Spencer, the president's chief of staff, and Mark Holloway, the secretary of state.

"Gentlemen," said the president, "good morning. What do we have?"

Spencer said, "Mr. President, we think we understand what China's motivation was for the Nantucket operation. We believe they infiltrated the Al Qaeda cell in order to influence your position on the Spratly Islands UN vote."

Starting in 2013, China began a major construction program to create a large artificial island in the area known as the Spratly

Islands, an archipelago in the South China Sea, with the undeniable purpose of exerting maritime control over the region.

In addition to the NATO countries, Russia, and Japan, protests had come from Brunei, Malaysia, the Philippines, Taiwan, and Vietnam over China's plan, making the islands one of the world's most heavily contested areas.

Furthermore, China's claim to the Spratly Islands was contrary to at least three treaties the US had with the Philippines, in which the US had agreed to defend the Philippines against China.

In spite of some recent tensions, the US and the Philippines had remained close partners in trade and in the War on Terror, with Washington sending thousands of troops and other resources to combat the Islamic insurgency in the Philippines in recent years.

The United States also maintained close relations with the Republic of China (Taiwan). The Spratly Islands issue was also a major concern to Taiwan.

The United States might very well be called by Taiwan to help defend it against China, as cited in the Taiwan Relations Act the US had signed with the Taiwanese in 1979.

In addition, China's assertiveness in the region had led Vietnam to look to the United States to counter Beijing's power and land grab. India also was involved in the dispute, worried about Indian companies currently drilling for oil in the territorial waters of Vietnam.

At stake was potential control over this major transit point for Asian trade and shipping.

There was a treaty in front of the UN that would attempt to settle once and for all that the Spratly Islands were Chinese.

The president turned to Holloway and asked for his thoughts.

"Mr. President," Holloway said, "it makes sense, but I do not think this was their primary motive. The State Department believes China became involved in this matter first and foremost to show they could be a good actor on the world's stage as a superpower. Beyond a doubt, I think that was their primary intent. That said, this operation cost them very little in terms of capital. Yes, if it went wrong it could have been catastrophic for them, but we don't think they would have taken the risk unless they were certain they could pull it off."

The president turned to his director of the NSA. "George?"

"Mr. President, I am not buying any of this. The thought that China has all of a sudden become our 'friend' gives me pause. Think about it. If they knew about the attack, why not notify us the day before? We could have flown you and your family off the island, and we would have our four Secret Service agents, your cook, and a US Marine alive today. How many times have the Brits or Israelis called us to inform us about an impending attack? No, sir, they did this to get something in return."

Holloway responded, "George is correct. They did want something in return, Mr. President. But had they just called us to inform us of the impending attack, it would have had much less impact. They sent two of their most advanced subs halfway around the world without us detecting them. Then, even with two subs and a carrier group close by, we still didn't detect them.

"I think they wanted to make a statement that, one, they have an intelligence org capable of infiltrating Al Qaeda; two, their navy is now a world-class navy; and three—and this is important—they wanted the claim of 'doing the right thing.' Remember, China is still striving for the world's respect and a seat at the grown-up table."

The president then asked, "What would we have done in the same circumstances?"

After a moment Holloway again commented, "Mr. President, if it were one of our close allies, say the Brits, French, or Germans, we would have told them in advance. If it were someone whom we thought couldn't handle the threat or might not believe us, then we probably would have done what the Chinese did. Although it is worth pointing out that the Chinese have told us they didn't know anything about the plan to infect your wife with the virus. That was closely held by the sheik's people and never shared with the Chinese."

The meeting had gone on for its allotted time of thirty minutes, and with that the president stood and said, "Thank you, gentlemen." Everyone knew what that meant.

❖

It was Friday afternoon and the president was golfing again. Kennedy Russell was upstairs in the residence when Andrew Jr. called from his room, "Do you know where my basketball is?"

"Did you check the hall closet?" she replied.

"I did—it's not there," came Andy's response.

The first lady started to look for the basketball. And no surprise, it was in the hall closet, where she'd told him to look.

"Andrew, its right here." Curiously, right next to the basketball were the president's golf clubs. *So much for him playing golf every Friday,* she thought.

❖

As week ten approached in the president's training cycle, he started his carrier qualifications or CarQuals. This is really where the rubber meets the road for any Navy pilot.

Landing a high-performance jet on a ten-thousand-foot runway is easy. Landing on an eleven-hundred-foot carrier is one of the most difficult tasks in all aviation. And it really isn't eleven hundred feet. The true landing area is more like 800 feet.

The USS *George H. W. Bush* (CVN-77) was assigned to the Atlantic Fleet, which meant its homeport was Norfolk, Virginia.

It would be the *Bush*—call sign Avenger (named after the call sign of the forty-first president)—where Rusty would CarQual.

At Pax River, as at most naval air stations, there was a runway painted up to resemble the flight deck of a US carrier. That's where pilots would do what is known as FCLPs, or field carrier landing practice, before "heading to the boat."

During weeks eight and nine the president focused on FLCPs. While it was helpful and gave the aviator the feel for the size of the flight deck and time interacting with the ball, or the Improved Fresnel Lens Optical landing System or IFLOLS, every pilot knew it was just not the same as landing on a carrier at sea. For Rusty that would happen this week.

It took some planning and subterfuge to get Rusty on the *Bush* incognito.

What worked in the president's favor was that once in his flight suit, with his helmet on, he easily looked like any other flag officer.

A very select few were aware that the president would be landing on the *Bush*.

Those in the Secret Service who knew about it hated the idea of POTUS flying again—the risks were just too great. When Dan Nicols went to the president to express his concern, President Russell summarily dismissed it with, "Dan, this is happening—get behind it."

❖

In Riyadh the sheik was assessing the aftermath of the attack in America. Contrary to public opinion, the sheik was quite pleased with the operation.

"Kaizad, we accomplished much, my friend," said the sheik to his security chief.

Kaizad nodded but added, "Yes, but we failed to get the children to the Chinese submarine. The SEALs thwarted our plans."

The sheik considered that statement for a moment before responding with, "Yes, the Chinese." He paused. "I am not convinced that all is as it seems."

Kaizad looked puzzled. "Your Highness, do you suspect the Chinese did not tell us the truth about the mission?"

"It doesn't matter what I think at the moment. I need you and your people to confirm the facts. Keep pressing our resources in China for more information. Did the SEALs rescue the Russell children on their own, or did they have help from the Chinese?"

"Yes, Your Highness, I will make finding out a priority."

"But, Kaizad, we have accomplished a great victory. Never again will an American president feel safe from our reach. We attacked the most secure family on the planet, on their soil, and we successfully penetrated their defenses. Their submarines, their aircraft carriers, all were powerless against us. It is a legacy I will be proud to leave to our Islamic brothers as they carry on the fight against the infidels."

"Yes, Your Highness. Had we wanted to, we could have killed his family, and the president knows that."

Both knew that as a result of the attack, never again would an American president's family ever feel totally safe. The operation had proven that the Islamic Front could get to anyone. A lesson that was not lost on any of the other world leaders, let alone the citizens of those countries.

Since 9/11 the world had entered a new reality where terrorism was a constant concern, and the psychological impact of that was something the sheik savored.

In addition, the attack showed how fragile American society was and how panic could be spread at a low cost with great effectiveness. The entire Attack on ACK cost the sheik a mere $30 million. The return on investment in terrorism was, indeed, very high.

The sheik said, "I now want to advance our plans for similar drone attacks on New York, San Francisco, and Disney

World. We will show the Americans what widespread panic really looks like. Alhamdulillah."

But the sheik was mindful of loose ends.

"Kaizad, what is the latest on La Rue's whereabouts?"

"Your Highness, I have confirmation that La Rue in now in US custody."

The sheik angrily replied, "We already knew that."

"No," replied his chief of security. "We suspected that, but now we know for certain."

"Good, now you know what I have known for two months. Where is she being held? Do you *know* that?"

He responded, "Either at a US black site, in Guantanamo, or in Colorado at their supermax prison."

"Kaizad, I pay you a small fortune to run my security organization. That means you should *know*. Find her." On that point the sheik was ready to conclude the meeting. It was late and he wanted to start his evening entertainment.

Ever since La Rue's disappearance, the sheik had had a vendetta against American women. To satiate these desires, which were becoming increasingly sadistic, his people provided him with American women for his pleasure several times a week.

Reports were making it back to the United States regarding the sheik's behavior, which only added to the urgency of the intelligence agencies to bring the sheik to justice.

❖

The president was now carrier qualifying, or CQing on the USS *George H. W. Bush* off the East Coast. The process required that he make ten traps and two touch and goes over a two day period in order for him to become current. The president would not be qualifying for night traps – which was a relief to him and everyone involved.

With a large SD on his jet's tail, designating the squadron the president was now a member of, "Rusty" Russell was now in the groove, a mile behind the US aircraft carrier on final approach. He called the Carrier Air Traffic Control Center or CATCC with the call, "123, Rhino, Ball, 9.5, Auto." This indicated that the president was flying jet numbered 123, it was a Super Hornet model, his fuel state was more than adequate with 9,500 pounds left and he was using his autothrottles.

Rhino was the name used to identify the jet as a Super Hornet. It was important for the flight-deck crew to know the exact model of the aircraft they were trapping on the deck. The individual model told the deck crew the weight and performance characteristics of the aircraft so they could safely trap it.

To aid with distinguishing between Hornets and Super Hornets, the Navy adopted Rhino as the call sign for a Super Hornet and used Hornet for the F/A-18A, B, C, and D models.

Furthermore, for night landings, the jets used a different pattern of strobe lights to distinguish the various jet models so the Landing Signal Officer or LSO could easily classify a Hornet from a Super Hornet simply by the pattern of their navigation lights.

The LSOs, stationed on the platform on the stern of the carrier were there to provide voice commands if necessary to assist Russell as he fine-tuned his approach. It had been more than twelve years since the president's last trap, and his rapid heartbeat was reminding him of that fact. That said, no LSO calls were made to Russell on his approach.

As the Rhino crossed the stern of the carrier, Russell made his final adjustments, and caught the number three wire. As he touched down Russell pushed his throttles to full power so if he missed the wire he would have had the power to go around for another approach. But that wasn't needed on this trap. *Shit hot*, he thought, *I haven't lost it.*

With that, Rusty Russell nudged the throttle forward, following the direction of the yellow-shirted flight-deck directors.

The president's heartbeat was beginning to return to normal as he lined up at the direction of the plane handlers on the deck for another takeoff.

On days like this the USS *George H. W. Bush* would be carrier qualifying as many pilots as possible. The president positioned his Super Hornet behind catapult number one for a cat shot off the *Bush*. This worked to Russell and Bartlett's advantage, for never leaving the cockpit greatly reduced the risk of the president being recognized.

The president was going to have a busy day. He wanted to get in six traps before returning to Pax River. The CAG made sure the air boss gave Rhino 123 priority, which did raise some eyebrows, but it was dismissed as the preferential treatment that any flag officer would get.

For the final catapult off the *Bush* the president gave command over to Lieutenant Commander Bartlett who flew the F/A-18 from the backseat for their flight back to Pax River.

The president was exhausted and knew not to push his luck in a high-performance fighter jet, where any mistake could end very quickly and very badly.

❖

The NSA was still working through the treasure trove of data they had obtained from La Rue. Much of the data related to the sheik's finances.

La Rue knew about all of his accounts and investments. She had the names of the banks and the bankers involved and as a result gave the NSA and CIA a very detailed picture of the inner workings of the sheik's finances. La Rue was also providing a lot of additional information on the sheik's partners and contacts.

La Rue had decided to come totally clean and share everything she had on the sheik and his colleagues.

She was in advanced talks with the Justice Department over a plea deal, by which she would provide additional information in order to avoid jail time and work for the NSA.

The US government was working with the governments of France, Great Britain, Germany and Switzerland to construct a detailed map of the sheik's holdings.

Swiss bankers were revered for two things: how well they protected their clients' privacy, and not cooperating with other governments on tax investigations where their clients' accounts were concerned.

The Swiss, as a matter of policy, rarely cooperated with foreign investigations, but in the case of the sheik and his involvement in the Attack on ACK, they knew if they didn't cooperate with the United States that President Russell would bring the full weight of the United States down on Swiss banks and the country of Switzerland.

The secretary of the treasury made this point to the Swiss authorities in person.

He said, "Should the Swiss banks choose not to cooperate fully with the US on this investigation, the Swiss would risk experiencing unexplained disruptions to their networks over the next few months."

The Swiss bankers quickly fell in line and implemented a plan that would get the sheik to Switzerland. With the disappearance of Ms. La Rue, the sheik's Swiss bankers had set up new accounts for him. But the Swiss bankers were adamant that the sheik come to Zurich in person in order to set up the encryption for these new accounts, which included biometrics such as fingerprints, handprints, retina scans, and voice verification.

The sheik, a person of extraordinary wealth, could live extravagantly for the rest of his life just on the funds he maintained in Dubai alone. But the Swiss bankers were correct in their insistence that they needed to set up new biometric access for the sheik and for La Rue's replacement, a Brit named Natalie Hurp.

After some back-and-forth it was agreed that the sheik would travel to Zurich from Riyadh the second week of November.

As always, the sheik traveled in strict secrecy and by private jet, in this case a brand-new Gulfstream G650.

Typically the sheik would not involve himself in the administrative minutiae of setting up security on his accounts. In the past he would have delegated this assignment to La Rue.

That said, the banks were adamant that given the mystery surrounding La Rue's disappearance, the aggregate amount of the sheik's accounts, and their newly implemented security systems, the sheik needed to come to Zurich in person to set up the biometric access on the new accounts.

The sheik was not happy about this trip in the least. And like most powerful people who are forced to deal with administrivia, he repeatedly let those around him know it. This included letting Natalie Hurp, La Rue's replacement, his Swiss bankers, and Kaizad Shehzad, his head of security, who was already making the plans for the sheik's protection while in Switzerland, know almost daily about his irritation over the trip.

The sheik, along with his security team, and Hurp, who would fly in from Dubai, would depart Riyadh and fly direct to Zurich.

As agreed in advance, the Swiss bankers passed the information regarding the sheik's itinerary back to the CIA. The trap was set.

❖

Fall had arrived in Washington. It had been eleven weeks since the Attack on ACK.

FLOTUS had recovered from the virus, but she and the children were working with a therapist to deal with the fallout from their ordeal.

The president's schedule had him attending the G8 meetings in Rome the following week.

The president asked his wife, "I have the G8 next week in Rome. Care to come?"

"I don't know, Andy. I think it is too soon to leave the kids."

The president wasn't surprised in the least and replied, "I understand. We could bring the kids and probably get a meeting with the pope."

"Andy, I don't want the kids traveling."

The president agreed with her, but he was surprised by the sharpness of her tone and how final she was on the subject. Ever since the attack, Kennedy had been dealing with post-traumatic stress, and her behavior reflected her difficulty in resuming a normal schedule.

The president agreed with her assessment. He would travel alone to the G8 meeting, but more than anything it was her tone that concerned him.

It was Monday, November 14, and the president would depart Andrews Air Force Base that evening, arriving in Rome early on Tuesday.

Sterling Spencer met with the president and Mark Holloway to discuss the agenda and schedule for the G8 meetings. The president informed them he would be traveling without his family to the meetings. Given everything that had happened, no one on the president's staff was surprised.

The president did make a point to meet with the therapist who was treating the first lady and his children. Without asking to betray any patient-doctor confidentiality the president inquired about the progress his family was making. He learned that the children were recovering quickly, as expected, but his wife was struggling in the aftermath of the attack. That wasn't unusual, he was told, but she would need more care to resolve the issues she was facing. The president asked what he could do to help. The reply came back, "Just be patient with her, Mr. President. This is going to take some time."

❖

Spencer began, "Mr. President, here is the schedule." He handed the president a folder that contained a detailed itinerary for the G8 trip.

He continued, "Once we arrive, we will settle into the American embassy, where we will be staying for the duration of the trip."

The president would get some rest and then host a private dinner with the British prime minister, the German chancellor, and the president of Russia. They had all provided support during the Attack on ACK.

Holloway spoke up. "Mr. President, the French president will feel offended if he is not included in this dinner, sir."

"I know," said the president, "but I will make it up to him with a one-on-one meeting that will give him a great photo op to assuage his bruised French ego."

He then added, "I think it is important that I meet with the leaders who helped with the Nantucket operation personally. Plus I need to talk to them about the Spratly issue."

That left Thursday and Friday for G8 meetings, with a return to Washington planned for Friday evening.

The president covered the other goals for the meeting with Spencer and Holloway and then moved on to his next meeting.

As was often the case, the president cleared his calendar on travel days so he could spend some time with his family before he began his trip.

The president went up to the residence, where Andrew was complaining again about the weak Wi-Fi signal that affected his

Xbox One video game performance. "Our bandwidth is the worst," he complained. "All my friends' Xboxes are better than ours."

The president responded by saying, "Maybe you're spending too much time on the Xbox. How about shooting some hoops or reading a book?" Andy just went back to playing his game.

The president turned to Katie and asked about her day, which she said was fine, as she always did.

He joined his wife on the couch in the family room and asked about her day. She was frustrated with the White House Christmas decoration planning.

She wanted the residence and the public spaces of the White House to look nice, but she just didn't have much energy for it. She would be happy to follow whatever recommendations her staff offered.

"Are the G8 meetings going to be difficult?" she changed the topic.

"No more than usual," said the president. "It will be good to spend some time with James, though." The president was referring to the British prime minister, James King, whom he considered a friend.

"What are you thinking about for Thanksgiving? Camp David?" he asked his wife.

"I guess so," said Kennedy. "Are you okay with that?"

"Sure," said the president, trying to be supportive of his wife. "Let's just take it easy this year. You know me—as long as we have a big flat-screen and cable, I'm fine."

She just shook her head. A moment later, the president's valet knocked on the door to announce that Marine One was ten minutes out.

The president grabbed his daughter with a growl and said, "Before I go, I need a big hug." He gave her a big squeeze and a hug. Then he gave a kiss to his son, who at twelve still didn't mind.

He then spent a few quiet minutes with his wife before he heard the knock on the door indicating it was time to leave.

"Take care," he said to them all. "I'll say hello to the pope for you." And with that he gave his wife three kisses, which was his ritual, one on each cheek and one on the lips. Then he was gone.

Chapter Twenty-Six

As the president got settled in his office on Air Force One, he opened his briefing book and took out a folder marked "Operation Warlord," with "PEO" on the tab. "PEO" stood for "President's Eyes Only."

He opened the folder and spent the next forty-five minutes reviewing the document.

When he finished, he put the folder in his safe and then moved to his lounge, picked up the remote control, and selected a movie from the Air Force One entertainment system, which was usually loaded with as yet unreleased new movies.

Once he finished the movie, he had dinner with his chief of staff and Senator Stephen Krone of Texas, whom the president had invited on the trip due to his expertise on the trade agreements that were part of the agenda for the meetings.

After dinner he went up to the cockpit to say hello to the flight crew. The command pilot was a full-bird colonel; the copilot was a major.

"Colonel, how is the flight progressing?" the president asked.

"Fine, Mr. President. Would you like to take over for a while?" the colonel asked.

He was referring to the fact that every once in a while the president would pilot Air Force One as a way to keep his hand in at flying. Of course, the colonel of Air Force One didn't know that the president was now getting plenty of "stick time" on F/A-18s.

The president replied, "Not tonight, Colonel. Maybe on the return." With that, he said good night to the flight crew and turned in for the night.

When Air Force One flies overseas it picks up a flight of US Air Force F-15Cs as a fighter escort—their call sign is Halo flight.

The F-15Cs joined up from Otis on Cape Cod along with a new KC-46 US Air Force tanker. It was a tough flight for the F-15 pilots, as it would take about seven hours to reach Rome, and that was a long time to spend in a single-seat cockpit. But they were used to it.

The next morning Air Force One landed on time at Rome's Fiumicino–Leonardo da Vinci Airport.

The F-15Cs also landed at da Vinci, but they stayed aloft until Air Force One was chocked.

❖

The *USS Theodore Roosevelt* (CVN-71), "The Big Stick," had completed its training and deployment prep off Nantucket in September, returned to Norfolk, and then left on its eight-month deployment to the 6th Fleet Area of Operation, or AOR, which was basically the Mediterranean.

During the deployment they would be based out of Naples, Italy. November 14 found the USS *Theodore Roosevelt* steaming two hundred miles south of Sicily conducting flight operations with the same squadrons of Air Wing 1 (CVW-1) that were on board during the Nantucket assignment.

Three fighters of VFA-211, the *Fighting Checkmates*, were getting ready to shoot off the USS *Theodore Roosevelt*—the makeup of the flight was three F/A-18Fs.

It was early morning on Tuesday, and today's mission called for the *Fighting Checkmates* of VFA-211 to fly to Rome, where they would billet close to the Rome airport. Curiously, one of the F/A18Fs had an empty backseat. The cover story was the backseat was left open because they would be flying an Italian Air Force VIP once in Rome. So the flight of three F/A-18s had only five crew members, three pilots and two NFOs. The flight would be led by Lieutenant Commander Bartlett who had been temporarily assigned to VFA-211.

The Super Hornets were loaded out fully, including AIM-9X Sidewinders, and AIM-120 AMRAAM air-to-air missiles. The missiles on these Super Hornets were painted grey and had a yellow and brown stripe indicating they had *"live"* rocket motors and warheads. These Hornets were loaded to fight. Operation Warlord was about to commence.

❖

The president always enjoyed visiting Italy.

Once he was settled in his suite at the US embassy, his secretary informed him there was a naval officer waiting to meet him.

"Mr. President, there is a Lieutenant Commander Bartlett here and he would like to speak to you." Sharply she added, "Sir, he isn't on the list."

The president smiled. He knew this sort of deviation from protocol drove her crazy. "Yes, Alice, I will see him. Bring him into my study in five minutes."

The commander was shown into the president's study. After getting comfortable, they started going over the material that Lieutenant Commander Bartlett had brought with him.

Before he left, the president said, "So we think it will be Thursday morning. Is that correct, Commander?"

"That's affirmative, Mr. President," the commander replied.

"Commander, keep me apprised as data comes in. Thank you."
That was Bartlett's cue to leave, and he did.

❖

The sheik was reviewing his schedule for the rest of the week with his staff. He was breaking in his replacement for La Rue, Miss Natalie Hurp.

It came as no surprise that it was another woman, this time a Brit, with an MBA from the London School of Economics who had worked for Goldman Sachs in their London office.

She came highly recommended, she was extremely smart and attractive, and most important, she was not an American. The schedule called for them to fly to Zurich on Thursday to set up the new accounts and biometrics with the Swiss banks. They would leave in the morning from Riyadh and fly directly to Zurich and spend the evening.

From Zurich, Natalie would go on to London to deal with some of the sheik's business there. There was no chance the sheik would step foot in either the US or the UK, as he knew he would be immediately arrested. The sheik would return to Riyadh on Friday morning as planned.

❖

The president's dinner on Tuesday evening with the British PM, the German chancellor, and the Russian president was a success, and, more importantly, it gave the four world leaders some unscripted time to openly discuss current events.

Not surprisingly, the entire first hour of the dinner was consumed with talk of the Attack on ACK. It was the first time these leaders had met face-to-face since the attack. It was not lost on any of them that their families could be next.

The leaders were unified that extra precautions would need to be taken to protect their families—especially when outside the protective bubbles of their primary residences.

As dinner gave way to after-dinner drinks, the topic of the Spratly Islands came up for discussion.

The Russian president, Alexei Vasiliev, began and was typically direct and to the point. "Mr. President, what will be your position at the UN vote on the Spratly Islands issue?"

The US president didn't pull any punches either, "The US is going to vote in favor of China's request for control over the Spratly Islands." He let the British prime minister, James King, Alexei Vasiliev, and the German chancellor, Sabine Reutemann, absorb the point.

The president added, "Related to our support of China's move on the Spratlys, the US is going to re-open and dramatically increase the size and scope of our naval and Air Force bases in the Philippines. In addition, we are also proposing the creation of a new major joint base in Vietnam."

After a minute during which no one said anything, the president asked, "What would your countries think of establishing a major base in Vietnam—a joint base—a major US, NATO, and Russian base?"

"By establishing a base in Vietnam along with the US presence in the Philippines, we would effectively bracket the Spratly Islands and the Chinese."

James King then spoke, having previous knowledge of the president's proposal. "My government has been in secret negotiations with Hanoi for months, and we have been given assurances that the Vietnam government will support this plan."

The German chancellor then asked King, "You have assurances from Hanoi that they will support this plan?"

King replied, "We are already working on transferring the Song Han Terminal to a British-controlled company as a first step."

The president said, "The choice is either to confront China on the Spratlys or to establish an equally strong presence in the area. Those are our options." The president added, "The Spratly Islands is a case where we need to meet force with force. It's the only thing the Chinese understand.

"That is my proposal, or rather, our proposal," said the president, looking over to James King, who nodded his agreement. Russell then added, "To resist the Chinese on this issue would set us back in terms of our bilateral relationship. However, we cannot allow China to exert control over the entire South China Sea. Imagine the reaction of the world to our announcement that the US and Russia along with our NATO allies are establishing a joint base in Vietnam."

"It would signal a new world order. Plus imagine the reaction of the North Koreans to this plan."

Sabine Reutemann said, "You are right to mention North Korea. They are unpredictable. Also, how will Japan react to this plan?"

The president said, "I am meeting with the Japanese PM tomorrow to discuss this specific matter. But first, of course, I wanted to get input from this room."

Vasiliev stated, "Your plan to bracket the Chinese between Vietnam and Philippines bases is the right move given the alternatives."

They all knew building the base would also cost billions, which both the Philippines and Vietnam would benefit from, further cementing the relationship with both governments.

Eventually, the president thanked his guests for coming and wished them a good night, knowing he would see them all tomorrow but in a more formal setting, where all of the conversation and comments were basically scripted.

❖

It was oh dark thirty on Thursday morning when a light knock on the president's bedroom door announced it was time for him to start his day. He showered, shaved, and got dressed, although this time in more casual clothes and without the help of his personal valet.

He came downstairs and said good morning to the Marine on duty in the front hall. The Marine said, "Good morning, Mr. President. Your car is waiting."

A few minutes later the president was in a hangar at a secluded portion of Leonardo da Vinci Airport.

There he changed into his flight suit and inspected his gear as he listened to the mission brief from Lieutenant Commander Bartlett along with the flight crew of the other VF-211 Super Hornets.

Lieutenant Commander Bartlett got in the backseat of the squadron's CAG bird, as the president got into the front seat of Nikel 200. The 200 jet would use the call sign of Nikel 11 for today's mission.

Dawn was just breaking. US Navy ground crews had completed the preflight checks and were now in the process of turning up the General Electric F414 turbojets on the F/A-18Fs.

As the pilots and NFOs got settled in their cockpits, each crew was inputting way points into their navigation systems. Then Commander Mike Bartlett got a call from Closeout, the Navy's E-2D Advanced Hawkeye, which was orbiting somewhere over Sicily.

"Nikel 11, Closeout, Orphan 1, Rock 010, 110, 28,000 thousand, track northwest" came the call.

Closeout was tracking the sheik's Gulfstream, which they had given the call sign of Orphan 1.

Based on the information just relayed from the E-2D, Lieutenant Commander Bartlett brought up the mapping system on the screen in the backseat of the president's Super Hornet and surveyed the situation.

He then touched the mike on his neck. "Mr. President, we have a problem." Bartlett then went on to explain the problem.

The president replied, "Commander, how did this happen?"

Bartlett's response referred to a combination of lighter-than-forecasted headwinds and an earlier-than-planned departure time for the sheik's Gulfstream.

A moment later the president popped the canopy and started to power down the Super Hornet.

Lieutenant Commander Bartlett made the radio call to the flight: "Nikel 11 to Nikel flight—mission scrubbed, I say again, mission abort. Cycle down and reassemble in the hangar for debrief."

Twenty minutes later, after speaking with Admiral Jacobsen and the Closeout crew, Lieutenant Commander Bartlett entered a private room in the da Vinci hangar and debriefed the president.

"Mr. President, it was something of a perfect storm. Orphan1 took off a half an hour earlier than expected, and then there were unusually light head winds over the Med—the result was they were forty-five minutes ahead of schedule and we missed our window."

The president didn't reply. He just put his forefinger and thumb on the bridge of his nose, closed his eyes, and grimaced as he thought for a moment.

"When are they planning to return to Riyadh?" he asked.

"Our G2 tells us tomorrow," responded Bartlett.

The president nodded and said, "Commander, no more mistakes. Do you understand?"

"Copy, sir."

The president then got back in his Suburban and rode back to the embassy.

This change in plans would wreak havoc with the schedule. Now the president would need to extend his trip by a day. He would return to Washington on Saturday instead of Friday as planned.

The typical way a president handles this sort of change in plans is to say he is feeling under the weather and to move everything out by a day on the schedule.

But in this case his Thursday afternoon would go as planned. He would inform his staff that he would like to extend his trip by a day in order to meet with the Holy Father on Friday afternoon.

Actually, this would not come as a surprise to his staff. They knew the president would like to meet with the pope during his trip if possible.

Now Russell needed the pope to cooperate and open a window in his Friday afternoon schedule.

The president was confident that the pope would comply, although he also knew his staff would hear a lot of complaining from the Vatican staff about why this wasn't arranged weeks ago.

Chapter Twenty-Seven

The sheik landed ahead of schedule in Zurich and made his way, along with Miss Hurp, to the various meetings.

There were retina scans, handprint scans, and voiceprints, which were all required by each bank for both the sheik and Miss Hurp.

As their day wound down, they traveled back to their hotel in a Maybach provided by one of the banks. The sheik was then escorted up to his suite by his head of security and six bodyguards, all of whom were heavily armed.

The sheik had reserved the entire floor of the Zurich Ritz-Carlton. This was not unusual for a VIP from the Middle East. Part of the reason for this was to provide enhanced security, but much of it was just for their egos.

As the sheik entered his suite, he asked in anticipation, "Kaizad, what do you have for me this evening?"

"Sir, a very exclusive selection from Russia and Croatia," Kaizad replied. He wasn't referring to the wine list.

As Kaizad opened the door to the suite's den, the sheik saw six completely naked women standing in a line. All were stunning.

The sheik looked them over one by one and then took three by the hand and walked them into his bedroom.

Just as he was ready to close the bedroom door, the sheik took another look at the remaining three and selected a fourth woman to join his group.

That left the remaining two for Kaizad.

❖

The president's team did a good job of juggling his schedule.

Again came a soft knock on the president's door before sunup on Friday morning, which led to a similar sequence of events as the day before.

Bartlett briefed the president on a late change in the plan. The CIA had a team in Zurich's Kloten Airport monitoring the sheik's departure. The team had confirmed that the sheik would not be returning in his Gulfstream G650 but instead had chartered a Dassault Falcon 900 under another name.

In addition, the sheik's security team had created an elaborate process to get the sheik to the airport and to switch jets undetected. But the CIA had anticipated the move and had all the necessary manpower and technology in place to overcome the ruse.

The CIA passed the information to the Navy, which informed Closeout, the E-2D Advanced Hawkeye, which again was orbiting over the Tyrrhenian Sea. The tail number of the sheik's Falcon jet was N8406E.

This time, while the president was seated in the cockpit of Nikel 11, came the call, "Nikel flight, Closeout, Orphan 1, Rock 190, 140, 29,000 thousand, track southeast."

The Closeout call followed the Navy's BRAA format that relayed bearing, range, altitude and aspect.

Lieutenant Commander Bartlett, in the backseat of the president's F/A-18F, entered the data just relayed from the E-2D into the Super Hornet's navigation systems, and replied, "Closeout, Nikel 11, Copy."

The Nikel flight then lined up for immediate takeoff. No radio calls were made; it was all covered in the mission brief. In addition, it was agreed the president would stay off the radio in order to remain incognito.

At commercial airports around the world, military jets are extended the courtesy of jumping the takeoff line upon request, and this morning at Leonardo Da Vinci Airport was no different.

Lieutenant Commander Mike Bartlett called the tower, "Da Vinci tower, Nikel flight of three requesting immediate clearance for takeoff."

A few seconds later came the response, "Stand by, Nikel flight." A minute later an update was provided: "Nikel flight, switch to departure, you are clear to taxi for immediate takeoff on runway 34Right. Take position in front of the Alitalia triple 7 that is holding short of the apron on 34R."

Bartlett responded, "Copy, da Vinci control. Nikel flight cleared for immediate takeoff on 34R. Arrivederci and thank you." During the mission brief Bartlett had briefed that they would take off one at a time.

The president, using the Super Hornet's rudder pedals, lined up on 34R with Nikel 12 and 13 in line behind him.

The president performed the wipeout checks of his flight controls, released his brake and performed the run-up on his engines.

He then advanced his throttles as his Super Hornet started its takeoff run down the runway, increasing speed until they reached the F/A-18F nose wheel liftoff speed (NWLO), or what is called rotation speed in other aircraft, which is fast enough for the jet to become airborne.

The president pulled back on the stick, or rotated, as the Super Hornet became airborne. Three seconds later he retracted the gear, cleaned up his flaps, and pulled slightly back on the throttle as the Super Hornet reached 350 knots for its climb out. The president held his climb as the other two Super Hornets of Nikel flight joined up. Nikel flight was under way.

A moment later came the call, "Nikel, Closeout, group, Rock 070, 100, 29,000, track southeast, bandit."

Five minutes later, Nikel flight was in formation at thirty thousand feet on a heading towards the target over the island of Portoferraio, which lies between Corsica and Italy.

The Nikel flight had picked up Orphan 1 on their radars causing them to signal a "commit" for the mission. With the commit issued Nikel flight switched from broadcast to tactical control.

"Closeout, Nikel 11, commit," called Nikel 11.

"Closeout copies commit," came back the call adding, "Orphan 1, BRAA 345, 110, 28,000, hot, bandit."

"Nikel 11, target, single," came the immediate reply from the Nikel flight leader.

Nikel flight moved into a combat spread formation as they were only sixty miles from the target.

As planned, the three fighters split into two sections of one lead fighter followed by a two fighter section. The lead F/A-18F was call sign Nikel 13 and the second section was call sign Nikel 11 and 12.

The Falcon was cruising at .8 MACH on a southern heading, while the F/A-18Fs were approaching from behind at .9 MACH. That gave them a closure rate of 17 miles per minute. With only sixty miles separating them, they would cross paths in four minutes.

The president's adrenaline was pumping as his concentration on the mission sharpened.

The mission plan had them approach Orphan 1 from behind and below. They would setup a stern conversion, by performing a climbing turn that would let them fall in right behind the target.

The mission plan called for Nikel 13 to perform a visual confirmation of the tail number on the Falcon without being detected.

Nikel 13 had now accelerated to approach the Falcon from behind to perform the ID. The Falcon did not have air-to-air radar so it could not detect the approaching US Navy fighter jet. In addition, the F/A-18Fs had secured their transponders to prevent the Falcon's TCAS (Traffic Collision Avoidance Alarm) from going off as the F-18Fs approached.

As planned, Nikel 13 advanced his throttles forward and came up on the Falcon about thirty feet below him approaching from his six o'clock.

Nikel 13 called, "Nikel 12, tally single, 12 o'clock 6 miles, 5 high."

A little more throttle and Nikel 13 was now twenty-five feet off Falcon's tail and about thirty feet below him. He looked down at his white notepad on his right knee, which read N8406E.

"Nikel 13, Nikel section, bandit, confirm, Nancy, Eight, Four, Zero, Six, Echo. Repeat, Nancy, Eight, Four, Zero, Six, Echo, copy."

Nikel 13 called, "Nikel 12, single group, hostile."

And with that Nikel 13 broke left and low and cleared the area as the mission brief had designated.

Perspiration covered the president's brow. He advanced his throttles a notch to close the ten-mile distance to Orphan1.

Fox is the code US and NATO pilots use to signal the release of an air-to-air missile. Which missile is fired dictates the variations of the Fox call.

Fox Two is the call used for the firing of a heat seeking AIM-9X Sidewinder, and Fox Three is for an active radar-guided missile like the AIM-120 AMRAAM and AIM-54 Phoenix.

Lieutenant Commander Bartlett had activated the air-to-air radar when they took off from Rome. He now called, "Master arm on," to the president. The flight checked that Nikel 13 had cleared the area. No one wanted to fire a heat seeking missile with their wingman out in front of them.

As the president's F/A-18Fs closed the range to Orphan 1, his right thumb pushed the selector switch on his control stick to select his AIM-9X Sidewinder missiles.

Three seconds later a solid tone was heard in the headsets of both the president and Lieutenant Commander Bartlett, indicating that the Sidewinder had locked on the heat signature of its target.

Now trailing Orphan 1 by seven miles, well within the Sidewinder's twenty-mile range, with its radar locked, the president depressed the trigger button on his stick as Bartlett called, "Nikel 11, Fox Two."

He released the trigger, then pressed the selector switch a second time and heard the tone begin to sound in his headset again. He depressed the trigger a second time and Bartlett called, "Nikel 11, additional Fox Two."

The second Sidewinder missile ignited and slid down the rail of the launcher from the left wingtip of Nikel 11. Once fired, the Sidewinder's tracker, which was already locked on the heat signature of the Falcon jet's engine, took over the guidance of the weapon.

The Sidewinder accelerated to 2.7 Mach and closed the range on the unsuspecting target in thirteen seconds.

The first Sidewinder honed in on the heat signature from the Falcon's port engine nacelle and exploded on target. The Falcon's left wing sheared off at twenty-eight thousand feet.

Lieutenant Commander Bartlett's call was simple and direct, "Nikel 11, splash."

Two seconds later the second Sidewinder hit what was left of the target and the entire jet exploded into pieces that fell into the ocean below, making the likelihood of recovery and ever finding out what happened to this jet extremely unlikely.

"I hope you enjoy hell, you son of a bitch," the president said over the internal communication system (ICS) – only Bartlett heard him.

Next the E-2D Hawkeye, which was monitoring the mission, checked in with the USS *Theodore Roosevelt*: "Rough Rider, Closeout, splash single, repeat, splash single."

Standing by in the Command Direction Center on the USS *Theodore Roosevelt* were Admiral Brian Jacobsen and Rear Admiral Mark Singer, who were monitoring the radio calls for the mission.

There were no cheers from the staff in CDC, as they didn't know any of the details of the mission.

Lieutenant Commander Bartlett got on the radio. "Nikel flight, RTB."

The Fighting Checkmates of VFA-211 flew now in a loose formation of three ships, picking up the USS *Theodore Roosevelt's* TACAN or tactical air navigation system, which would lead them back to "The Big Stick." Overnight the carrier had steamed to a location one hundred miles north of Palermo.

The Nikel flight would land in twenty-five minutes according to their mission plan.

Admiral Jacobsen left the CDC and went to the admiral's bridge along with Rear Admiral Singer.

Once on the flag bridge, located on the 08 level, one deck below the captain's bridge, the admirals called and asked the captain to send the on-duty signalman down.

A minute later the signalman knocked on the bulkhead.

Admiral Jacobsen, a four-star admiral and COMFLT-FORCOM, handed the signalman a package wrapped in brown paper and said, "I want you to fly these flags now and keep them up until thirty minutes after we recover the last VFA-211 bird. Do you understand?"

The signalman repeated the admiral's order verbatim and nodded his understanding. He then made his way to the platform above Vulture's Row—the area just off the bridge that provides an optimal vantage point for observing Flight Ops.

Just above Vulture's Row was the access ladder to the area where signalmen raise and lower flags on the carrier's masts.

The signalman opened the brown paper package and removed two standard-size flags from the package.

The on-duty lookout said, "Lenny, what's up?"

"Hell if I know, dude. A four-star and a two-star just told me to fly these until we recover our last Rhino."

The first was a flag with the Seal of the President of the United States, which consisted of the presidential coat of arms on a dark blue background.

As ordered, the signalman attached the flag to the line and started to run it up the mast.

The signalman, assisted by the lookout, then put a twelve-foot spacer and attached the second flag. The second flag, of a size similar to the first, was a skull and crossbones—the pirate flag.

"Have COMFLTFORCOM and COMCARGRU-12 lost their shit?" said the signalman.

On the bridge of the USS Nitze (DDG-94), an Arleigh Burke destroyer attached to the carrier group, the lookout called to the officer of the deck, "Sir, the flagship just raised some new signals."

On hearing that, the captain and the officer of the deck both raised their binoculars and trained them on the flag mast of the USS *Theodore Roosevelt*. The officer of the deck was the first to speak, "What the . . ."

It didn't take long until every ship in the carrier group was talking about the flags.

What many people might be surprised to learn is the role music plays on military ships.

While at sea, ships play music over their loudspeakers for many reasons—to motivate their crews, to announce various activities, and to improve morale. And the music of choice, by far, on US Navy ships is AC/DC.

COMFLTFORCOM's next order—another unusual one—was to the on-duty bosun's mate on the bridge of the USS *The-*

odore Roosevelt. "After Nikel 200 traps, I want you to play AC/DC's 'Thunderstruck' on the 1MC, understood?"

"Copy, Admiral," was the bosun's mate's reply. The rest of the bridge crew looked at one another. Captain Fraser just smiled and let out a quiet chuckle.

As planned, Nikel 11 was the last aircraft of the flight to land.

As the president's Super Hornet entered the pattern behind the ship, he called "200, Rhino, Ball, 5.5, Auto, Bartlett."

That call indicated the pilot, Bartlett, was flying a Super Hornet, number 200, had the IFLOLS, or meatball, in sight, and his remaining fuel state was 5,500 pounds. In reality the pilot flying the Super Hornet was President Andrew "Rusty" Russell but by agreement Bartlett was handling all the radio calls.

President Russell, in Rhino 200, lined up for his approach, adding power to correct his rate of descent as needed. As the Super Hornet hit the deck, his tailhook caught the Roosevelt's three wire. Sierra Hotel.

Once the arresting wire disconnected from his tailhook, the yellow shirted deck crew directed Nikel 200 to the area on the deck where the blue shirts would chock and chain the Super Hornet. Once secure, the brown shirt plane captains instructed the crew to fold the Super Hornet's wings and execute the shutdown process.

Once powered down, Russell popped his canopy, swung his leg over the side of his fighter and raised his helmet visor.

Once on the flight deck, the president shook the hand of his backseater, Lieutenant Commander Bartlett.

The president then took off his helmet and put it in his helmet bag. From the bag he grabbed a ball cap that simply read VFA-211, and pulled it low to keep his presence a secret. It was then that he heard AC/DC playing on the 1MC. He looked up to the bridge and saw the two flags flying from the mast. The president shook his head and smiled.

Only a very few knew the details of the mission, but the crew was betting that some sort of Al Qaeda strike had occurred.

That conclusion was supported when the red shirt ordnance deck hands noticed that the sidewinder rails on Checkmate 200 were now empty.

As AC/DC continued to play, a safety officer in a white vest escorted the crew of Checkmate 200 to the captain's outboard cabin.

There Admiral Jacobsen, COMFLTFORCOM, Rear Admiral Mark Singer, COMCARGRU-12, Captain Tom Fraser of the USS *Theodore Roosevelt*, a past squadron mate of the president's, and CAG, Captain Kent Benson, congratulated President Russell and Lieutenant Commander Bartlett on the success of the mission.

After a short debrief, the president asked, "Whose idea were the flags and the AC/DC?"

Admiral Jacobsen smiled and responded, "Sir, you just made history. I thought some subtle celebration was in order."

The president laughed and remarked, "Yeah, subtle as a sledgehammer. Anyway, we just made history that no one will ever be able to write about."

The president changed into a fresh flight suit. He noticed a new patch on the right shoulder that read "Gunslinger."

Thirty minutes after landing, POTUS, wearing his fresh flight suit and helmet, which was standard for a flight on a COD, along with Lieutenant Commander Bartlett and several other passengers, all undercover Secret Service agents, made their way out to the flight deck.

There they boarded a C-2A Greyhound from VRC-40, the Rawhides, for their flight back to Leonardo da Vinci Airport and Rome.

A short time later the captain of the destroyer Nitze sent an email to Admiral Singer with a photo of the USS *Theodore Roosevelt* flying the "unusual" flags. Admiral Singer forwarded the email to Admiral Jacobsen, Captain Fraser, and CAG Benson.

It was a secret that would not stay secret very long.

An hour later the president and his detail landed at da Vinci. The president changed into a suit and along with his Secret Service detail boarded three black Suburbans for their trip back to the embassy, where he would prepare for his meeting at the Vatican.

Lieutenant Commander Bartlett would stay in the embassy and fly back to Washington as a guest of the president on Air Force One.

❖

Ninety minutes later the pope greeted the president at the Vatican, surrounded by cardinals and his personal aide.

After they had discussed an array of topics, the pope took the president on a tour of the recently restored Sistine Chapel.

Then the pope invited the president into his private study. As they sat together, the pope's eyes met the president's—and in them he recognized the familiar look of guilt and remorse that every parish priest knew well.

The pontiff reached into the drawer of his side table for a stole and placed it over his neck.

He then turned to Andrew Russell and said, "My son, would you like to make a confession?"

The president of the United States knelt before the pontiff, made the sign of the cross, and began, "Bless me, Father, for I have sinned. . ."

❖

Later, on Air Force One, the president had time to reflect on the mission and his actions. There was no doubt the US was going to avenge the attack that transpired on ACK. That was clear. But the president was now wrestling with post-mission remorse, which was not unusual for any fighter pilot.

The intensity around the training and planning of the mission was so consuming that it rarely, if ever, left time for any analysis or soul searching. But post mission was when the chaplains always earned their pay. In the stillness of the long flight home, the president was alone with his thoughts.

The president resolved that his actions were justified, although if he were being honest, he knew that he'd "wanted" to exact revenge on the sheik for what he had done.

As the president sat alone in the quiet of Air Force One, he thought of all the sweat he had expended in the mission and its work-up. He recalled the stinging feeling in his eyes. Now in the solitude of his private cabin, his eyes were responding again, but this time it wasn't from sweat; it was from tears.

Chapter Twenty-Eight

The Birth of the Gunslinger Legend

It is said there are no secrets in Washington.

It was just a matter of weeks before all of Washington was talking about the rumor that President Russell had flown a fighter on a secret mission that shot down the jet carrying Sheik Abdul Er Rahman, the mastermind of the Nantucket plot to kidnap his children and infect his wife with a deadly virus.

And it didn't stop there. Every major intelligence organization around the world was hearing variations of the story. The Brits, French, Russians, Germans, Israelis, and Chinese were all filling in whatever missing details they could provide.

It was about a week later that the name Gunslinger came to light and it stuck.

The most important data point regarding the story was a private one.

It was two weeks after the president returned from the G8 meetings. Andrew Russell had just gotten into bed and was about to turn off the light when his wife turned to him and said—she didn't ask, but said—"I want you to know, I would have pulled the trigger myself given the chance."

The president didn't respond. He paused for a moment, didn't say anything and then turned off the light. Then in the darkness he reached for Kennedy's hand and held it until they both drifted off to sleep.

For the American public, eager for a leader who was a hero, the story took root and continued to grow. And that is how the Andrew Russell Gunslinger legend was born.

Epilogue

Nantucket Strong

In the spring of 2018, less than a year after the attacks, a ceremony was held on Nantucket to coincide with the Daffodil Festival, which occurs on the island every year in late April.

Main Street was closed and platforms were erected in front of the Pacific National Bank building.

There the president, the first lady, and the governor of the Commonwealth of Massachusetts, as well as Massachusetts state officials, presented awards and medals to those who came to their nation's and the Russell family's aide. First and foremost the president honored those who lost their lives or were injured in the attack. Next the president recognized Billy Herbert, Ron Orden and John Munson, as well as the members of the Nantucket Police and Fire Departments.

The ceremony began with a prayer by the pastor, Monsignor George V. Fogarty of St. Mary, Our Lady of the Isle. The monsignor also remembered the six individuals who lost their lives in the attack as well as those who were injured

Next the president spoke of his affection for the island and its people. He recalled fondly the time he spent on the island both before and after he became president.

The president announced the government was going to construct what amounted to a new Camp David on the grounds of the old Sconset Coast Guard station.

Going forward, instead of renting private residences for presidential vacations, the president and first family would stay in a presidential retreat to be built on the island.

The government still owned the land at the Coast Guard station, which was a perfect location for the new presidential retreat. The location was set well away from the rest of the village of Sconset, which would allow for the installation of all the necessary security and technology required in this day and age.

Most important, the location of the Sconset Coast Guard station would not upset the fragile ambience of the village or run afoul of any HDC zoning regulations.

It would take three years to complete the construction of the compound, which suited Kennedy Russell just fine. She needed some time to pass before her family returned to Nantucket.

For their next vacation she was thinking of Aspen, Vail or Telluride. The Russells were very fond of Colorado, too.

The president made a few closing remarks and the event came to an end. But it felt more like a beginning. After all, it was springtime on the island, with daffodils everywhere and a fresh ocean breeze.

The people of New England were descendants of countrymen who, when also confronted with threats to their liberty, did not hesitate to respond to the call to duty. Like their president, they were citizens who could be counted on to act, and act with courage.

You could say the residents of Nantucket were patriots and you would be correct. They were New England patriots.

Acknowledgments

For their aid in contributing to technical accuracy, the author wishes to thank the following individuals.

For technical advice, local Nantucket color, and initial encouragement, the author wishes to convey a special thanks to the distinguished Caltech alum Dr. Philip M. Neches.

Additional Nantucket color was provided by Maryann Wasik, executive director of the Nantucket Lightship Basket Museum. Carol Bunevich and John Merson provided assistance and guidance on the Sconset portion of the story.

I owe a debt of gratitude to the many dedicated members of the United States Navy, both past and present, who contributed technical input and authenticity to the plot.

For carrier and aviation expertise, I am indebted to Rear Admiral Thomas "Chain" Zelibor USN (Ret.); Rear Admiral Mark "Guad" Guadagnini USN (Ret.); Captain Rob "Ice" Ffield USN (Ret.); Captain Craig "Clap" Clapperton, Commanding Officer of the USS *Theodore Roosevelt* USN, Captain Richard "Twig" LaBranche USN; Captain Thomas J. Fraser USMC (Ret.). For submarine accuracy and color, Lieutenant Commander Michael Smith USN (Ret.) was invaluable. Captain Aaron Stachel US Army (Ret.) provided details around the US Army and its Apache attack helicopters.

For guidance on the story's pace and cadence, I am indebted to my *wingman* since grammar school Richard Assaf.

In terms of entering the muddied waters of writing and publishing, Mark Dane, Amy Waters Yarsinske, and Richard Herman provided encouragement and practical advice.

This effort could not have been completed without significant editorial and production assistance provided by Jennifer Fisher, Eileen Chetti, Gail Kearns and Deborah Perdue.

Anita Moseley provided valuable legal counsel and moral support.

Graphic design was provided by Austin Hollywood as we vetted many cover designs. Website design and development was provided by Divami UX Design and Innovation.

And lastly, to Jean, Andrew, and Katie who make my existence—be it in Colorado, New York, or Sconset—complete.

CPSIA information can be obtained
at www.ICGtesting.com
Printed in the USA
LVOW11s0233150417
530772LV00002B/21/P